I0452999

The Fall
by
Dylan Neville

"The Fall" is a work of fiction. All characters in this book are fictional and create d by the author, Dylan Neville. Names, characters, places, and incidents are either a product of the author's imagination or used fictitiously. Any resemblance to actual persons, living or dead, events, or locales is entirely coincidental.

"The Fall" by Dylan Neville ISBN- 978-0-9845362-9-0

Published 2014, by Fire Pit Creek Publishing, 31208 E Heidelberger Rd. Buckner, Mo 64016 US.

Manufactured in the United States

<u>Acknowledgments</u>

When I began writing this book, I did it with absolutely no intention of publishing it. In fact, I let a large portion of it sit for months without doing any writing at all. I simply wrote it when I felt like it, and because I enjoyed it. It wasn't until I finally allowed a few people to read parts of it or in its entirety that I decided to publish it. At first I felt like it would never be good enough to publish, and no one else would enjoy it the same way that I enjoyed writing it. It turns out that I was wrong. I almost let my modesty and lack of self-confidence prevent me from doing something that I always dreamed of doing. While I will most certainly never be compared to the literary giants who came before me—such as Ernest Hemingway, William Shakespeare, Tom Clancy, etc.—I find satisfaction in the fact that my creation (and hopefully many more to come) has been enjoyed by a great many of those who read it. The aim of everything I write is to spark inspiration, whether it is a full book or a short story. Nearly every element of my tales has some sort of symbolic importance, and that symbolism is for you—the reader—to decide. It can mean a great many things to a great many people, and no one can ever be right or wrong when it comes to their interpretation. I invite you to read my work with an open mind, and look for hidden meaning deep within its pages.

While I greatly appreciate everyone who has read *The Fall* and given me feedback (both while I was still writing it and after its completion), there are several individuals whom I must acknowledge outright:

My wife, Sarah, for being patient and understanding while I spent days and days preoccupied with writing, often for hours at a time. There were only a couple of times during the whole thing when she

3

got frustrated enough to express it.

Amela Celic, for being my number one fan. Amela read my work before it was completed, and was the first person to convince me that more people needed to read it. Though I was humble and doubted her belief that others would enjoy it as much as she did, it turned out that I was indeed very wrong. She always offered feedback and encouragement, and spoke about my book with others. Without that initial prodding from her, I probably would have never finished *The Fall*. I certainly would not have had it published.

My mother, Jayne, for giving birth to me and blessing planet Earth with a really awesome person. It can be said with absolute certainty that I would not have written this book and published it if it hadn't been for her. On a more serious note...I want to thank her for always offering guidance and encouraging words. No matter what happens, I have always known that we will be there for each other.

My grandmother, Joyce, for truly teaching me from little on how to be "proper". I may not always act it, but I certainly know what it means to be civil and well-mannered. And to my friends who will undoubtedly be thinking that I am *never* proper or well-mannered, don't forget that *you* were the ones who often encouraged my poor behavior.

A great man, the late Edward B. Neville (more commonly known as "Junior"), my grandfather. He was tough and certainly rough around the edges, but he was very humble and had a kind heart. He was known by most as a man of few words (and when he did speak, his words were often harsh and to the point), but his words were always true. Most importantly, he taught me how to be tough and kind at the same time. My grandfather was the only person on the planet who could swat me across my backside and I would always know that I deserved it. He taught me to always do what is right, even when it

4

hurts. People like him are a dying breed, and the loss of men like him is a loss to many.

My publisher, Angie Chapman, for helping me get through this process and devoting so much time to it. Her support and guidance has been much appreciated.

My friends, Brandon and Mary Lewis, and their son Trevor Lewis. Trevor helped me out by being "Charlie" for the book's cover photo. He did a wonderful job.

My friend Rick Failing, who was involved in a terrible motorcycle accident while I was in the process of writing this book. The doctors said there would be a lot of things that he would never do again, but Rick proved them wrong. After a long, rough road, Rick prevailed and came out on top. He's tough as nails, and because of that he continued fighting through all of it. Rick is surely a source of inspiration for many.

Last but most certainly not least, I would like to thank you, the reader. In this crazy, fast-paced world, it is often challenging to find the time to read a book. I thank you for finding the time to read mine, and I encourage you to pursue your goals and wish you good fortune in all your endeavors.

--Dylan Neville

Prologue

James Vance walked along the road, alone. It was cooler this evening than it had been the last few nights. The September air was crisp and fresh. He had traveled over twenty miles in just a day, all the way from the big city of Boston to the small town of Millis. He still had a very, very long way to go. He had traveled from Albuquerque, New Mexico, to Boston, Massachusetts, just to deliver a package. But the journey to Boston hadn't been too difficult. He had taken a train most of the way. Trains were one of the only modes of transportation still operational. Or at least, they were. After The Fall, people had taken it upon themselves to restore order and commerce. In a lot of ways, it had been good for humanity. Most of the world was in the same situation. After the United States fell, the rest of the world shortly followed. Of course, there were many countries that weren't affected too much. Countries like Afghanistan, Somalia, Peru...mainly developing or third world countries...made it out okay because their people didn't notice much difference. They had relied on each other and the land from the very beginning.

But countries like America...everyone had been so dependent on the system. Everything from food, to water, to jobs...without the system, the people were left with nothing. A lot of people didn't survive. Most starved to death, or were killed by bandits and thieves. A lot of others were killed by the military while they were trying to restore order. Five grueling years passed before there was peace. It took that long for the military to fall apart, for people to come together, for a somewhat stable system of trade to be set up. Vance didn't really play a part in it, besides helping a friend form a regional government back West. Now he was just a courier. Couriers were paid well, but it was a tough and dangerous job. People always wanted packages delivered to their loved ones across the state, or across the country. Merchants needed armed guards to escort them, and couriers were usually the employee of choice. Most couriers were former military or law enforcement. It took training like that to make it out in No Man's Land. Others were just gung-ho, wanting to score some "easy" goods. But guys like that didn't get the difficult jobs. Vance had gone on three low-priority assignments across the state and two more across the country before he got the higher paying jobs. Now he was the most recognized courier in the West. Or at least, he used to be. Now he wasn't sure what was left of back home.

After arriving in Boston, Vance had learned that bad things were happening back West. Chaos had erupted. Gangs of bandits were supposedly coming in and stealing food, water, and pretty much anything else. People were being killed in the streets. Albuquerque was basically gone, or so he had heard. He had waited in Boston for nearly two months, being pulled along by reoccurring promises that the railroad would become operational soon. He finally gave up hope and took off on his own. Now he needed to complete one more assignment before throwing in the towel. Just one more package to be delivered, and then he would find some other kind of work to do. That was assuming anything was left back West.

So, now the only modes of transportation were horse and carriage, or feet. The railway had been shut down. Resources weren't accessible. People weren't showing up for work. The value of goods fluctuated like Vance had never seen before. Hopefully what he had with him would get him all the way back to New Mexico. Over twenty-two hundred miles. But this package was worth it. He had fought and killed countless times for packages before, and he would do so again to defend this one. This package was the most important package he'd ever carried.

Everything about James Vance looked military, except for his goatee and mustache. His personality was cold and largely devoid of emotion, and his face never hinted at what he was really thinking. He kept the sides and back of his head shaved down almost to bare skin, and the top was not much longer. He was muscular and athletic. Sunglasses covered his eyes nearly all of the time. He wore a tactical

7

vest, with a bullet-proof vest underneath. For pants he wore tan or black BDUs. His shirt was a black or tan t-shirt, pulled tight across his muscles. His pants were bloused into his boots, which were made for tactical operations. For weapons, he had a 5.56mm M4 assault rifle, a .40 caliber Glock, a .38 caliber snub-nose revolver, a sawed-off 12-gauge pump-action shotgun, a tanto knife, and a short tanto sword that he carried on his back. All of these things he had acquired long before The Fall. It would have been nearly impossible to get them afterward, and that fact alone made all of his equipment very valuable. He could have easily traded his M4 for a horse and a week's supply of food and water. But the weapon meant a lot to him. It had seen him through some tough situations, and it was his friend out here in No Man's Land. His rifle and his backpack were his most valuable items. Inside his backpack, he carried whatever package needed to be delivered. He also carried a vast array of supplies and tradable goods. James Vance was not a man to be trifled with, and it showed on his face. Only the most foolish crossed his path. Or the most unlucky.

James Vance had spent fifteen years in the Army. Seven of those years were spent in the Special Forces. He knew how to survive in every way, shape and form. He had done two tours in Syria, and one in Iran. Now here he was...43 years old, been out of the Army for ten years, been living in this hell for nine years. He often thought back to the good times, back in the late 20's. He had just joined the Army, was getting ready to get married, enjoying life. Now it was 2050, and the whole world had gone to shit.

Vance kept marching along. There were only about two hours left of daylight, and the closest town was about three and a half miles away. He could easily make it before sundown, but he needed a breather. He took off his backpack, sat his rifle down against a tree, and took a knee. After taking a few big gulps of water and eating a slice of bread, he picked up his things and kept walking.

***

Medway, Massachusetts, appeared to be more of a rural community. It wasn't really a town, per se. It was more of a collection of communities. Vance had never been to this particular area before. He saw a large building—possibly a shopping center—and headed in that direction. There would more than likely be merchants set up around that area, and there were probably rooms to be rented inside the mall.

After arriving at the mall, Vance saw that there were quite a few people meandering about. Most were calling it a day, sitting around fire pits and conversing with one another. They looked like travelers, mostly. There appeared to be a whole market set up outside the shopping center, selling food and drink and general goods. Vance headed to the nearest food vender and took off his backpack.

"Hello there, stranger. What can I get for you?" the portly merchant asked.

"What do you have?" Vance asked.

"Squirrel and rabbit, mostly. I do have some venison as well, if you're interested." The merchant wiped his hands with a rag and threw it over his shoulder.

"I'll take a squirrel," Vance said as he began rummaging around in his backpack.

"Alright. Let's see what you've got in that bag of yours," the merchant replied, as was tradition.   Various metals were commonly used as currency for larger merchants. They would accept pretty much any metal, because they could then melt it down into whatever they wanted. Smaller merchants, however, would not accept metal as currency. It wasn't feasible for them to melt the stuff down. Instead, they would trade and barter with pretty much anything. The value of most items was established by the two people doing business.

"I've got a couple AA batteries here," Vance said as he set them up on the counter. The merchant looked them over.

"I suppose that will do," he said as he took a cooked squirrel off a

9

stick and handed it to Vance.

Vance threw his backpack over his shoulder, let his M4 dangle at his side from the combat sling, and began eating the squirrel as he walked away. Everyone here seemed pretty content. No one appeared to be starving, no one appeared to be fighting. If he didn't have more pressing matters, he might consider calling this place home. But since he couldn't do that, he would call it home for one night only.

Vance stepped inside the old shopping center, where people were congregating. The "host" was sitting behind the counter—which looked to be the old information desk of the mall—sipping from a glass.

"Want to rent a room?" he asked.

"Just for one night. I'll be out shortly after sunrise. Barter or money?" Vance asked.

The question was ubiquitous. For larger business owners and merchants, it simply meant, "Want me to show you my goods, do some work for you, or pay you in metal?"

"Barter only," the host replied.

Vance once again dug through his backpack. He pulled out two plastic lighters, two pairs of wool socks, and a pack of cigarettes. The host's eyes lit up, assuming that Vance was naïve or desperate, or both. Socks and cigarettes were worth quite a bit to most people. The plastic lighters were of moderate value.

"I expect two canteens-worth of water as well," Vance told him. The host's eyes returned to normal and he smacked his lips.

"Fine," he said after briefly looking over the items. He handed Vance a paper card and told him where to go.

Vance made his way up the non-functioning escalator. His feet hurt and he was in desperate need of sleep. He approached the guard and handed him his card. The guard looked at it, taking note of the big "1" drawn on it, as well as the room number at the top. He wrote both down on a piece of paper and allowed Vance to pass.

"Third one on the right," the guard said.

The area used as motel rooms looked like it used to be an office

10

section of the mall. Vance entered his room, closed the door, and took off his vest. He left his thigh rig with his sidearm on. After waiting several minutes, there was a knock at the door.

"Water," the boy said after Vance opened the door. Vance handed him his two canteens and the boy ran off.

A short while later, the boy returned. The two canteens had been filled to the brim. Vance tipped the boy with a pack of matches and shut the door. The water smelled and tasted good enough. After determining that the water was good enough to drink, Vance downed half a canteen and prepared for bed.

He had taken everything off except for his boots, pants, and shirt. He laid his weapons and backpack on the far side of the bed, furthest away from the door. After sitting the only lamp in the room next to his bed, he pulled out an old book from his backpack and began reading *The Old Man and the Sea*. Vance had read it probably five times during all of his travels. It was one of only two books he had. The other, *The Three Musketeers*, he had probably read five times as well. It wasn't so much the content as it was the book's ability to pull him out of his current world. If an author could manage that, he didn't really care what he was reading. He had once owned a copy of *Little Women*, and didn't much care for the storyline at all. But the way it was written had briefly pulled him out of the world in which he lived. He had lost the book when he was attacked by raiders in the middle of the night. It wasn't a huge loss.

After reading for awhile, Vance turned off the lamp and laid down. Within moments, he was asleep.

***

Vance woke up suddenly, and was unsure how long he had been asleep. He looked at his watch. It was 5 AM. There was no window, as this area of the mall had no exterior walls. Vance gathered his things, dumped the two canteens into the hydration pack inside his backpack, put his gear on, and left the room. He nodded his head to the guard—it

11

was a different one than before—and handed him his card. The guard crossed him off his list and kept the card.

Vance exited the mall and looked out across the gray landscape. The sun hadn't yet risen, but its rays were wrapping around the earth and shedding just enough light to transform everything to grayscale. He took in a long breath of fresh air to clear his lungs (the inside of the mall was little more than a thick fog of cigarette and cigar smoke) and looked around for vendors who were preparing to open up shop. There were very few—most didn't like getting up this early after working from sunup to sundown. One food merchant was preparing his business for the day, and hadn't even unlocked the wooden flap on his stand.

"I was wondering if I could get something to eat?" Vance asked.

"Why of course. Give me a few more minutes to get the burner going," the jolly merchant replied.

Vance opened up his backpack and looked around for stuff to trade. He settled on a few possible items, but waited for the merchant to be ready before pulling them out.

"I've got fresh eggs, if you're interested," the merchant said as he unlocked the flap on his stand.

"That would be great. Will you take these?" Vance sat a few wet wipes on the counter.

"Those will work for two eggs. Nothing more," the merchant said.

"That's fine. Scrambled, please."

Vance waited for the eggs to get done. When they were, he quickly gobbled them up and washed them down with a few draws from the tube of his hydration pack.

"I've got tea as well," the merchant said with a smile.

"That would be fine. A small cup. Let's see here," Vance dug around in his bag, "How about these?"

The merchant looked at the small bag of trimming nails. It was an odd item, admittedly. But Vance picked up just about anything he could find along his way.

"Those will do, but only because you bought something else to start with. Got a cup? It won't be very much, for what you gave me."

Vance handed the merchant his tin cup and watched him pour some tea into it. After taking a drink and determining that it was barely strong enough to be considered tea, he thanked the merchant and took off walking.

The sun was just barely beginning to peek over the horizon. Vance finished his tea in only a couple of drinks, and hadn't made it more than a hundred feet from the merchant's stand when he heard a horrific scream. He quickly turned around, but saw nothing.

"Oh my god!" the merchant who had sold him the eggs and tea yelled. He was looking around the side of the shopping center, where Vance couldn't see.

Vance ran over to the merchant and sat his cup on the counter.

"Get down!" the merchant yelled at him. Vance remained standing.

Around the corner, he saw three men who appeared to be raiders. They were sacking another vendor. A woman—presumably the merchant—was being held down on the ground by one of the men.

Vance wrapped his M4 behind his sidearm, locking it in place so it was out of the way. From over his shoulder, he pulled the sawed-off shotgun from his backpack.

"Don't go over there! They'll kill you!" the merchant said to him. Vance ignored him.

"Get away! Leave me alone!" the woman screamed.

"Fuck you, bitch!" one of the raiders shouted.

"Leave her alone," Vance said casually as he approached.

The raiders looked up to see a man dressed in tactical gear, and he was heavily armed. He was about six feet tall, probably two hundred pounds. He didn't looked like the kind of man to cross.

"Fuck you!" said the raider who was holding the woman down. His two buddies stopped digging through the stand and pulled out their weapons. One had a machete, the other held a metal pipe.

"You think you can take all three of us, you piece of shit!?" one

13

of them yelled.

"You may kill one of us, but we're close enough to gut your ass before you get off another..."

Vance fired his shotgun, quickly pumped another shell into the chamber, and fired again. The two closest men fell to the ground. One's head was split in half, the other had a gaping chest wound. The third man froze in fear, his hand still tightly gripping the woman's arm. Vance slowly and decisively racked another shell into the chamber.

"Let me go!" the woman yelled as she kicked and flailed.

Vance slid the shotgun back into its makeshift sheath on his backpack.

"You...you fucking killed them..." the only remaining raider stuttered.

Vance grabbed him by the throat, kicked the arm that was holding onto the woman, and forcefully threw the man down onto the concrete. The back of his head hit the ground with a loud "thud".

"There's no room in this world for people like you. Never was." Vance pulled out his tanto knife from his vest and held it close to the man's face. Blood began forming on the concrete from the back of the raider's head.

"Son of a bitch!" the woman yelled as she kicked the raider in the face. It wasn't a very good kick, but it surprised Vance nonetheless.

"I think he's learned his lesson," the woman said after taking a few calming breaths.

"Let him go. He'll carry the message back to the rest of his crew," the original merchant—the one who had sold Vance the eggs—said as he walked up behind them. Vance stared at the raider for a moment.

"Looks like I got outvoted. Don't come around here again, or I'll hunt down all of you and cut you up into pieces," Vance told him with his raspy voice. The man's nostrils were flaring and his eyes were wide with fear.

Vance sheathed his knife and pulled the raider to his feet. He pushed him away and kicked him in the ass as he did so, causing him to fall to the ground once more. The man quickly got back up and took off at a dead sprint.

By this time, more people were starting to come outside. Business was about to begin for the day. Only a handful had witnessed the scene that took place. The two dead bodies were obviously a sign for concern.

"What's your name, stranger?" the first merchant asked.

"Vance. I have to get back on the road now." Vance didn't even make eye contact with anyone as he turned and began walking away.

"Thank you..." the female merchant said from behind him. Vance didn't reply.

1

James Vance continued his determined march down the road. Several days had passed since he had been in Medway. It was midday, and he was now entering Hartford, Connecticut. He had walked the whole way. He had joined the Army as a Combat Engineer, and had gone to Sapper school before joining the Special Forces. Vance knew how to keep walking, and he knew how to do so as efficiently as possible. It sounds dumb, really, to make walking seem like some sort of art. But when you're walking a long distance—especially carrying a load—an art is exactly what it is.

Home. That was the only thing on his mind right now. He didn't even want to think about the current state of affairs. So much had changed just since he traveled to Boston. He had left Albuquerque with a world in his mind that was beginning to stabilize. Now he might be returning to a wasteland. He wasn't even sure what exactly had happened back West. No one was. Just one more package to deliver. That was what he really needed to focus on. He was just delivering one more very important package...

Vance stopped at a diner in Hartford. It was a rundown dump, but most everything was these days. There were a few small communities scattered across the nation that had managed to create a local power grid. They were limited, but having electricity made life much easier. Of course, those towns were usually targeted by raiders, or became overcrowded because everyone who needed hope flocked to them. He had heard rumors that there was a large community in Canada that had established trade and commerce, as well as a stable power grid and a security force. But it was probably just a rumor. He had heard things like that countless times before. Hell, before traveling to Boston, he had heard that they had crab boats out on the ocean. When he got there, he quickly discovered that it had just been a dream. A hope, lost in the wind. Luxuries like crab weren't going to happen anytime soon. It cost way too much in resources to power those big boats. Trains had barely been functioning, and they only operated on a very limited schedule. But now there weren't even any trains. The ones on the East Coast had been ordered to stay put, for fear of what was going on back West. The trains back West...well, they probably weren't around anymore.

After ordering a very basic sandwich and handing over some goods, Vance quietly sat at his table and stared at the empty seat across from him. Memories flickered into his mind. He fought to keep them out. He tried and tried, but images flashed like bright lights every time he blinked.

"What are you hungry for, Daddy?"

Vance got up from the table and headed for the door.

"I'll be right back," he told the waitress. She nodded her head in acknowledgment.

Vance went outside and walked around the side of the building. Leaning up against an old dumpster, he pulled out a pack of cigarettes and lit one. He took the opportunity to briefly look through the dumpster, though he was sure that he wouldn't find anything but trash. To his surprise, he actually found an old pair of sunglasses. Some drunk probably threw them in there.

After putting the shades in one of the pockets on his backpack, he let his cigarette hang from his mouth and went back inside. His sandwich was waiting for him. After quickly eating his meal, he

17

pulled out his book and decided to read a couple of pages, just to escape reality for a short while and give his legs a break.

"Hey Diana, let me have a sandwich," a young man—probably in his late teens—said as soon as he walked in. Vance thought nothing of it at first.

"You know how it works, Jimmy. You gotta give me something," the waitress told him.

"I'll give you something...a fucking black eye if you don't give me some food!" the man—"Jimmy"--said with a raised voice. Vance continued to ignore him, and kept his focus on his book. Outbursts and anger were common in the world nowadays.

"Go on Jimmy, don't cause any trouble for yourself," the cook said as he came walking out of the kitchen. He was a large man, but didn't appear to have much fight in him.

"Oh I'll cause all the trouble I want to!" Jimmy said as he pulled out a handgun from his waistband and pointed it at the cook. Diana the waitress screamed, and the cook stumbled backward.

"Yeah! That's right! Now give me some goddamn food! I'm starvin'!" Jimmy continued.

"That thing loaded?"

Jimmy jumped a little and whirled around to see a very scary looking individual standing about three feet from him.

"Bet it's not," Vance said as he cocked his head to the side. His face remained expressionless.

"Fuck you, man! Get the fuck outta here!" Jimmy yelled at him as he pushed his gun forward to add emphasis to his words.

Vance slapped the gun from the man's hand quicker than anyone could have believed. The gun flew over the counter. Before Jimmy knew what hit him, he was bent backwards over the counter with Vance's hand wrapped tightly around his neck. He looked up at Vance, and immediately became terrified. This man's lack of emotion scared Jimmy. His face was stoic and hard like stone.

"Jimmy...why do you want to cause trouble? All I wanted to do was read my book and head down the road. But I can't do that when

18

there's a lunatic waving a gun at people." Vance's words were calm, cold, and quiet. Jimmy didn't fight at all...he was too terrified.

"It's not loaded," the cook said as he held up the gun and empty magazine.

"This guy's from around here, I take it?" Vance asked, without taking his eyes off Jimmy. His sunglasses were on, like they usually were. That probably added a little bit to the fear factor for whoever was on the receiving end of his smite.

"Yeah...unfortunately. He's just a young punk who wants everything given to him," the cook answered.

"Aren't they all like that?" Diana put in her two cents.

"That's how we got into this mess in the first place. We bred generations of people who wanted everything handed to them. They didn't know how to work for it. You'd think The Fall would have changed people, but it didn't." Vance spoke softly. Not with malice, or even frustration, but as if he were stating a simple fact. He loosened his grip on Jimmy's neck, but didn't let go.

"Don't bother these people anymore. If they let you back in here, expect to pay for your food," Vance told him. Jimmy nodded his head as much as he could with being pinned down to the counter. Vance let him go and he ran out of the diner.

"Thanks," Diana said to him.

"Yeah...thanks..." the cook said as well.

Vance walked back over to his table.

"Take this. Not much use to us," the cook said as he placed the handgun on the counter. Vance grabbed it, shoved it in his backpack, and started heading toward the door.

"Don't you want some sort of payment? Something we can give you as a thank you?" the cook asked as Vance put his hand on the door.

"Shouldn't thank someone for doing the right thing. It's like everyone's forgotten their humanity," Vance said without looking at them. He pushed the door open.

"Wait," Diana said.

19

She grabbed something and ran around the counter.

"Take this," she said, and grabbed Vance's hand. In it she placed a tea towel with something wrapped inside it.

"Two biscuits and some jelly," she said with a smile. Vance looked down at his hand. He wasn't so much focused on what she had placed in his hand as he was on the fact that another human being was touching him out of kindness. He wasn't used to much human interaction anymore.

"That isn't necessary, but thank you," he said, then walked out of the door.

"That's one scary son of a bitch," the cook said.

"Yeah...he is. Good thing he's not a bad guy," Diana replied as she stared at the door.

***

Vance trudged onward down the road. He was about two blocks away from the diner when he heard shouting behind him.

"That's him! That's the mother fucker!" Vance turned around and saw Jimmy about half a block away. He was accompanied by four other young men.

"Stop!" one of them yelled.

Vance continued walking until he heard the footsteps getting closer. He then turned around and pointed his M4 at the group of men.

"Fuck!" Jimmy yelled.

"We don't even have any guns!" another shouted.

"So I'm just supposed to let you mug me? I'm on a mission, and there is *nothing* that is going to stop me." Vance raised his voice a little and swept his M4 from left to right, giving all of the boys the opportunity to look down the barrel of his assault rifle.

"Fuck it man...let him go..." Jimmy said after feeling that same fear as before consume him.

"Fuck that! Get this mother fucker!" said one of the braver—or less intelligent—members of the group.

20

The young man rushed forward empty-handed, presumably to tackle Vance. He probably assumed his comrades would follow him into battle. It didn't happen. Vance struck him hard across the face with the butt of his rifle. The boy fell to the ground like a rag doll. The other boys stepped back, eyes wide.

"The next one to charge me gets a fucking bullet..." Vance said matter-of-factly.

"He's fuckin' lyin'. He could've shot Dustin but he didn't! Rush him!" one of the boys said.

"No...no...he's tellin' the truth," Jimmy managed to spit out. He stared into Vance's eyes, and he saw something inside him that turned him pale as a ghost. Vance continued keeping his M4 trained on the boys.

"Let's...let's just go..." Jimmy said as he backed up even more, then ran off. The other three boys backed up as well, but didn't run.

Vance lowered his M4 and took off walking again. He looked over his shoulder and saw them dragging their fallen comrade out of the road.

***

Two days had passed, and as the sun lowered itself in the sky Vance realized he was tired of sleeping out on the road. Vance passed the road sign for Somers, New York. He was nearly out of water, and would have to find a place to sleep soon. He didn't want to spend another night out on the road. Obviously, he couldn't afford to keep paying rent every night. He would sleep out in No Man's Land for a couple of nights, then usually tried to find somewhere to lay his head for a night so he could get some good rest. This lifestyle was not new to him. There were plenty of places he had traveled to on foot as a courier. Unless he was traveling across the country, or across a couple of states, he always went out on foot or on a horse. It was more economical that way. Train tickets were extremely expensive, and only metals were accepted as payment. For his train ticket from

Albuquerque to Boston, for example, he was forced to pay fifty pounds of scrap iron. Of course, he didn't personally pay that. The company he worked for did.

Vance entered the town proper of Somers, or what was left of it. This particular town had been hit hard. Or rather, it hadn't been built back up like other places had. For whatever reason, it closely resembled a ghost town. The inhabitants all looked like bandits and raiders. Some carried guns, and Vance had a sneaking suspicion that a lot of them were loaded. Somers looked more like a large town that had been taken over by a war lord.

"Gotta pay the toll," a man said as he approached Vance. Two more men followed him. One had a shotgun. Apparently Vance's suspicion had been correct, at least in part.

"Toll?" Vance asked.

"To pass through our town," the man told him.

"And what's to stop me from walking around this shit hole?" Vance asked as he looked at the three men.

"You're here now, so that means you gotta pay the toll." The man had a heavily worn toothpick hanging out of his mouth.

"What's in this town that makes it so spectacular?" Vance asked.

"We got a brothel, a bar, an inn, and a couple merchants," the guy said.

"Do you have clean water?" Vance asked him.

"Yeah."

"You like toothpicks?" Vance asked abruptly. The man looked at him funny.

"Toothpicks?" the man asked.

"I see you have a toothpick in your mouth. Looks like you've had it awhile," Vance said as he pulled off his backpack and dug through a pocket, "Here."

He handed the man a small box of toothpicks. The man opened up the box, saw the toothpicks inside, and briefly smiled.

"What if this isn't enough to get you in?" the man asked. He was obviously testing the outsider.

"Then I kill all three of you and take my payment back. Better stick with the toothpicks," Vance quickly replied. The man lost his smile, but quickly recovered.

"Let him pass," he said, then chuckled.

Vance stepped past the three men, not overly enthusiastic about being in this town. It looked like its only inhabitants were scum. No matter...he would get his water, sleep through the night, and leave at first light. He wouldn't worry about other people's problems here. Worrying about other people's problems in a place like this could get him killed.

Vance stood in front of the bar/brothel/inn. The guard had failed to mention that all three of the establishments were in the same building. More economical that way, or so Vance assumed.

"What'll it be?" the barkeep asked as Vance walked in.

"Just some water and a room for one night," Vance told him as he pulled out the sunglasses and a handful of wet wipes.

"You'll have to do better than that, cowboy," the old barkeep growled.

"And these." Vance sat a pack of cigarettes on the counter. The barkeep opened the top of the box and looked inside.

"This pack is only half full," he complained.

"Consider that as me being generous," Vance told him.

"I like that little flashlight you got there on your vest," the barkeep said as he pointed.

"Not a chance. Take what I offered," Vance said, without looking down at the flashlight.

"Alright, alright...fine. Here's your key." The barkeep handed Vance a room key. This place was fancy, keys to the rooms and all.

After getting one of his canteens filled, Vance walked upstairs to room number two. There were stains all over the wallpaper in the hallway, and the entire place reeked of stale cigarettes, rotten food, and sex. After opening the door and stepping into the room, Vance noticed a woman sitting on the bed. She wasn't an attractive woman, either. Not that that made much different to Vance.

23

"Hi there," the woman said.

Vance opened the door to his room and motioned for her to leave.

"No way...you're not getting rid of me that easily," she said with a smile.

"Yes I am. Get out," Vance told her.

"What you got there in that bag? I'm real cheap..." she began.

"I have no doubt that you are, miss. Now please leave," Vance said to her. He had even said please.

"You want me to go down there and tell them that you're not paying for me?" the woman asked.

"That's exactly what I want you to do. Now go." Vance pointed toward the hallway once more.

"No one pays for a room here and doesn't buy a girl!" she complained.

"I do. I pay for a room and don't buy a girl. Now leave. That's the last time I'm telling you," Vance said.

"Fuck you, asshole! Give me something and I'll leave..."

Vance sat down his backpack and M4 and headed toward the bed.

"Get off me!" the woman yelled.

Vance picked her up, walked out into the hallway, and dropped her flat on her ass.

"You mother fucker! I'm telling Ricky!" she screamed. Vance slammed the door shut and locked it. He didn't know who Ricky was, nor did he care.

Soon enough, a man started yelling and banging on the door. He was going on about how Vance had assaulted one of his girls, and had refused to buy her. Vance told him to go away several times. Finally, after almost fifteen minutes, the man went away. Apparently it wasn't worth it to the man to break down the door and confront whatever was on the other side. Vance fell asleep shortly after, his M4 laying across his chest.

***

Vance woke up the next morning a little later than he had expected to. His watch said it was 7:30 AM. He got everything together and left the shitty motel room. After walking downstairs to return the room key, he quickly realized that he wasn't going to be able to simply leave. Five men and the bartender all stopped what they were doing and stared at him. Vance handed the key to the barkeep, who glanced at the room number attached to the key and said, "That's him."

"So, you're the one who tried to beat up my girl," a man said as he rose from a table. His four goons got up as well. All of them had cigarettes in their mouths.

"I don't want any trouble. I didn't beat her up. I just didn't want a prostitute, that's all," Vance said as he backed up a bit. It wasn't that he was scared...he just wanted a larger reactionary gap between him and the bad guys.

"My name's Ricky," the guy began.

"I figured as much," said Vance.

"I own this place, and I own all the girls," Ricky continued.

"Quite the nobleman, aren't you?" Vance said.

"At the Red Palace, everyone pays for a girl when they stay the night. Everyone." Ricky had a devilish smile on his face. He didn't look like he was any older than 25 or so.

"'Red Palace'? What is this, the Soviet Union?" Vance asked. The men looked at each other, obviously confused. While no one in the room was old enough to have been alive during the Soviet Union's existence, Vance had at least studied history extensively before The Fall. He even studied it afterward, when he got the chance.

"Who the fuck do you think you are? A tough guy? Just because you got guns? That might make you a tough guy most places, but around here it just makes you a target," Ricky slowly started stepping closer. Vance casually moved his right hand just a little closer to his sidearm, his M4 gripped tightly in his left hand and hanging by his

25

side.

"Drop everything and we'll let you walk out of here. Consider it payment for assaulting one of my girls and refusing to pay for service." Ricky pointed at him with one hand and flicked his cigarette on the floor with the other. Apparently he didn't take too much pride in keeping his establishment clean.

Vance took another step backward. The four goons standing beside Ricky started reaching behind their backs. Vance quickly drew his Glock and started pumping rounds into them from right to left. Two of the thugs recoiled back at the gunshots, but Vance rewarded their hesitation by putting them down anyway. He skipped over Ricky, who wasn't grabbing for a gun. All four of the goons dropped to the floor, all four either dead or horribly injured. Vance heard a noise to his left, and out of the corner of his eye he saw the barkeep reach for something behind the counter. Vance turned his attention to the bartender, who came back up with a shotgun. Vance fired two shots into his chest. The bartender fell backwards to the floor, inadvertently pulling the trigger as he did so and putting a nice hole in the ceiling. Vance holstered his Glock and approached Ricky, who was frozen from shock. One of the goons—who had two holes in his abdomen—slowly brought up a handgun and started to point it at Vance. Vance drew his Glock once more and fired a round into the man's head, barely looking at him to aim before doing so. It was all muscle memory for him. Point and shoot.

"I...I..." Ricky stuttered.

"Can't I go anywhere without having problems?" Vance asked rhetorically.

"Just...just go..." Ricky told him.

"Yeah...like you're giving me permission? Sit down." Vance pushed the muzzle of his Glock into Ricky's chest, forcing him down into a nearby chair. He then went over and locked the front door and stuck a chair in front of it.

"Now...you and I are going to have a little bonding time," Vance told him as he approached Ricky once more.

26

"Yeah...right..." Ricky said. He was starting to sweat.

"Where do you keep the goods?" Vance asked.

"Behind...behind the counter..." Ricky was nearing a state of panic.

"Good boy. I'm going to take a look through it, and if you move I'm going to put a round through your skull. Understand?" Vance made his way behind the counter.

There was a large footlocker with a padlock on it sitting behind the counter. Vance took a quick look around, but saw nothing of value.

"Toss me the key. I'm sure it's around your neck or in a pocket," Vance ordered. Ricky pulled a key from around his neck and threw it in Vance's direction.

Vance caught the key and removed the padlock. Inside the footlocker was a plethora of goods. Bottles of water, a few handguns, some ammunition, jewelry, gloves, socks, knives...it seemed to be an assortment of very valuable items. People apparently paid good money to sleep with Ricky's whores. Vance removed a handgun, almost a full carton of cigarettes, the only two bottles of water, several bars of lye soap, several pairs of socks and two pairs of gloves, a handful of jewelry, and a nice hunting knife. He placed them all on the bar in a somewhat organized fashion, then he sat his backpack beside them and began placing his newly acquired goods inside. Just as he was about to walk back around the bar, he spotted the sunglasses he had traded last night. He grabbed them and stuffed them in his backpack as well.

"Fuckin' asshole..." Ricky said to himself as he dropped his head into his hands.

"What was that?" Vance asked as he turned his attention on Ricky.

"Nothing..."

"Nothing? I'm a fucking asshole, but that's nothing? You're scum," Vance began, though he did so without raising his voice or showing much expression, "You prey on the weak, you make money off of slaves, and to top it all off, you think you're a bad ass. You're the fuckin' asshole, and you're lucky I don't slice your fuckin' neck open."

Ricky leaned back in his chair, eyes wide and mouth hanging open. He was terrified. Vance stepped a little closer to him and drew his tanto sword from his back. He placed it right up against the side of Ricky's neck. Ricky began to beg, but it sounded more like a whine.

"Please...God please...no..."

"God? God doesn't have anything to do with this, kid. It's just you and me." Vance pulled the sword back. Ricky closed his eyes tightly and began openly weeping. After several moments, he opened his eyes and the man in front of him was gone, the front door wide open. Ricky fell out of the chair, down onto his knees, and cried like a little kid whose dog had just died.

***

Vance was making a fast exit. He was walking as quickly as he could, nearly pushing people out of the way in the process. The logical side of him knew without a doubt that he should have killed Ricky.

In the distance behind him he could hear yelling. He had a good head start, assuming they didn't keep a vehicle or two filled with fuel sitting around. Ricky may have been a blubbering mess when Vance had left, but he would surely get his courage back when his people came to his rescue.

Vance was now just outside of town. He moved off the road and down into a tree line. If no one came after awhile, then he was probably safe. About half an hour passed and Vance hadn't seen anyone, so he followed the tree line further away from town.

This was his life now, it seemed. Or at least it would be for awhile. The long trek back to New Mexico would be dangerous. As he continued on, he could see how whatever had happened back West was affecting life around these parts as well. The bad news had put more fear into people. Goods from back West weren't being brought East anymore, and the normal traffic had gone away almost completely.

28

Vance stopped on the side of the road and pulled out a map of the United States. He briefly looked it over, getting an idea of the route he was going to take. He had to avoid the Midwest as much as possible—nuclear bombs had gone off in Missouri years ago, and the whole place was radioactive. The fallout from the blasts had affected the entire area. Nearby states like Indiana, Tennessee, and Arkansas were relatively safe, though no one really ventured toward the borders of Illinois or Missouri.

Vance marked his tentative route in pencil, sticking to highways as much as possible. He then folded up the map, placed it back in its plastic sleeve and continued on his journey. It was going to be a rough road, walking all the way across the country. He had never walked the whole way before. Perhaps with any luck, he would find someone traveling West by way of horse and wagon, maybe hitch a ride with them. But that wasn't likely. Horses were quicker, but they were in very short supply. Most of them had been killed off for food when The Fall happened. The other disadvantage when traveling by horse was feeding them. Horses, of course, required food and water just like people do. Both of those things weren't easily acquired. Every once in awhile, you would see people getting around on motorcycles. Since they were easy to maintain and required a lot less fuel, they were the obvious choice. But pretty much the only people who had those were bandits and raiders who worked for some powerful mayor or governor. Certain areas had a form of government. Towns were ran by mayors, and larger areas were ran by governors. But the feeling of order was usually an illusion. Most of the mayors and governors did little for the people, and instead focused on swinging business in their favor. Most were the leaders of bandit and raider groups.

So Vance continued on, determined with completing the mission. There wasn't much left to live for, but what was left was certainly valuable to him.

29

2

James Vance was entering Charleston, West Virginia. Nearly two weeks had passed since he had left Somers, New York. Those two weeks hadn't been overly enjoyable, but they hadn't been terrible, either. He had only been messed with once, and the small group of bandits had regretted it. Other than that, the journey had been peaceful.

Vance made his way into Charleston, which was the seat of the regional government. Again, this particular government was crooked as a dog's hind leg. Vance had been here once before, when he delivered some family heirlooms to a man who had just lost his father. The government here was a large group of "former" bandits, ran by a mysterious man whom everyone called, "Wild Bill". But Wild Bill and his group of thieves ensured a steady supply of clean water, and they protected most of the merchants in the area. Ironic, really— bandits who were protecting merchants, rather than robbing them. But make no mistake...you did what they told you to do, or you weren't protected anymore.

The city was bustling with merchants and potential customers. Everyone had a goal in mind for the day. Some were more enthusiastic than others, but everyone had something that they needed to get done. Vance walked on past the merchants and into a rundown motel. Inside there were a few people playing cards, and the front desk had been converted into a small bar.

"Drink?" the barkeep asked.

"Just water," Vance replied as he pulled out his two canteens and opened up his hydration pack.

"That's a lot of water," the barkeep commented.

"Yeah. Give me a minute to pull out some goods," Vance said.

Vance pulled out Jimmy's 9mm handgun and placed it on the counter. He then pulled out half a box of 9mm ammunition as well.

"I also want a room for two nights," Vance said.

"Does it work?" the barkeep asked as he looked inside the box of ammunition. Vance quickly disassembled the 9mm.

"All the parts are there. I've never fired it, but I don't see why it wouldn't work," he said.

"I see. Well, you look like you might know a thing or two about firearms," the barkeep said, looking at Vance's gear, "You have a deal. Hang around for a few and I'll have my boy get you all the water you need."

Vance had no use for the 9mm, and it was weight he didn't need to carry. He still had one more extra handgun in his pack—the one from Ricky's bar—and he would eventually trade that off, too.

A boy—no older than 10 or 11—was pushing a cart with a cooler on it. He wheeled it up to the bar and started filling up Vance's canteens and hydration pack. When he was done, Vance took a drink from one of the canteens and pulled his head back a bit. The water was ice cold.

"Cold water?" he asked.

"Yep," the boy said, "We have a little power. Dad put a couple windmills on top of the motel."

"That's good," Vance said as he took another drink, "Wish more people would be that resourceful."

"Dad is definitely resourceful," the boy said, and wheeled the cart away. Pretty soon the barkeep—the boy's father—came back and handed Vance a room key.

31

"I see you met my boy. How do you like that water?" he asked as he wiped down the counter.

"It's fantastic. He told me you put some windmills on top of the motel." Vance stuffed his hydration pack into his backpack.

"Yep. It's not a perfect system, but it gets us a little power. Enough for cold water and to light this place up occasionally." The barkeep seemed to be a good enough guy. He was in his late forties, balding on top, and had a portly belly.

"Business good?" Vance asked.

"We fair pretty well. Folks around here appreciate an honest businessman, as well as cold water." The barkeep pulled up a stool and sat down in front of Vance.

"What's your name, stranger?" he asked.

"James Vance. Just call me Vance."

"Nice to meet you. I'm Bob Frederick." Bob stuck out his hand. Vance shook it and continued sipping on his water.

"Pleasure to meet you," Vance said.

"Where are you from?" Bob asked.

"Back West. New Mexico."

"Heard there was nothing left back West," Bob said with wide eyes.

"Yeah. I heard that too." Vance looked down at his canteen, trying not to think about the state of affairs back home.

"Where you headed?"

"Back West."

"I see. Hope the rumors are wrong," Bob said with a comforting smile.

"So do I, but they're not. People wouldn't be acting this way if the stories weren't true," Vance said to him.

"You might be right about that. So what brought you all the way to West Virginia?" Bob asked as he placed his elbows on the counter and leaned forward.

"I'm a courier. Had to deliver a package to Boston."

"A courier? Hell, I've got a lot of respect for you guys," Bob said.

32

Couriers were usually looked upon pretty highly. They transported goods, delivered messages, sometimes protected people...they were a big reason why society had been able to continue as it had. They were one of the few elements of the New World that still represented at least some level of normalcy.

"Thanks," Vance replied.

"What company do you work for?" Bob asked him.

"Rocky Mountain Courier Service. Or at least, I did. Not sure if it's still around anymore."

"That's a fine company, or so I've heard."

"Yeah." Vance took a few large gulps from his canteen.

"Hungry?"

"A little. What do you have?" Vance asked.

"Eggs, squirrel, rabbit, venison...the usual stuff," Bob told him.

"I'll take a venison steak, if you got it," Vance eagerly said as he began rummaging around in his pack.

"I'll tell you what...I'll cook you up a fine steak if you do a little something for me," Bob offered.

"I suppose that depends on what the job is," Vance said as he stopped looking through his backpack.

"I've got a little problem with a couple hooligans. They come in here and threaten me, get drunk, start fights...I want them to know their place around here. Wild Bill—he's the governor—he won't do anything about it. I understand, of course. It's a small concern for him. But we don't have much security around here, at least not enough to patrol the streets. The two boys are brothers, young guys. What do you say?"

"What did you have in mind?" Vance asked.

"Just scare 'em off. Maybe rough 'em up a little if you have to. You look like you can handle that," Bob said. Vance thought about it.

"Fine," he said.

"Great. But no guns...I don't want them killed," Bob said as he left the counter and walked to the back room, presumably to cook up Vance's steak.

33

A short time later, Bob came back with a beautiful looking steak. He sat it in front of Vance and took his seat on the stool across from him. Vance began cutting up the steak, preparing to savor the flavor.

"Good?" Bob asked.

"Definitely. It's very good. You know...I hardly miss steak sauce anymore," Vance said, trying to make small talk. Bob laughed a little.

"I do," the barkeep said.

Vance finished his steak while the two conversed back and forth. He took his time, enjoying the wonderful cut of meat as well as the company of a kind individual. Bob's boy joined them—his name was Charlie, and he was 11 years old—when Vance was about halfway through his steak.

"Those troublemakers should be showing up pretty soon now," Bob said, about an hour later.

"Billy and Brad..." Charlie said with a sigh.

"Our new friend here is going to take care of them, Charlie. He's going to scare them off," Bob said to his son, placing his hand on the boy's head and ruffling up his hair. Charlie smiled and pulled away.

"Let me put my things in the room, then I'll be back down." Vance got up from the bar.

The motel room was clean enough. It had a single oil lamp in the corner, a bathroom inside the room (which obviously didn't work), and a nice queen-sized bed. It wouldn't be a bad place to stay for a couple of nights. Vance surely needed the break. After leaving everything in his room except for the handgun on his thigh, Vance made his way back downstairs. It felt good to move around without all that extra weight. With his two vests, his rifle, the back pack with the shotgun and all the goods inside, and the tanto sword, Vance was weighted down nearly all the time. Walking around with nothing but his t-shirt, BDU pants and thigh rig on was a godsend.

Downstairs, people were making their way into the motel. Bob was busy serving drinks and haggling with people. Vance took a seat at the bar and Charlie served him a glass with alcohol in it.

"What is it?" Vance asked.

"A guy across town makes it. Whiskey," Charlie answered. Vance took a small sip. He didn't normally drink, at least not when he was on the road.

Pretty soon, two loud young men entered the motel. Vance assumed they were Brad and Billy, the two hooligans Bob had hired him to take care of.

"There they are," Charlie whispered to him. Vance looked over at Bob, who nodded his head at him. He would wait until they became a problem.

***

A couple of hours passed, and Brad and Billy were getting a little loud. Thus far, Vance hadn't seen them do anything that would qualify them as a nuisance. Everyone needed to let loose every once in awhile, and this was a bar, after all. Just as Vance thought that he might make it out of this without having to do any real work, Brad threw a chair across the room and challenged everyone to a fight. Most of the patrons laughed, but it seemed like Brad was pretty serious about it. Billy joined him in his attempt to pick a fight.

"Come on! Come on!" Brad yelled.

Vance slowly stood up and approached the brothers.

"We've got a taker!" Billy shouted with a smile as he tapped his brother on the shoulder.

"You two need to leave," Vance told them calmly. The brothers looked at each other, confused.

"Wait...you're telling us that we need to leave?" Brad asked.

"That's right. The owner of this place doesn't want you here." Vance stood about four feet away, ready to pounce on one or both of them if it was needed.

"How's that different than any other night?" Billy laughed.

"You boys need to go!" Bob shouted, "You come in here and start fights, tear up my stuff, threaten me and my patrons...you're not welcome here!"

"Shut up, old man!" Brad yelled across the room.

"Have some respect. Find somewhere else to drink," Vance said.

"And who the hell are you?" Billy asked as he began circling Vance, "You've got some nice boots there. Nice holster, nice gun. I'd like to have some nice things like that."

"So go find them or buy them," Vance said.

"I've already found them. I just gotta take 'em." Billy smiled.

"I'm going to tell you boys one last time to leave, then I start breaking things. Leave," Vance said, calm as ever.

"You hear that, Brad? He's going to start breaking things! He must be talking about chairs and shit, because I know he's not talking about us!" Billy was getting angry now.

Vance grabbed Billy by the neck and tossed him to the side. The young man tripped over a chair and fell on his ass. Brad charged forward and took a wild swing at Vance, who stepped to the side and dodged it. Patrons started getting up from tables to make room for the brawl that they believed was surely going to ensue.

Vance stood his ground and allowed the boys to regroup. If he was really going to teach them a lesson, he needed to do it the right way. Billy picked up a mug and Brad grabbed a chair. They were ready to fight now. Vance stood in front of them nonchalantly, arms down by his side.

"You're gonna die now, old man," Billy said through gritted teeth. Vance held his hands out, as if saying *Come on, then*.

Billy rushed forward, and was met with a boot to the chest. He fell to the ground once more and began gasping for air. Brad wildly swung the chair from side to side as he approached Vance, who didn't even move. Vance grabbed the leg of the chair as it flew toward his head. He threw it straight down, ripping it from Brad's hands and bouncing it off the floor. He then grabbed Brad by his shirt collar, threw the boy's head forward, and connected his knee with Brad's nose. The young man fell to the floor like a rag doll, blood gushing from his face. Billy got back up, still a little winded, and pulled out a large pocket knife.

"Sure you want to go there, boy?" Vance asked him. The stakes had been raised now that Billy was holding an instrument designed to kill.

"Drop the knife!" Bob said from across the bar. Vance looked over and saw him holding a shotgun. The other patrons dove for the floor in case gunfire erupted.

"You mother fucker!" Billy growled as he ran toward Vance.

Vance stepped to the side and kicked Billy in his knee, causing him to collapse once more. He then stepped on the hand that was holding the knife, twisting his boot as he did so. An ugly crunching noise was heard. The knife rolled out of Billy's hand and the boy screamed. Vance formed his hand into a fist and struck Billy in the face several times. A cut formed above his left eye, another on his lip. He then grabbed the boy by his foot and dragged him outside. He did the same with Brad, who was just now starting to come around a bit. Both boys were out of commission for awhile, and Bob wouldn't have to worry about them causing any problems for at least a couple of weeks. Just to be on the safe side, Vance decided to give them another message.

"You think you're tough," Vance said as he knelt down beside Billy, "But you're not. You're both just scared little boys. You know what I did before The Fall? I was in the Special Forces. You fucked with the wrong guy tonight. And I'm not the only one who could end you...there are many other older guys all over the place who have a lot less control than I do. Before long, you're going to get killed. Settle down."

Vance casually walked back inside and the patrons began clapping. Whether it was because they were glad the two problem children were gone or because they enjoyed the show, he wasn't sure.

"Thank you," Bob said to him.

"One question. Why didn't you pull the trigger when he had the knife?" Vance asked.

"No shells. I ran out a few weeks ago when raiders came into town," Bob told him.

"I see."

Vance hung around the bar for a few more minutes, then retired for the night. His feet hurt, and so did his head. Not because he drank too much—he had only taken a few sips of the whiskey. His head hurt because of lack of good sleep. That would be fixed tonight.

<u>3</u>

"Come play with me, Daddy!"
"What are we playing?"
"Hide and seek!"
"Hide and seek? You always beat me at that."
"So? You've been gone forever! I've missed you!"
"I've missed you too, sweetheart..."

Vance abruptly sat up in bed. He was breathing heavily and sweating. Memories were haunting him in his dreams again.

He got up, drank some water, and decided to make a journey to wherever the closest pond was to wash up. It had been three days since he had bathed, and wet wipes only got a man so far. Especially when he was constantly walking and sweating. Vance put on all his gear and went downstairs. After speaking for a minute with Bob and learning where the closest pond was, Vance exited the bar and began the journey. After about thirty minutes of walking, he had finally arrived at a small pond. It was situated in the middle of a circle of houses. Not a bad place to live, really. Too bad most houses had been burnt to the ground or destroyed in some other way.

Vance put all of his gear into a pile and sat his sawed-off shotgun on a nearby rock. After stripping all of his clothes off, he got in the water and began scrubbing himself with a bar of lye soap. The water was cold, so the bath was quick. He then dried himself off with a towel and changed into some clean clothes. After washing out his other pair of clothes, he put on all his gear and headed back to the motel.

Once inside, Vance hung his wet clothes up in his motel room and read his book. He pulled out a couple slices of bread and ate his breakfast while he read. Quiet times like this were cherished. Being on the road all the time, Vance rarely got the opportunity to relax.

The rest of the day passed by all too quickly. Vance talked extensively with Bob and Charlie, though they did most of the talking. Vance listened intently and drank cold water (which Bob gave him for free), ensuring he was properly hydrated for the journey ahead. He planned to walk a couple hundred miles before staying in another town. When the day was over, Vance passed out on the all too comfortable bed in his motel room. He surely wished he could call this place home. There was little doubt that Bob would allow him to stay permanently. The man seemed to like him quite a bit, though Vance couldn't figure out why. He was quiet and calculating, not someone who made friends easily.

***

Vance awoke to gunfire. For a moment he couldn't tell if it was a dream or reality. He quickly jumped out of bed and put on all of his gear, grabbing his backpack in case he needed to make a quick exit. The gunfire was getting closer, and as he made his way down the hallway it began to sound like it was right out front of the motel. He shouldered his M4 and tactically made his way down the stairs. Bob was hiding behind the bar, holding the handgun Vance had sold him two days ago. Charlie was knelt down beside him.

"Vance! Get down!" Bob yelled over the gunfire.

Vance took cover behind the wall at the bottom of the stairs. The battle was certainly right out front. He couldn't see anything through

40

the windows, but he heard screams and the familiar chatter of gunfire within fifty feet or so.

"Bob! You and the boy need to get upstairs!" Vance said from around the corner.

"Goddamn raiders! Trying to burn the whole town down!" Bob yelled to himself.

"Bob! Come on!" Vance said again, raising his voice a little more.

Vance peeked around the corner and saw Bob running toward him, Charlie directly in front of his father. At that moment the front door burst open. Bob and Charlie were blocking Vance's line of sight, but they were nearly to safety. The window broke and a Molotov cocktail came flying in, setting the room ablaze. Bob stumbled and fell as the flames consumed half of the bar. Charlie kept running, finally reaching Vance. Vance pulled him behind him so that the child was safely behind the wall. Bob started to get back up, but raiders poked their heads inside through the front door. Muzzles from their firearms could be seen bobbing around.

"Get down!" Vance yelled to Bob as he aimed his rifle and fired. The round caught one of the raiders right in the forehead, dropping him like a ton of bricks.

"Holy hell!" Bob screamed. He was flattened against the floor. The portly man rolled over onto his back and started firing his handgun in the direction of the door.

"Just come on!" Vance screamed at him, "I'll cover you!"

Bob got to his feet, but another Molotov cocktail flew in through the doorway. It hit about five feet from Bob, setting his legs on fire and causing him to fall down once more.

"Shit!" Vance yelled as he started popping off rounds in the direction of the doorway and carefully advancing toward Bob.

Bob screamed as he swatted at the fire.

The bar was beginning to fill with smoke. In a very short amount of time, flames had made their way across the bar and had completely consumed it. As the vicious fire approached Bob, Vance grabbed a

41

hold of his collar and dragged him toward the stairs. The fire on his pant legs went out as Vance pulled him. Charlie was poking his head around the corner, terrified.

A gunshot was heard coming from behind them. Vance felt Bob jerk violently. Looking down, he saw a blood spot spreading across Bob's chest.

"We need to get out of here!" Vance yelled to Charlie.

"What...what happened...?" Charlie stuttered.

"We need a way out! Now!" Vance growled.

"The...the back door..." Charlie answered, his eyes fixated on his father. Vance began dragging Bob down the hallway.

Raiders flooded into the hallway, presumably from the back door. Vance squeezed the trigger on his assault rifle as fast as he could, firing from the hip so that he could keep moving forward and drag Bob. Within seconds, a small pile of four or five bodies had formed in the hallway.

"Grab a gun!" Vance said to Charlie. The boy picked up a sawed-off shotgun that had been dropped by one of the raiders.

Vance dragged Bob toward the back door, holding his rifle up as best he could. He wasn't sure how badly injured Bob was. The man was still moving and groaning, so at least he wasn't dead yet. The three of them made it out of the back door, the fire following them as they went. Vance dragged Bob off to the side, behind a wooden privacy fence. Charlie stood in front of his dead father, bouncing back and forth.

"What happened!? What happened to my dad!?" Charlie began to panic.

"Calm down! Keep your eyes out there...watch for raiders! Don't turn around!" Vance said to him, physically turning the boy's body toward the road.

Raiders were running around like wild men, screaming for anarchy and looting as much as they could. Apparently the anarchy that had occurred just nine years prior hadn't been enough for them. They were shooting down people in the streets, setting buildings on

42

fire, and laughing the whole way.

Vance rolled Bob onto his back and looked at the wound. The bullet had hit him just below his sternum. Blood was gushing from it. Vance rolled him onto his side and saw a gaping exit wound on his back. Bob was spitting up blood now, gurgling as he did so. Vance instinctively applied pressure to the wound, but then noticed the trail of blood they had left from the back door. Reality hit him, and he realized that there was no saving this man. He had maybe another minute before he died.

"Is he okay?" Charlie asked anxiously, his eyes still looking out toward the road.

Vance opened a pouch on his backpack and dug through it. He pulled out a morphine syrette—one of only two he had—and jammed the needle into Bob's thigh. Within seconds, Bob stopped thrashing about and relaxed. He looked around for a few brief moments, then his final breath exited his body. There was no need to let him live the last moments of his life in horrible agony.

Vance got up and looked over at Charlie, who was rocking from side to side. He was still keeping watch, though. Vance walked over to him and looked out on the street. The raiders had passed, and were now down the road quite a ways. It sounded like they were in a gunfight with another group.

"Charlie...listen to me..." Vance said after deciding it was safe to let his guard down. He took a knee in front of the boy.

"My...my dad..." Charlie said as he looked over at his father's body.

"He's dead, Charlie. I did everything I could, but the raiders got him good," Vance told him. He removed the shotgun from Charlie's hands, knowing that the boy was likely to have an emotional meltdown.

Instead, Charlie just dropped his head and began quietly crying. He showed considerable control. After wiping away a few tears, he once again looked over at his father. Staring at him only made it worse, for the boy dropped down to his knees and began weeping.

43

***

Vance loaded up Bob's body in the back of a small cart, then started pulling it out toward the pond. There was a small graveyard there, filled with bodies from after The Fall. Charlie accompanied him.

"Too bad we don't have anyone to help us," Charlie said after ten minutes or so.

"That's alright," Vance grunted as he kept pulling the cart over the rough terrain.

"We didn't have a whole lot of friends around here. The two good ones we had were killed by the raiders, too," Charlie continued, "And Reggie...the guy who guarded our water for us...no one can find him. I doubt he would have helped us anyway. All he cared about was getting paid with whiskey."

Vance didn't answer. He just kept leading the cart to the pond. They were about halfway there.

"Reggie was alright. He never did anything bad. It's just all he cared about was drinkin'," Charlie said.

Vance sat the cart down and took a short break.

"Want me to help?" Charlie asked.

"That's alright, boy. I can manage," Vance replied.

"You look tired."

"I'm fine. Just needed to catch my breath a bit." Vance placed his hands on his head and breathed deeply.

"Bet it's not easy pulling that over this rough ground," Charlie commented. The boy was obviously trying to avoid the thought of his father dying.

Vance grabbed the handles of the cart and started pulling again. Before long they arrived at the pond. The small cemetery sat off to the right just a little ways.

"Where do you want him?" Vance asked.

"Right here is as good a spot as any," Charlie said.

Vance started digging. It was grueling work, but luckily the ground was pretty soft. After about an hour of digging almost non-stop, Vance stuck the shovel in the ground and sat down.

"Want me to dig for awhile?" Charlie asked as he reached for the shovel.

"No. Sit down," Vance quickly replied.

"I can help..."

"No. A boy shouldn't have to dig his own father's grave," Vance said sharply. Charlie sat down next to him and started playing with a blade of grass.

After a few minutes of rest and about half a canteen of water, Vance got up and resumed digging. Almost another full hour passed, and he was nearly done. After another break and another thirty minutes of digging, Vance finished the grave and took a step back to see if it was satisfactory. The hole was about four feet deep, three feet wide, and six feet long. It would serve its purpose.

Vance pulled Bob's body out of the cart and threw it over his shoulder. Charlie remained sitting in the grass, staring at the ground. Vance placed Bob's body in the grave as gently as he could, then began shoveling dirt over top of him.

"Wish we could get a casket or something..." Charlie said after a couple minutes.

"Why's that?" Vance grunted as he shoveled dirt into the grave.

"I dunno...just seems like it would be better..."

"His body's going back to the earth either way," Vance said.

"That's kind of a mean thing to say right now," Charlie quickly responded. Vance stuck the shovel into the ground and looked at Charlie.

"No, it's not. We all go back to the earth, boy. It's just a matter of time. We came from all this. Everything around you is connected. The trees, the grass, the animals...hell, even the water in front of us. A casket only delays the reunion. To me, it only seems proper to let someone go back where they came from as soon as possible. That way they start living again that much quicker." Vance picked up the shovel

45

and went to work again.

"What do you mean 'start living again'?" Charlie asked.

"Well...not the same way as they did before. But their body goes back to the earth, and they become part of it. Then flowers grow, grass grows, trees grow...see what I mean?" Vance explained.

"Not really," Charlie said.

"I'll explain it another time."

Vance shoveled as much dirt into the grave as he could. When he was done, he took a few drinks of water and wiped his brow. Charlie stood up and approached the grave. Vance walked over to the cart and pulled out the small cross they had made, then stuck it in the ground. Carved into the wooden cross were the words, "Bob Frederick – 2004-2050".

"Want to say something?" Charlie asked as he turned to Vance.

"No...I'm no good at stuff like that," he said.

"Well we've got to say something," Charlie told him.

"Fine..." Vance placed his hands in front of him and looked down at the ground, fighting back the awkward and uncomfortable feelings that the situation caused him. He was by no means a religious person, so everything he was about to say was for Charlie's benefit, "Bob, I didn't know you very well. But I learned quickly that you're a hell of a nice guy. I appreciate everything you did for me the past two days— all of the pleasant conversations, the delicious steak, the free water— but most of all I appreciate the fact that I had the pleasure of meeting you. You were a fine man, and a good father. You've raised a fine boy. He's strong and full of life. It's unfortunate that you won't be able to see him grow, but he'll do just fine. He'll be alright, Bob. I've placed you here, next to the pond. I hope that's alright with you. I figured it was a good spot. You're in the earth now, where we all came from and where we all shall go. It was nice to know you, Bob."

A few tears ran down Charlie's face, and he quietly whispered "*I love you, Dad*," under his breath. Vance placed a firm hand on Charlie's shoulder, and the boy abruptly wrapped his arms around Vance's waist and buried his face in his side. Vance blinked several

46

times, not used to physical contact and taken aback by it. He quickly got over it, and staring at the grave, he felt an overwhelming sense of calmness. Perhaps it was just the moment, or perhaps he was simply realizing that someday he would be in the ground as well, away from all of this.

"I'm ready to go now," Charlie said as he wiped the tears from his face.

"Hop in the cart. I'll pull you back to town," Vance told him.

Charlie jumped up in the cart and Vance pulled him all the way back to town. People were cleaning up the mess that the raiders had caused. A strong force of armed guards were walking the streets. Too bad they hadn't been around when the raiders had passed through. Wild Bill probably hadn't known about the raid until it was too late. Damned raiders.

"Hey you!" one of the guards yelled, pointing at Vance.

"What?" Vance yelled back.

"You want to go with us to hit the raiders?" the guard asked.

"Don't go! They'll kill you!" Charlie said as he tugged on Vance's shirt.

"Ain't nobody killin' me, boy," Vance said to him, then to the guard, "How far out?"

"Just a few miles. They got themselves a little camp up on a hill." The guard was making his way over to Vance.

"How many are there?" Vance asked.

"We're not exactly sure. This is the first time they've ever came around here with such force. We're guessing maybe twenty or so."

"And how many men do we have in our posse?" Vance looked around the guard and saw a good-sized group standing in the street.

"About fifteen at the moment. Hoping to recruit some more. It's hard...nobody really has the know-how or the fire power. But you...you look like you could take them on yourself." The guard chuckled slightly.

"Seventeen is enough," Vance said.

"Seventeen? I told you we only have fifteen," the guard said.

"Yeah, but I'm joining you. And I'm good for at least two men," Vance quickly said with a smirk, then began putting on his gear. It never hurt to build up morale a bit.

"Good deal," the guard said with a laugh.

"You can't go!" Charlie told him.

"I *can* go, and I *will* go," Vance said to him as he finished getting everything on.

"No! They might kill you! Don't go!" Charlie begged.

"Don't you want them to pay for what they did to your father?" Vance asked.

"Killing them isn't going to bring Dad back. You're the only one I trust now. Everyone else is gone. If you die, then I'm all alone." Tears welled up in Charlies eyes.

"Listen kid, I hate to tell you this, but I'm an Outlander. I spend most of my time out in No Man's Land. I travel alone. I'm a courier, and I have a very important package to deliver back West." Vance almost felt bad for basically telling the kid that he wasn't going to take him under this wing.

Charlie looked down at the road, then back up to Vance.

"Please don't go," he said.

"I have to, boy. It's the right thing to do."

"But what if something happens?" Charlie asked, his lip quivering.

"Sometimes, boy, it's just about doing the right thing, and to hell with the consequences."

4

"How do we do this?" one of the guards asked the leader, Paulie. Paulie had been the same one who had recruited Vance.

"We're going to sneak up the hill, then once we're up close, we open fire and wipe those bastards out," Paulie said with confidence.

"No...you're going to sneak up that hill and get yourselves killed," Vance interjected.

"And who the hell are you?" one of the guards asked him.

"Hang on...let him tell us what he thinks," Paulie said.

"I didn't know I was going with a group of rookies. Good thing we still have a good mile to go," Vance said as he shook his head.

"Alright, let's think about this. Most of you have shotguns and handguns. A handful of you have hunting rifles. We're expecting to be outnumbered, but we have the element of surprise. I need someone who knows the area to draw the layout in the dirt." Vance crouched down and waited for someone to do as he said.

One of the guys took a stick and dragged it around, forming the hill and some rocks.

"How far is it from these rocks to the camp itself?" Vance asked the man.

"Probably about fifty yards," he answered.

"Alright...those of you who have rifles, go with me. We'll sneak up this side of the hill and take cover behind this area," Vance pointed to the rocks, "The rest of you who have shotguns and handguns, go with Paulie up this side and wait for us to open fire. When you hear us start shooting, wait for about ten seconds before advancing further up the hill and making your assault. This way we'll eliminate our chance of creating a crossfire scenario and we'll have two points of attack. Everyone focus on the sectors in front of you and don't get in over your head."

"What the fuck did you do before The Fall?" Paulie asked. Nearly everyone's eyes were wide and their mouths were hanging open.

"I was in the Special Forces. Now look, this part is very important. Don't rush in. Take cover behind whatever you can and be smart. These guys probably don't have any training, but I'm guessing most of you don't either. Keep your eyes and ears open, and listen for my orders. Our plan depends on them initially focusing on those of us behind the rocks. When I give the word, start advancing. Don't do so until I give the order. Like I said, keep your ears open, it's going to be noisy." Vance stood up and checked his weapon. Almost in unison, the others began doing the same.

"Glad you're on our side," Paulie said as he patted Vance on the shoulder.

"Let's do this. We only have a couple hours of daylight left," Vance told everyone as he began walking toward the hill.

***

The group split up at the base of the hill. Vance led his team of about five men toward the left, and Paulie took his team of ten toward the right. The hill wasn't very steep, but it was steep enough that the camp wasn't visible. Vance had fought on worse terrain.

Vance's group approached the rock formation. He motioned for everyone to stay low and be quiet. He would wait a little while before acting, to give Paulie's group time to get into position. They didn't have the benefit of having a seasoned veteran leading their team.

Vance took the time to scout the camp. A handful of raiders were sitting around a fire pit. A few more were scattered around talking. None of them appeared to be on guard duty, and a lot of them didn't even have any firearms. A few makeshift tents were placed here and there, and the raiders' remaining force was probably inside.

"Take out the ones who have firearms nearby first," Vance said quietly, "Line up your shots, and wait for my order."

Vance brought his assault rifle to his shoulder and looked down the sights. His men did the same with their scoped rifles. Vance gave them about thirty seconds to line up their shots.

"Do it," he said, and started throwing lead downrange.

His men all opened fire at almost exactly the same time. Vance's shots were precise and lethal. There was no return fire until he had dropped three raiders. Then bullets whizzed past.

"Take cover and wait for Paulie!" he told his men. They obeyed, and ducked down behind the rocks with him.

Soon enough, a barrage of gunfire was heard coming from the other side of the hill. Raiders started screaming out orders to each other. There appeared to be very little control.

"Now!" Vance said when the bullets stopped flying past them.

The group popped back up over the rocks and started firing again. Raiders were dropping left and right, and they were returning very little fire. Paulie and his men had followed the plan to the letter. From Vance's position, he couldn't even see most of the other group.

One of Vance's men let out a sharp cry. Vance ignored it and kept firing. The raiders were running around, taking cover behind anything and everything. One even tried to take refuge behind a folding chair, and received a bullet for his trouble.

Most of the raiders were lying on the ground, so Vance popped up around the rocks and slowly advanced toward the camp.

"Move up!" Vance yelled.

Paulie's group appeared from the brush, and Vance's men began following him closely.

"You guys stay here. Take care of the wounded and provide cover from a distance," Vance ordered. His group went back behind the rocks and did as they were told.

Vance met up with Paulie's group, and the team began searching the camp. A few raiders were alive, but they had surrendered. A couple more were found in tents, but they surrendered as well. The group rounded everyone up and placed them in the middle of the camp. The handful of raiders were forced to their knees, and ordered to keep their hands behind their heads. There were eight in total.

"Who's in charge here?" Vance asked with his authoritative voice. No one answered, but several looked toward the end of the line.

"You, huh?" Vance asked as he approached a rough looking man in his late thirties.

"Fuck you," he said.

Vance struck him across the face with the butt of his assault rifle.

"You have to pay for the crimes you have committed," Vance said calmly.

"Which crimes?" the man asked with a smirk.

"Your group killed a lot of people," Vance said, still in a calm tone.

"We're already dead, so what the hell? You all won't let us leave here. Or will you? I know of a great place nearby that has all kinds of supplies..." the leader began.

"I don't care about your supplies. I care about retribution." Vance pulled out his handgun and aimed it at the man's head.

"Wait, wait, wait...!" the leader said as he waved his hands in front of him.

"We should take them all back to town, let the folks see their executions for themselves," Paulie said.

"No. Knowing that the threat has been eliminated is enough," Vance said to him.

"Wild Bill wants them at the town square by sundown," Paulie told him.

"I don't care what Wild Bill wants," Vance said, and pulled the

52

trigger. The round hit the gang leader in the left eye. He fell over, completely limp.

"Jesus Christ!" the nearest raider screamed.

"Christ ain't got nothin' to do with it, son," Vance told him, and shot him in the head as well.

"Hey! What am I supposed to tell Wild Bill?" Paulie complained.

"You tell Wild Bill that James Vance doesn't have the time or the give-a-shit to take these worthless bastards back to town." Vance moved on to the next man, holstering his sidearm as he did so.

"Wouldn't want to waste good bullets, now would we?" he said as he drew the sword from his back.

"Fuck!" the raider screamed as Vance swung the short tanto blade at the man's neck.

The blade had nearly cut his head off. The man fell over on the ground, head flopped over to the side and blood gushing out. Vance walked around behind the rest of the men so they couldn't see him.

"Shit!" one of the raiders said, and took off at a dead sprint.

Vance drove the sword into the soft soil and brought up his rifle. A single shot was fired, and it hit the man between his shoulder blades. He dropped to the ground and writhed around a bit before he bled out. Vance pulled his sword from the ground and swung it at the next guy, hitting him between the neck and shoulder. The blade cut deep, lodging itself in the man's chest cavity. The man bucked and fell to the ground, kicking his feet and waving his arms. He was dead within seconds. Vance finished off the remaining three in this manner. Paulie's men stood off to the side, most averting their eyes. It was a horrible sight, to see a man execute unarmed people in such a terrifying manner. Raiders or not, it was gut-wrenching. A couple of Paulie's men expressed how bad it was by throwing up their supper. Once Vance was done, he cleaned off the blade of his tanto sword on a dead man's pants, then sheathed it.

"Let's go," Paulie said.

53

***

The group arrived back in Charleston after sundown. There wasn't much talking along the way. Vance had stayed at the front of the group, not wanting to deal with the terrible looks they might give him. Once they were safely inside the town proper, Paulie confronted him.

"You did a hell of a thing, helping us out. I appreciate it," he said.

"Didn't do it for you, or this town, really. There's a boy who lost his dad to those men, and his father was a good man. Bob Frederick," Vance told him.

"Don't know him. Whatever your reasons were, thanks for helping us. We might not have made it back," Paulie said.

"Probably not. Speaking of which, your injured guy looks like he needs some water." Vance pointed. One of the men on his team had taken a bullet to the arm. It was only a flesh wound.

"Yeah, we'll take care of him. Thanks again. You stayin' around here?" Paulie asked.

"No. I'm a courier. I've got an important package to deliver back West," Vance replied.

"Too bad. We could use someone like you around here. Hell, you'd probably take the governor's position before long if you stayed," Paulie laughed.

"I'm not one to lord over bandits and thieves," Vance said.

"Right. Well, thanks. You're free to have whatever you want in this town, within reason. I'll put the word out that anything you want to buy is on Wild Bill."

After the two men parted ways, Vance walked over to the cart that was parked outside of Bob's burned down motel. Charlie was still sitting on the end of it, kicking his feet.

"I didn't die," Vance said. Charlie looked up and smiled.

"I was worried. I...I don't have anywhere to go, so I just stayed

54

here." Charlie hopped down from the cart and stared at Vance.

"Well, I'm sure you can find someone to take you in," Vance told him.

"Nobody will. I'm just another mouth to feed, and all the people we were friends with died in the attack," Charlie said to him with sad eyes.

"Let's find somewhere to sleep," Vance said as he took Charlie by the arm.

***

They found refuge inside an old, abandoned business. Several others had found the place as well, and were settling in when they got there. Vance pulled out a blanket from his backpack and threw it out on the ground.

"Try to get some sleep. You've had a long day," he said to Charlie.

"What about you?" Charlie asked as he laid down on the blanket.

"Don't worry about me, boy. Just get some sleep."

Vance stepped outside and lit a cigarette. The cool air was comforting. This part of town was quiet, and most everyone who had been here yesterday was now elsewhere trying to find shelter. A large portion of the people probably left town all together. Vance sat down on the sidewalk and enjoyed his cigarette. Life out this way seemed less orderly. Back West, the governments were a little more organized...and less crooked. They were primarily set up around trade, so most of the people in power were businessmen. Perhaps that was why they were so easily taken by the bandits or raiders or whoever it had been. Vance still wasn't sure what had happened back West. He dreaded finding out, but he had no other choice. The package had to be delivered.

Vance was still a little on edge after the day's events. He pulled up an old chair and sat next to Charlie. Keeping his eye on the door, his mind began to wander. Home. Such a wonderful place compared to here. But when his mind started to call upon certain memories, Vance shook his head and dismissed them. It was funny, really...he just watched a kind man die, a son lose his father, a town get sacked, and he wasn't even focused on any of that. Furthermore, he had assaulted a raider camp and brutally executed eight unarmed men. Again, none of that bothered him. He was broken when it came to matters of death. After witnessing so much of it, a man becomes dull to it. Of course, that mentality was what kept him alive. He obviously had no qualms with killing a man who got in his way. Vance was all for justice, but in today's world justice was hard to find. The thief who would normally get arrested and go on trial in the Old World would get brutally beaten or killed since The Fall. It was just how things had to be now. But Vance had no problems with that. The consequences were well known to everyone. If a person wanted to violate the Laws of Man, then so be it.

***

Vance woke up the next morning to Charlie shaking his leg. The two of them headed out into town, and Vance picked up some supplies. Paulie hadn't been lying about everything being on the house. Vance got a box a shotgun shells, two boxes of .223 ammo, two loaves of bread, a small sack of fruits, an extra backpack, and four bottles of water...all free. The people who sold the items to him just smiled, thanked him, and assured him that the governor would pay them back.

Vance placed the backpack on Charlie's shoulders and made him carry some of his lighter items. He wasn't overly enthusiastic about having Charlie along with him, and he hadn't even outright told the boy that he was taking him with him. He was another mouth to feed, another person to take care of, and he was a child. There was rarely any benefit to having a companion with him, and in this instance it would probably be a hindrance. But Vance felt an obligation to take care of the boy. Bob had been a good person, and Charlie was a good

56

boy. Vance couldn't leave him in Charleston without anyone to watch after him. As much as he hated the situation, he had to follow his code.

"So I'm going with you?" Charlie asked as they headed out of town.

"Yes," Vance answered.

"Thank you!" Charlie said with a smile.

"We need to lay down a few ground rules, boy," Vance began, "First, you do everything I say. No exceptions. Second, you keep your ears and eyes open. Third, no complaining."

"Got it," Charlie said as he happily walked beside Vance.

The two walked and walked, and Charlie's pace began slowing. Vance realized that the boy was having to nearly run to keep up with him. He slowed his pace down a little, cursing inside his head. The boy was going to delay him even more.

"Can I carry a gun?" Charlie finally asked.

"No."

"Why not?" Charlie whined.

"Because you don't know how to use one. You're just a boy. No arguing." Vance continued walking, not even looking at Charlie as the boy threw his arms out in frustration.

"Besides, you can barely keep up with me as it is. A gun would just weigh you down even more." Charlie didn't object. Vance's words made perfect sense.

"Can we take a break?" Charlie asked after several more minutes.

Vance blew some air out of his mouth in frustration, then looked down at Charlie. The boy was sweating bullets and breathing heavily.

"Fine," Vance said.

The two took cover from the sun under a tree. They swapped a bottle of water back and forth, sitting in relative silence while they did so. Finally, Charlie started talking.

"Did you kill those men?" he asked.

"Yes," Vance answered.

"Did it help?" Charlie asked.

"Help what?"

"Help how you felt?"

"It's not about emotions, boy. It's about retribution." Vance kicked his legs out straight in front of him, enjoying the moment of relaxation.

"What's retribution?" Charlie asked.

"Payment for crimes someone has committed. Punishment. Those men committed horrible crimes. They needed to be eliminated," Vance explained.

"Oh. So will they go back to the earth, too?" Charlie was full of questions.

"Yes. Everything and everyone does."

"You told me you'd explain all that a little better." Charlie turned his body toward Vance, who frowned a little as he finished his bottle of water.

"Everything comes from the earth. Nutrients are given back to the earth by many processes. Rain, decomposition of bodies, minerals, etc. When someone or something dies, their body decomposes and goes into the soil. Then plants grow using those nutrients. Animals eat the plants, other animals eat the animals that eat the plants, and it all continues."

"The circle of life," Charlie said with a smile.

"Basically, yes."

"I saw that in a really old cartoon once. Something about lions." Charlie started picking at grass.

"We are all connected. We look up at the stars at night, but we feel so distant from them. Few people know that we are connected to the stars as well." Vance decided to turn this into a brief lesson. Charlie seemed to enjoy learning.

"The stars!" Charlie exclaimed.

"Yes. You see, all life can be traced back to the stars if you go back far enough. Everything is essentially star dust...the elements of life were created from dying stars. One thing ends, but another begins." Vance stood up and got another bottle of water from his backpack.

"That's so cool!" Charlie said.

"Yes it is. Now come on, let's get moving. I'll tell you more later."

The two walked for hours, taking more breaks than Vance would have liked. They arrived at Milton, West Virginia, at almost dusk. Instead of venturing into the town, Vance made camp just outside of it. He didn't want anymore problems or anymore delays. The two ate bread and crackers for supper, and sipped on water.

"Why do we have to eat both? They're basically the same thing," Charlie asked.

"The crackers have salt. Salt has electrolytes, which help keep you alive. Without salt, drinking water is pointless," Vance explained. The boy ate his crackers and bread without further complaint.

"Now we get a little something extra. It's been a long day," Vance said as he pulled an MRE out of his backpack. He saved a few for emergencies.

"What is that?" Charlie asked.

"It's an MRE—a meal ready to eat. They used to give these to people in the military."

Vance opened the main course of the MRE—beef stew—and dumped the contents into a cup. He then placed the cup over the fire and waited for it to heat up. It didn't take long. Within minutes the two of them were sharing the beef stew. Charlie thought it tasted wonderful. For Vance, it made him nostalgic. He had survived on nothing but MREs for months when he had been in Syria. But it wasn't the long, hard months in Syria that caused his nostalgia. It was simply the thought of the past, and how things used to be. Combat was nothing to get nostalgic about, although Vance would have jumped at the opportunity to do another tour if it would mean everything going back to the way it used to be.

The two fell asleep early, both tired from the long day. They hadn't traveled as far as Vance would have liked—only about twenty miles—but it wasn't too bad for having a boy accompany him. He had

59

actually expected to travel a lot less.

***

Vance woke up early in the morning. His neck was stiff and his lower back was sore. Charlie was nowhere to be found. Vance stood up and looked around. Nothing. The boy's backpack was still sitting by the tree. After briefly searching the area, Vance became a little worried. He saw a merchant in a covered wagon riding down the road.

"You seen a boy?" Vance shouted to him. The merchant stopped his wagon and looked in his direction.

"What's that?" he yelled back.

"A boy," Vance said as he walked closer to the road, "A boy was traveling with me, and I don't know where he is. Have you seen him?"

"Afraid I haven't seen no boy," the merchant said. He remained stopped in the roadway.

"Shit," Vance said to himself.

"Looking for me?" Charlie asked as he appeared behind Vance.

"Where were you?" Vance asked him.

"There's a stream over that hill. I went down there to wash up a bit," Charlie answered.

"Don't do that. New rule: you don't go anywhere without me," Vance told him sternly.

"But..."

"I'm responsible for you now. We're out in No Man's Land...crazy people are everywhere. Don't go anywhere without me." Vance pointed his finger at him.

"You all need a ride?" the merchant asked. Hospitality was hard to find these days.

"I'd appreciate that," Vance said. Him and Charlie gathered their things and placed them in the back of the wagon.

"You ride back here. I'll be up front," Vance told Charlie.

Vance climbed up next to the driver and started digging around in

60

his backpack. After a short while he pulled out a bar of soap.

"Will this suffice?" he asked the merchant.

"Oh I don't need no payment. I'm heading this way anyway. Milton's just up here." The merchant was an older man, with long, gray hair. He wore a straw hat and overalls.

"Thank you. Are you stopping in Milton, or continuing on?" Vance asked.

"Naw...I gotta go on through it past Huntington. Where are you all headed?" the old man asked.

"Back West. New Mexico," Vance said.

"That's a long way to walk."

"Yeah it is. But we'll manage. I appreciate your generosity." Vance looked over at the old man and nodded his head. The old man ignored it and kept his eyes on the road.

After about half an hour, they were on the other side of Milton. The old man didn't speak much, other than to tell Vance that the two of them could keep riding with him, and Vance was okay with that. It was a nice change of pace to travel by horse and wagon. Seeing everything pass by so fast—and thinking about how slow it would be passing if they had been walking—made him feel relaxed.

The road beneath them passed by quickly. The old man was still silent, and Vance could see another town up ahead. Had to have been Huntington, the town the old man had mentioned. Vance pulled out his map, just to make sure they were still going in the general direction of his destination. They were still traveling West, but they would have to make a detour South to avoid the mid-western states. Radiation levels were higher than they should be practically all over the country from the fallout, but not enough to do any real harm. But the Midwest was off limits. They probably wouldn't even make it a quarter of the way through Missouri before they fell over and died from radiation sickness.

"Where you heading?" Vance finally asked the old man.

"Just West of Huntington, right across the Kentucky border. Got a camp there with a couple friends." The old man kept his eyes on the road.

As the wagon kept moving, Vance became tired. He forced his eyes to stay open. There was no way he could sleep out in No Man's Land during the day, wagon or no wagon. Especially now that he had a boy to look after. Vance grunted. A *boy*. Of all the things that could have happened to him, he just *had* to be responsible for taking care of a *kid*. But the situation had been forced on him, and now he had to deal with it. Nothing could be done about it.

Huntington seemed to fly past. There didn't appear to be much there...just a few merchants and a small motel. Once they were outside of town, Vance looked in the back of the wagon to check on Charlie. The boy was asleep. He could have that luxury, but Vance could not.

"Thirsty?" the old man asked.

"No thanks. I have my own water," Vance told him.

"I got plenty of it back there. Help yourself," the old man insisted.

"No thank you. I wouldn't want to take any of your water." Vance was trying to be polite. Hopefully the old man would leave it be. Vance didn't normally take water from people out on the road.

"Go on, son. Drink up. With how far you got to walk, you're gonna to need to save your water." The old man became a little more animated now.

"No thank you. I'm really not thirsty." Vance didn't want to be rude, but he wasn't going to drink this man's water. The only water he drank was his own, or from merchants in towns.

They continued on, and the camp came into sight. It was small, with a tiny shack and a couple of tents sitting off the north side of the road. A small fire was going, and before long Vance could see that a woman was cooking something over it.

The old man pulled the wagon into the camp, put the brake on, and slowly dismounted. Vance walked around to the back and shook Charlie. The boy groaned a little and rolled his head to the other side, but he didn't wake up.

"He's fine. Let him nap," the old man said. Vance grunted and let the boy sleep, but didn't stray too far from the wagon.

"Come over here and get you some food," the old man offered.

"No thank you. You've already been more than generous," Vance said politely.

"Come on now...we've got plenty," the woman said. She wore a dress, which was most uncommon in these days. Her face was pale and her brown hair was wiry. She looked like she was in her thirties.

"I appreciate it, but no thank you. We'll be leaving as soon as the boy finishes his nap," Vance replied.

"Want some water?" the old man asked as he presented Vance with a tin cup.

Just before Vance declined the water, he noticed the liquid rippling back and forth in the cup. The old man was shaking pretty bad. Of course, he *was* old. Vance took his eyes off of the cup and looked at the man's face. His skin was pale, his eyes were wide and red. He looked down at the old man's free hand, which was shaking almost as bad as the one holding the cup.

"I might take some food after all," Vance said to the woman. She smiled and poured some stew into a bowl.

"Here you are," she said as she held the bowl out for Vance to take it.

Just as Vance had suspected, the woman had the shakes, too. The stew jostled around in the bowl, the metal spoon rattled against the side. The woman's eyes were wide and red as well.

"Sir, thank you for your generosity. We must be going now," Vance quickly said as he turned toward the wagon. These people were cannibals.

"Thought you wanted some food?" the woman asked as she followed him.

"No thank you," he said, "Charlie!"

"He probably ain't gonna wake up for awhile," the old man said from behind Vance.

Vance turned around and saw the old man holding a double-barrel shotgun. Vance brought up his M4 and pointed it at him.

63

"What the hell did you do!?" Vance yelled.

"I didn't do nothin', boy. He must have drank the water." The old man grinned, showing the only four teeth he had in his mouth. A young man appeared from a tent behind them, holding a machete.

"I'll kill all of you! Tell me what you did to him!" Vance demanded.

"It's just got some passionflower in it. Nothin' to be concerned about. It relaxes people." The old man spoke as if Vance was the crazy one.

"If you cannibals come near me, I'll kill you. We're just going to get our things and go." Vance told them calmly.

"I'm afraid not, boy. My family's gotta eat somehow." The old man raised the shotgun, and Vance squeezed the trigger on his assault rifle three times. The old man went down hard. One round had hit him in the chest, the other two in his abdomen.

"No!" the woman screamed. The boy from the tent ran up to the old man.

"You son of a bitch!" the young man yelled at Vance.

"I'm not dying! And neither of you have to, either! Just let us go!" Vance told them, his M4 still raised.

The young man grabbed the shotgun from the old man's hands. Vance gave him the benefit of the doubt, but as soon as he started pointing it in Vance's direction, Vance dropped him with two rounds to the chest.

The woman ran at him with empty hands, screaming as she did so. Vance grabbed her by the arm and tossed her to the ground. The woman rolled through the grass, her dress wrapping around her legs. She got up again, rushed Vance one more time, and got thrown to the ground again.

"Stop!" Vance yelled at her, "I'm not going to die, and you don't have to either!"

The familiar sound of a gunshot and a bullet whizzing past Vance's ear forced him to take cover behind the wagon. He poked his head out and saw a middle-aged man standing in the doorway of the shack, a rifle in his hands, about forty yards away. Vance blindly fired a round in his direction, then ran for a log on the other side of the camp fire. He wasn't going to use the wagon for cover with Charlie inside it.

Vance dove behind the log. The woman was still screaming, and he kept an eye on her to make sure she didn't try to get in the wagon. If she did, Vance would drop her. He didn't care that she was unarmed...Charlie had to be protected.

"Come on out, fresh meat!" the middle-aged man yelled as he fired at Vance once more. The bullet hit the log Vance was hunkered down behind, "Kill my kin, will ya'!?"

Vance quickly raised up, placing his assault rifle on the log to steady his aim. He fired a single shot at the man. From this distance he couldn't tell exactly where he had hit him, but by the way he fell it looked like it had hit him in the neck or head.

The woman dropped to her knees and screamed. Tears ran down her cheeks, and she wailed loudly. But the wail was not simply out of grief. It was horrifying, full of hate and violence and malice. Vance approached her and stared at her for a moment.

"Anyone else left?" he asked her, coldly. The woman buried her head in her hands and continued crying.

Vance looked in the wagon and saw that Charlie was still sleeping. That passionflower must have been some powerful stuff, to make him sleep through a firefight. Vance looked down at the woman just in time to see her pull something out of her waistband. It was a small snubnosed revolver, hidden by the fold of her blouse. Vance turned quickly to shoot her, but she fired first. At almost point blank range, the round hit him square in the chest. Vance doubled over and dropped to his knees. He mustered all of his strength and lifted his assault rifle with one hand. The muzzle was only a foot or so away from the woman. Vance fired, hitting her in the neck. He clenched his chest with his left hand, and fired once more. That time he hit her in the side of the head. Vance forced himself to his feet, grabbed the little .38 caliber revolver that had just been used to shoot him, and crawled

65

into the back of the wagon.

After taking a few deep breaths, he unzipped his tactical vest and placed his fingers on the spot where the bullet had hit. His bullet-proof vest had held, surprisingly. Vance removed both vests and his t-shirt and sat them off to the side. He looked down and saw a huge whelp forming on his left pectoral. A small amount of blood oozed from the circular wound. The bullet hadn't gone through at all, but the kinetic energy left one hell of a mark. This wasn't the first time Vance had been shot, but it didn't make it any less dramatic. He had taken a bullet when he was deployed in Syria, and had taken two more prior to that when he was in Iran. Two of those times he had managed to walk away with nothing serious. One of those times the bullet had missed the trauma plate in his vest and went through his side. Luckily it had entered through his abdomen, tore right past his kidney, and exited clean on the other side. It had been a hell of a flesh wound, but it was nothing serious. Vance glanced down at his exposed torso and saw the scar on his left side. He then looked over on his right pectoral and stared at the other scar he had, from one of the bullets his vest had stopped years ago. It had been a hell of a hit; he had walked away with a giant bruise and a cracked rib. He probably wouldn't have a scar from this most recent bullet, but that didn't make it hurt any less.

Vance rummaged through his pack and pulled out some alcohol wipes, gauze and tape. He cleaned the wound up with a couple alcohol wipes, ignoring the sharp pain it caused. He then placed some gauze over the wound and taped it to his chest on all four sides. Now his chest was starting to hurt immensely, but he couldn't tell if he had a fracture or not.

Charlie was still asleep, and Vance decided that the time to sleep was over. They needed to get away from here, in case the old man had any other members of his group still out and about. The shack hadn't even been cleared.

"Wake up, Charlie," Vance said as he shook him hard. Charlie groaned a little, but didn't open his eyes.

"Goddamn it, Charlie! Wake up!" he said a little louder. The boy

66

still didn't come to.

"Fuck," Vance said to himself.

He put all of his gear on, dragged Charlie to the back of the wagon, and threw him over his shoulder. It caused him much pain, but pain was something he could ignore. Vance tucked his M4 behind his thigh holster and pulled out his sawed-off shotgun from the makeshift holster on his backpack. It would be much easier to shoot than his assault rifle, and obviously had a larger spread. Vance twirled around, checking his surroundings, then ran off toward the woods. It was a horribly painful task, but he had no other choice. Taking the wagon would have made them too vulnerable. It was safer to move on foot. If the horse and wagon were still there later in the day, and no one else had come back to the camp, then Vance would consider taking them.

The brush was thick, but Vance barreled through it as if it wasn't there. He was terrified that someone might show up back at the camp and go on a witch hunt. As he rushed through the timber, Charlie bouncing around on his shoulder, he realized that he hadn't been this scared in a long time. And it wasn't his safety that he feared for...it was Charlie's. Without the kid, Vance would have been perfectly okay. But with the boy over his shoulder, Vance found that he was feeling a slight twinge of panic. He ran and ran through the thick timber, across a creek, and through more timber. He finally ran out of breath and stopped in a small opening in the middle of the woods. He kicked at the twigs and dirt at the base of a tree, clearing a spot to put the boy. After getting rid of any insects or sharp sticks that may have been there, he sat Charlie down and leaned him up against the tree. He then squatted down and listened carefully. There was no screaming, or the sound of horses. They were safe for now. Vance sat his M4 against the same tree Charlie was leaned up against and knelt down in front of the boy. He pulled one of his eyelids up, and Charlie turned away. Vance rubbed one of his knuckles firmly against the boy's sternum. Charlie blinked once and started to roll away. Vance did it once more, and Charlie opened his eyes briefly and with a groggy voice said, "Stop..."

"Wake up," Vance said to him.

Charlie opened his eyes a bit and looked around. He was obviously confused. Vance grabbed him by his face and forced him to look into his eyes.

"You've been drugged. You need to fight it. Keep looking into my eyes," he said.

Charlie's eyes were half open, but he did as he was told. A couple of times his eyelids fluttered, but the boy managed to come around. In that moment, while Vance was staring into his eyes, he realized that this boy was connected to him now. For whatever reason, his conscience had decided that Charlie was his to keep. He would not abandon this boy for any reason, and he would take him with him until he could find a safe place for him. Vance's nerves relaxed a little, the adrenaline subsiding. He swallowed the huge lump in his throat and took his hand off of Charlie's face.

"What happened?" Charlie asked as he rubbed his eyes.

"Those people were cannibals. They were going to eat us. Here, drink water." Vance took the lid off of a canteen and thrust it into Charlie's hands. The boy drowsily started sipping on it.

"Why...why are we in the woods?" Charlie asked.

"I had to kill them. That water you drank had an herb in it that made you sleepy. The old man took us back to his camp, where there were others, and they intended on turning us into food," Vance explained.

"What happened to your vest?" Charlie said as he stuck his finger in the hole of Vance's tactical vest. Vance quickly grabbed his finger to keep it from putting any pressure on the wound.

"I got shot, but my bullet-proof vest stopped it. I'll be alright," he said.

"They shot you?" Charlie came to life a little bit more.

"I said I'll be alright. Just keep drinking water," Vance told him. Charlie did as he was told.

Vance got up and listened a bit more. Still no signs of trouble. They had to be nearly a mile into the thick timber, so even if there had been someone out looking for them they were still relatively safe.

Vance sat down on a log and began picking thorns and sticks out of his pant legs. Charlie sat up a bit more and shook his head. The passionflower had really hit him hard, probably because he was so small.

"So what do we do now?" Charlie asked.

"We wait here for a few hours, get our wind back. Then we go back to the camp, take what we need, and move out on the wagon. That's assuming nobody else goes back to the camp."

"There's more of them?" Charlie asked.

"I'm not sure. That's why we're waiting. If no one is there after a few hours, we can be pretty sure everyone who belonged there is dead." Vance took off his two vests, lifted up his t-shirt, and peeled off the gauze covering his wound.

Now that he had the time, he would clean up the wound a little better. It had bled considerably more since putting the gauze on. Vance pulled out a small bottle of iodine and swabbed the wound. Now that the action was over, simply touching the wound caused a great deal of pain. He didn't have the benefit of adrenaline anymore. The circular tear in his skin was still oozing blood, and the area around it was dark red from the bruising.

"That looks terrible," Charlie said as he woke up a bit more.

Vance wiped off the iodine and put some triple antibiotic ointment on the wound, then placed a fresh gauze pad over it. He taped it on all four sides again, this time making the pad tighter and the tape placed a little better. His biggest threat now was infection. Hygiene wasn't an easy thing these days, especially out in No Man's Land. With all of the traveling they would do, sweat could easily run down his neck and be absorbed by the gauze. The sweat itself wasn't really a threat, but the bacteria it might carry down to the wound could create some serious problems. Fortunately, Vance kept a few bottles of antibiotics in his backpack. They were by far one of the most valuable items since The Fall. Vance had only used them a couple times in his travels—once when he had pneumonia and once when he had cut open his forearm and it got infected—so he still had a fairly large supply of them. For now he would rely on the triple antibiotic ointment, which was nearly as valuable as the antibiotics. There was no need to waste his precious supply of pills if he didn't have to. All except one of the bottles were still unopened, so they would stay good for quite some time, albeit with decreased potency.

The two sat quietly for a long time. Charlie got up and sat back down beside Vance. Vance still had his vests off, giving himself a much needed break. Charlie leaned his head against Vance's shoulder and took his hand in his. Vance wasn't big on things like that, but he allowed it. The boy felt bad for what had happened. Not just for Vance getting shot, but for everything. The only thing he knew how to do was show affection, and Vance found it quite beautiful in its own right. The young boy had no one now, and neither did Vance. The two had become close companions simply due to traumatic events, and in only a couple of days. Vance squeezed Charlie's hand a little, to let him know he was accepting of the boy's loving gesture. Charlie kept his head rested on Vance's shoulder, and remained there until Vance got up two hours later.

"Let's get ready to move," Vance said.

After Charlie slowly picked himself up and prepared for the journey ahead, Vance led them back in the general direction of the camp. He didn't take the same path as which they came, though, in case someone was out in the woods trying to track them. They moved much slower than they had before- Vance kept his M4 shouldered and crept forward, scouting out their surroundings. Charlie did a good job of staying on his heels and keeping quiet. Every once in awhile he would accidentally snap a twig or trip, and Vance shot him a quick glare to remind him how important it was to remain silent.

They finally arrived at the tree line, and Vance could see the camp across the road. There didn't seem to be any activity whatsoever. The two horses were still hooked to the carriage, a couple of bodies were visible, and the fire had died down quite a bit.

"All right, let's move forward. If anything happens, you find something to hide behind or flatten yourself against the ground if there isn't any cover. Then keep your ears open for my instructions," Vance said to Charlie. Charlie nodded his head in acknowledgment.

The two crossed the road, and there were still no signs of life. As they got closer, Vance's heart started beating a little faster. Again, this was due to the fact that he had Charlie to protect. If anything happened, the boy's safety would be his utmost concern. He briefly thought about how this was a perfect example of the boy being a hindrance, but he banished it from his mind. Nothing could be done about it.

Vance swept through the camp quickly, checking the two tents as he went. After clearing the small shack, he determined they were safe. It had been about three hours or so since the situation they had here, and there was still no one around. Besides, Vance counted the sleeping areas. Three beds in total- one in the house and one in each tent. The bedding area in one of the tents was larger, which indicated that the woman and the man who had shot at Vance were together. The shack was presumably the old man's since the younger man had came out of the other tent. More than likely, the young man was the offspring of the woman and the middle-aged man. The old man was probably a father or an uncle to one or the other of the middle-aged people. But none of that mattered now.

Vance sorted through the cannibals' belongings. There were a plethora of items, some of which were fairly valuable. Now that Vance had a wagon he would be able to take a lot more things, but it would also make him a bigger target. Hopefully a man dressed in tactical gear and carrying an M4- completely unlike the normal merchants who looked like old farmers- would deter any bandits or raiders. He would try to stick to the larger roads and highways where there was more traffic, to decrease the chance of something happening.

Vance and Charlie started loading up the goods. They didn't take a whole lot- you had to be careful when scavenging from cannibals. Water was obviously off limits. There were plenty of bars of soap, but Vance had a bad feeling that they were made out of human fat. About all they took were the few firearms laying about, the ammo, several

71

blankets, a few pairs of socks, two pairs of boots, some pots and pans, as many water jugs as they could find, some rope, two axes, two hatchets, and an old trunk (which they emptied; it contained various useless items).

Once the wagon was loaded, Vance led the horses down to the pond behind the shack. He checked it out to make sure there weren't any bodies or waste in it, then unhitched the horses and allowed them to drink from it. While they got their fill of water, Vance emptied all the jugs and filled them up with fresh water from the pond.

"Don't drink any of this until we purify it," he told Charlie.

After giving the horses about half an hour to graze, Vance hooked them back up to the wagon and off they went. It was late afternoon now, so there was still plenty of daylight left. Charlie took a nap in the back to sleep off the residual effects of the passionflower. Vance daydreamed, but kept his wits about him as they made their way down the road. They would make great time this way. With the two horses and a wagon, Vance would be able to nearly double his distance traveled in a day. Since traveling with the boy decreased the amount of miles he walked in a day, the horses and wagon would make up even more time. The first opportunity he had to pick up another horse, he would do so. That way he could swap out horses and increase his distance even more. The wagon wasn't that big, nor was it weighted down at all. Vance figured that the wagon weighed about 1,200lbs or so, load and all. Each of the Quarter Horses probably weighed close to 1,000lbs. Which meant that, together, they could probably safely pull 4,000lbs or so. Before The Fall, when equipment was better kept and living conditions were better, they could have pulled more. But now—with their only supply of nutrients being whatever they happened to stumble across, and water not being readily available—Vance wouldn't push them too much. Vance had grown up on a farm, so he knew quite a bit about living off the land and taking care of animals. He hadn't needed to use much of that knowledge out in No Man's Land, but now that he had horses to take care of it would come in handy.

While thinking about all of this, Vance realized that he hadn't eaten yet today. Charlie hadn't either. Evening was approaching, so Vance pulled out his pack and dug around while the horses followed the road. He woke up Charlie and handed him half a loaf of bread and a bottle of water. Charlie was still a little drowsy, but not bad. Vance ate from the other half and gulped down the water. When he was finished he pulled out two apples, handed one to Charlie, and ate the other one. It tasted pretty good, even if it was starting to go bad.

After two more hours, Vance pulled the wagon off of the road and set up camp in a clearing. He left the horses hitched while he wove together several lengths of 550 cord—extremely strong cord typically used for parachutes—into one, thick rope. He then strung it up between two trees and hooked the horses' leads to it. That way they could walk back and forth between the two trees and feel some freedom. It wouldn't keep them from tearing away from it if they really wanted to, put these horses seemed to be trained quite well. Vance felt nostalgic as he thought back to his childhood. He had had a horse that was so well trained and calm, all he had to do was throw the reins or the lead over a fence or something and the horse would stay.

The horses immediately began grazing, and Vance threw a handful of apples to them. He told Charlie to go get two jugs of water and fill up a few pots for the horses. Charlie did as he was told, and seemed to enjoy the task. He gently patted the horses and ran his hand down their sides as they drank from the big pots.

There was still a couple hours of daylight left, and Vance had some things he needed to do. First there was the matter of getting a fire going. He sent Charlie out to pick up kindling and tender around their campsite, while he chopped down a nearby small tree. After chopping a few logs up, he placed them on the small fire and let it get going. Then he pulled out the socks and blankets and hung them up around the fire, to let the smoke clean them out. Next, he began purifying their water supply. He ran the water through a clean rag and into a pot, then did it once more. He then placed the pot over the fire. While he was waiting for that to boil, he did the same thing with

73

another pot and jug of water.

The sun had been down for a good hour, and Vance had three big jugs of relatively clean water. That would keep them going for quite awhile. They still had five more jugs of dirty water in the wagon, so Vance had Charlie give each of the horses one more of them. When the chores were complete, Vance and Charlie sat around the fire and made small talk. The boy was extremely interested in the horses, because he had never really had an opportunity to be around them before. He informed Vance that he had touched a horse only once before, but he still really liked them. Vance listened to the boy talk and talk, once again feeling a bit nostalgic. Every once in awhile, the boy would break from rambling and ask Vance some random question. Vance would answer, and actually didn't mind the boy's energy. It made him feel comfortable, somehow. Normal.

"So...you're a courier?" Charlie asked after he had been silent for ten minutes or so.

"Yeah."

"You got a package now?" the boy asked.

"Yes," Vance said.

"Can I see it?" Charlie's eyes brightened up a bit.

"It's nothing that would be interesting to you," Vance told him.

"I wanna see it," Charlie insisted.

"No. It's time for us to go to sleep now." Vance kicked at the fire a bit to spread it out and lower the flames. Charlie pouted.

The two laid out under the night sky, and Charlie talked about which stars he thought were the brightest. Vance had intended on going to sleep, but the boy was too full of energy. Instead of scolding him and making him be quiet, he patiently conversed with him and told him all he knew about the stars. The boy had a million questions, many of which Vance couldn't answer. He asked what star that one was, or how old that star over there was. Then he began talking about traveling in space and all the planets he wanted to visit. He told Vance that he wanted to go to Jupiter because he had heard it was so big, and Vance had to explain to him why he would have a hard time landing

74

there. After awhile, Charlie's voice began trailing off as he fell asleep. As best Vance could tell, the boy had been trying to talk about aliens before dozing off. Vance smiled slightly, then closed his eyes and drifted off to sleep as well.

5

The next day, Vance and Charlie rode all the way to Mt. Sterling, Kentucky. It was about 6 o' clock, so they had plenty of time to take care of business before the day was over. Having a wagon meant that Vance wouldn't have to rent a motel room; they could just sleep in the back of it. The town was pretty small, and looked like it hadn't been much bigger before The Fall. A few merchants were scattered about along the main road, and there was a bar, a diner, and a motel. Everything else was vacant or destroyed. Vance parked the wagon right outside of the diner, and sent Charlie in with some goods to trade for a couple of hot meals. The two sat at the back of the wagon and ate their squirrel stew. It was rather good for being made in a small, rundown diner. The portions were fairly generous, too. Vance had only traded a bar of soap and a pair of gloves for the two meals, so he had expected less.

"This is good," Charlie said as he shoveled the food into his mouth.

Vance nodded his head in agreement and continued eating. Him and Charlie drank copious amounts of water to wash down the stew, and by the end of it they were both extremely full. Charlie hopped down from the wagon and kicked at some rocks in the road, looking around as he did so. Vance could tell that the boy wanted to go

76

exploring, but it was out of the question. He wouldn't let him out of his sight.

"Vance..." Charlie began.

"No," Vance replied, already knowing what the boy wanted.

"But I just want to go down the road. There are hardly any people here. Let me go take a look," Charlie begged.

"Absolutely not," Vance told him.

"Then go with me," Charlie said.

"No. I can't leave the wagon. Besides, we need to get the horses unhitched and let them stretch a little. They still need food and water." Vance motioned for Charlie to climb up onto the front bench, then the two took off down the road.

If it hadn't been for the few merchants and businesses, the place would have looked like a ghost town. Nearly every house they came across appeared vacant, but most of them were relatively intact. Vance stumbled upon one that had a privacy fence going around the back yard. He pulled the wagon up to the gate and checked it out. The whole yard was fenced in, so Vance unhitched the horses and led them inside. Charlie found a couple of buckets in the yard, so he filled them up with the impure water for the horses. The yard was good sized— big enough that the two horses could trot around and stretch their legs a little. Most of their time was spent grazing and drinking. Vance threw each of them two apples. They really needed some feed, or something to supplement the nutrients they weren't getting. But that was hard to find. Grass and apples would have to do for now. But Vance only had a few apples left. Perhaps they would find some fruit along the road.

The wagon was too big to pass through the gate, so Vance left it parked next to it. Him and Charlie sat on the front bench and talked about their plans. Vance informed him that he still very much intended on going back to New Mexico, and Charlie told him he would go with him. Vance didn't reply, and it was because the issue had been nagging at him all day. He had no idea what was waiting for him in New Mexico, and he didn't want to drag Charlie into the middle of a war

77

zone. It would be better if he could find a nice little community that would take Charlie in, but that bothered him as well. Charlie would not be happy about it, and Vance wouldn't really be either. The two had become close in just a few short days. But Vance knew that emotions should be left out of it...he needed to do the responsible thing. Charlie needed structure and normality. Or at least as much structure and normality as a kid could get in this new world.

"We need names for them," Charlie said.

"Huh?" Vance looked down at him, confused.

"The horses. We should name them."

"Alright...well what do you want to name them?" Vance asked.

"They're both girls, right?" Charlie stood up in the wagon and looked over the fence.

"Yes."

"Let's name that one Maggie," Charlie said as he pointed to the all-brown one, "and that one Daisy," he said as he pointed to the one that was brown with a white patch on its head.

"Maggie and Daisy...alright," Vance chuckled a little.

"Do you think they're happier now? Now that they're not around those mean people?" Charlie asked him. Vance looked at him and smiled.

"I think they're happy, yes." Vance patted Charlie on the shoulder.

"I'm glad we have a wagon now. All that walking was making my feet hurt," Charlie said.

"I'm glad, too." Vance jumped down from the wagon and walked around to the back.

After getting the bedding situated and making sure they both drank plenty of water, Vance had Charlie go refill the horse's buckets. They really weren't getting enough water for how much they were working, but they would manage.

Vance and Charlie crawled inside the wagon and laid down to sleep. The sun had just gone down, but they were both tired from a long day of riding. Charlie was out almost immediately, but Vance stayed awake for quite some time. He thought about the past, both

78

recent and long ago. He thought about things that he would have rather not thought about, but he couldn't help it. James Vance rolled over, shook the thoughts from his mind, and went to sleep.

***

Vance woke up early the next day. Charlie was already awake, sitting up and rubbing the sleep from his eyes. Vance immediately got dressed and jumped out of the wagon. The horses were still in the back yard, which was Vance's chief concern. He was afraid someone might steal one, whether it be to use as a working horse or as food. Vance walked up to the horses and petted them both, knowing how important it was to bond with your working horses. He refilled both buckets about halfway and let them get their morning food and drink. They were now down to one jug of impure water, and one jug of clean water. It wasn't a huge concern, though—Vance could easily find a creek or pond once they left. Just in case, he would purchase some clean water before they left town.

After giving the horses about an hour to graze and drink, Vance hitched them up to the wagon and they took off down the road. Him and Charlie ate some bread and an apple each. When they were done, Vance sent Charlie inside the old diner and had him get two jugs full of water. It wasn't cheap; Vance had to give up a pack of cigarettes and two pairs of socks for roughly two gallons of water. After that was done they headed West out of town, starting their journey once more.

"What's New Mexico like?" Charlie asked after they had gone a few miles down the road.

"Hot," Vance replied.

"How hot?" Charlie asked.

"In the summer it can get up above 100 degrees." Vance kept his eyes one the road, thankful that he had a good pair of sunglasses. The sky was clear today and although the sun was behind them, it was extremely bright this morning.

"That's hot," Charlie said. He had probably never experienced a

79

climate even close to New Mexico's.

***

They rode all day long, only stopping three times to give the horses a break. The work was starting to show, as the horses were slowing down quite a bit. They reached Bardstown, KY, about half an hour before sundown. It was a crowded dump. There wasn't much there, but for some reason people had chosen to call this place home. Barrels of trash burned in the streets, gangs of men roamed around as they pleased, and the locals were wearing little more than rags. The merchants didn't seem to be very kind individuals, either. Vance decided to push the horses a little more and get them through the town quickly. They would set up camp just West of this shit hole.

"Vance, look!" Charlie exclaimed as he pointed toward an alley off to the right.

A woman was being assaulted by a gang of men. It seemed that the gang was simply doing this because they enjoyed it. They were laughing and throwing her around, grabbing at her breasts as they did so.

"Look away," Vance told the boy.

"You gotta do something!" Charlie said.

"Too many of them, kid. We can't get involved." Vance felt a twinge of guilt, but his logic was not misplaced. There were five men in that gang, and they all looked tough as nails.

"Vance! We can't let them do this! Retribution!" Charlie parroted as he tugged on Vance's arm. Vance let out a frustrated sigh and stopped the wagon.

He set the brake and told Charlie to crawl in the back. One of the gang members was now restraining the woman from behind, while another tortured her by holding a knife close to her stomach. They were about a hundred feet away.

Vance fired off five quick shots with his M4, hitting two of the men and dropping them like rocks. The horses jumped a little, but

80

didn't try to pull the wagon after feeling that the brake was applied. The other three scattered, leaving the woman in the alley. Vance lowered his M4 and waited to see if the woman was going to get up and run off. Before he could do anything, Charlie jumped out of the back of the wagon and took off toward her.

"Charlie! No!" Vance screamed, but the boy was nearly halfway to her.

Vance jumped down and ran after him, keeping his M4 at the ready in case someone jumped them. Charlie reached the woman and knelt down beside her. Once Vance had made it over there, he remained on guard while Charlie checked her out.

"Are you okay?" Charlie asked her.

"Thank...thank you..." the woman—who looked more like a girl now that they were up close—said shakily.

"Vance...she needs help," Charlie said.

Vance had his back to them, providing security.

"We need to get out of here, Charlie. This place is trouble," Vance said in an angry tone.

"We can't just leave her!" Charlie told him. Vance groaned.

"Come on!" Vance growled as he pulled the girl onto her feet and led her back to the wagon. Charlie tried to help as well, though he wasn't quite big enough to really handle any of the weight.

Once they made it back, Vance loaded her up into the back of the wagon. Charlie jumped in with her, and they got moving again.

Vance kept his wits about him as they passed through the town. No one seemed too worked up about the shots being fired. Perhaps it wasn't anything out of the ordinary for this place. Vance kept going until they were about a mile out of town. The sun was just barely peeking over the horizon now. Vance drove the wagon off into a field and didn't stop until they were well out of view of the road.

Vance looked over the girl, who was probably 22 or 23 years old. She was a beautiful girl, with a slim, petite figure and long, blonde hair. She had a few superficial cuts and bruises on her, appeared to be close to starvation, and was probably dehydrated as well. She was conscious, but not very alert. After determining that she needed no immediate medical attention, Vance left her and Charlie in the wagon and started searching for firewood.

After only twenty minutes, Vance had a real good fire going. He fed it a few more branches to ensure it would grow a little more, then checked on Charlie and the girl. Charlie was sitting on the tailgate of the wagon, and the girl was sitting up inside it. She was sipping on a canteen of water.

"Thank you," she said, this time with a little more strength.

"Come over here by the fire, if you can. I need to check you over a little better," Vance told her.

The girl slowly crawled out of the wagon and limped over to the fire, favoring her right leg. Vance grabbed his backpack and sat down next to her. The first area to evaluate was her right leg, since it was obviously causing her some pain. After determining that she merely sprained her ankle, he moved on. After cleaning her up a bit, he treated the small cuts and scratches with triple antibiotic ointment and band-aids. She had four tiny cuts on her face from being thrown down in the street, and a few more on her arms, elbows and knees. Most were too small to really treat, so Vance only dealt with the "larger" ones. She really wasn't beat up that bad, but she'd probably feel worse in the morning. He gave her some ibuprofen pills and a vitamin.

"Thank you very much," the girl said again.

Vance ignored it, and instead unhitched the horses and attached them to the line he had tied up between two trees. He then went off in search of water, since they were running so low. About two hundred yards to the north was a treeline, and Vance was betting that a small creek ran through it. Once he got into the timber, he pulled out his small tactical flashlight and carefully navigated the brush. Sure enough, the ground started angling down into the treeline a bit, and at the bottom was a small creek. Vance made his way back to camp, to enlist Charlie's help and pick up some jugs.

"Her name is Angela," Charlie said when Vance had made it back.

82

"Everyone calls me Angie," the girl added quietly.

"Great," Vance said sarcastically, "Come on Charlie, we need to go get water."

Vance and Charlie grabbed two jugs each and some towels. They navigated the field and timber back down to the creek. Vance soaked up the water with the towels and squeezed them into the jugs, and had to explain to Charlie that doing so would help keep debris out of the water. It took awhile to fill up the four jugs, but by the end of it Vance felt satisfied. They carried it back to camp and found Angela sleeping beside the fire.

Vance's watch said it was 10 o' clock, but he needed to purify the water so they could have plenty of time on the road tomorrow. He would have to do the same thing again in the morning anyway, since they still had three more jugs to fill up. They only had one jug of clean water left, after watering the horses. Vance began the process of filtering the water and boiling it. After a couple of hours, all four jugs were filled with potable water. Vance sipped on some water and leaned up against a tree. Life was full of surprises. First he had picked up a boy, and now he was stuck with a girl against his wishes. He was still angry with Charlie for running off like that and disobeying him, but that would have to be handled another time. Both him and Angela were sound asleep. After thinking for awhile and smoking a cigarette, Vance fell asleep as well.

6

The next morning, the group woke up early and started cleaning up the camp. Vance sent Charlie down to the creek once more with two jugs, and would have sent Angela as well if she hadn't had a bad ankle. He put her to work folding up blankets and getting everything organized inside the wagon. Once Vance had purified the water that Charlie had collected, he put out the fire and hitched the horses back to the wagon.

The group traveled another two days to Bowling Green, KY, about 25 miles North of Tennessee. They were heading in a more southerly direction now to bypass Missouri and stay away from its borders.

"We need food..." Charlie moaned.

"I know this," Vance said to him.

"I'm starving, and I'm tired of bread," Charlie complained.

"Quiet," Vance said sternly. Charlie stayed quiet.

The group entered Bowling Green just before sundown. The city was rather large, but like most cities nowadays the vast majority of it was unused. Judging by the number of people, Vance figured there were probably 15,000 inhabitants in Bowling Green. That hopefully meant that there was some level of civilized order here. Everyone seemed to get along fine, and there were armed guards patrolling the streets. Finally, a city that wasn't full of degenerates.

Vance pulled the wagon in front of a general goods store, and was happy to see it actually being used for its intended purpose. He walked inside, keeping his eye on the wagon, and asked the owner about somewhere he could keep his horses for the night. The owner told him there was a football field that was fenced in about a mile down the road, where people were using it for just that purpose. Vance thanked him, gave him some goods in return for a large sack of apples, and hopped back in the wagon.

"I like this place," Charlie said as he looked around. Vance ignored it.

Vance quickly spotted the football field, and noticed that a good quarter of it had no grass at all. Luckily, the field at least contained several large troughs of water. A few horses grazed in the field, while people stood around its perimeter and made small talk. Vance pulled his wagon inside and paid the guard with two bars of soap and two packs of cigarettes. The guard placed twine around each of the horses necks, and attached to the twine were pieces of paper with numbers written on them. He then tore both of them in half, and gave the pieces to Vance. Vance unhitched the horses and put them in the football field, then pulled the wagon off to the side and started setting up camp.

The football field was fairly secure. Two armed guards stood at the gate, and several patrolled inside. All of the people standing around and setting up camp seemed quiet enough. They all looked like travelers, just wanting a safe place to stay the night. Vance left the wagon, and made Charlie promise he wouldn't go more than ten feet from the camp. He then went over to a food vender on the other side of the football field and ordered three rabbit kebobs, along with a jug of fresh tea. Next to the food vendor was a fresh produce vendor. Vance picked up a small sack of corn to go with their meal. It all cost him a pretty penny—three packs of cigarettes, a pair of socks, and a silver ring, between the two vendors. That jewelry he took from Ricky's bar was coming in handy.

85

Vance made a small fire in the already existing fire pit and hung a pot filled with water over it. Once it started to boil he placed a few ears of corn in it. While he waited for those to cook, he walked over to the fence surrounding the football field and called his two horses over to him. Maggie and Daisy trotted over to him, and he gave them each an apple. Once they were finished, he rubbed their noses for a few minutes and then headed back to his small camp. Angela and Charlie were sitting around the fire, watching the water boil. Vance sat down beside Charlie and nudged him with his elbow.

"I know you just wanted to help this girl, and I'm not saying you shouldn't help people. Hell, I'm not even saying that you did the wrong thing. I can't say that. But don't ever disobey me again. Got it?" Vance spoke quietly and calmly.

"Sorry..." Charlie said.

"That being said...I can't ignore the fact that it was a very noble thing you did, making me stop those guys. I know Angela here is very grateful as well. But that doesn't excuse you for running off like that. You could have gotten seriously hurt. Everything I do is for a reason. I was going to make sure she was okay, but I needed to wait to be sure we weren't going to get jumped by those guys. Luckily that didn't happen this time, but next time might be a different story." Vance was stern with his words but not unkind.

Vance pulled the pot off of the fire and sat it on the ground. He then placed the kebobs over the fire to warm them up a bit, and when they were done he served everybody their food.

"This is great!" Charlie said as he gnawed at an ear of corn.

"Thank you, this is really good," Angela said as well.

The three ate their supper, savoring the flavor. The rabbit kebobs were nothing special, but eating corn on the cob was really a treat. The tea tasted great to everyone, although Vance found it a little weak. But then again, he was the only one in the group who remembered drinking tea before The Fall. Angela probably would have been 13 or 14 when everything went downhill and Charlie would have only been 2 years old. Vance was 34 when everything came crashing down around him. Some days it seemed like forever ago, some days it seemed like it was just yesterday. Vance picked up the cores of the corn cobs and took them over to Maggie and Daisy. The horses ate them up quickly, though they had very little nutritional value without the corn on them. After rubbing their noses some more, Vance sat back down beside the fire and disassembled his M4.

Angela—who was sitting about three feet away—watched intently as Vance cleaned the rifle. Charlie was starting to doze off. Once he was finally asleep, Angela found it appropriate to take up conversation with Vance.

"I want to thank you again for helping me. I feel much better," she said.

"Good," Vance replied without looking at her.

"Charlie told me all about you. Said you were in the Army before The Fall," Angela continued.

"That's right. How old are you?" Vance asked, changing the topic.

"Twenty-five," she answered.

"All you young people...and none of you seem to know how to take care of yourselves," Vance said, though not in a rude manner.

"We haven't had a lot of time to learn," she replied, "It all happened so fast, without much warning."

"There was plenty of warning, it was just that no one wanted to pay attention. I saw it coming from a mile away." Vance got a little irritated when he thought back to the time leading up to The Fall.

"I have no doubt that you did," Angela said, but not sarcastically.

"Where are you from?" Vance asked her.

"Lexington, Kentucky. You?"

"Albuquerque, New Mexico. At least, that's where I've lived since The Fall." Vance meticulously cleaned the inner workings of his M4 as he spoke.

"What are you doing all the way across the country?" Angela asked him.

"I'm a courier. Had to deliver a package." Vance closed up his

87

M4, satisfied with the quick field cleaning.

"Now you're going back home?"

"That's right."

Angela rubbed her bruised arm and stared at the fire.

"Do you have anymore medicine for the pain?" she asked.

"On a scale of one to ten, how bad is it?" Vance looked at her.

"About a five," she said.

"When it gets to a seven, let me know." Vance sat his M4 inside the wagon. He did not give her anymore ibuprofen.

"Wish I could get cleaned up..." Angela hinted.

"You'll have to wait until morning. Everything is closing down for the night. But unless you have goods to pay with, you're going to have to wait until we find a pond or something." Vance was going through their supplies, sorting it all out and taking inventory.

"Oh..." Angela said. Vance became slightly irritated.

"Listen, girl," Vance said as he turned around and pointed, "life isn't fun out here, and nothing's free. I've already killed two people to save your ass, I've cleaned up your little scratches, given you medicine, *and* given you food and water. If you expect me to pay for you to take a shower, then you're sadly mistaken."

Vance turned back around and continued what he was doing.

"You want me to...pay you?" Angela said hesitantly, fear in her tone.

"What? No!" Vance waved his hand at her in frustration and walked around the side of the wagon.

He lit a cigarette and thought about what he had said. Had it been uncalled for? No, not really. The girl needed to know that she couldn't take advantage of him. If that wasn't her intention, then oh well. Vance had more important things to do than worry about a girl's emotions.

***

Everyone woke up feeling refreshed the following morning. Charlie was full of energy, and Angela actually looked a little better after another good night's sleep. Vance was stiff, like usual, but felt fine. After cleaning up the camp and retrieving the horses, the group left the football field behind. Vance stopped the wagon on the main road and turned around to face the back.

"This is where we part ways," he said to Angela, "Take this."

Vance handed her a gold necklace—a piece of jewelry he had taken from Ricky's place—so she could have some starting money. She'd be able to open herself up a line of credit with the owner of the general goods store, and that would sustain her until she could find a job.

"I'm...not going with you?" she asked.

"No. I'm a courier, not a babysitter. Sorry for your luck, but I have to get back to New Mexico as soon as possible." Vance held the necklace out for her to take it.

"Please..."

"No. Take it and go. I don't mean to be an prick, but I have important shit to do. I'm not running a daycare out of this wagon."

"Vance...please? She's a good person," Charlie said.

"No. Now either take this and get out, or just get out. I'd advise you to take it, though." Vance shook the necklace to add urgency to his words.

Angela slowly took the necklace and crawled out the back of the wagon. Vance snapped the reins and Charlie waved to her with tears in his eyes as they pulled away. Vance shook his head and gritted his teeth. He hated the New World.

"Pass me up some water," Vance said to Charlie once they were about a mile out of town.

There was no answer.

"Charlie...pass me up some water," he said again.

Still no answer. Vance turned around and looked in the back of the wagon. Charlie was sitting there, arms folded, staring at the inside of the wagon.

"What the hell's wrong with you?" Vance asked, though he knew what was wrong with him.

89

"You made Angela leave!" Charlie yelled at him.

"We don't need another person with us, Charlie," Vance said as he rolled his eyes.

"She was nice and hurt and you made her leave! I'd rather have her than you!" Tears ran down Charlie's face.

"Come on...really? We can barely keep ourselves healthy, we don't need another person," Vance argued.

"Sometimes it's just about doing the right thing, and to hell with the consequences!" Charlie yelled at him.

Vance pulled back on the reins, causing the horses to stop abruptly. This was the second time Charlie had thrown Vance's own ideology in his face. The boy apparently listened very well. He cursed under his breath as he pulled the wagon off the road, turned it around, and headed back toward Bowling Green.

"What are we doing?" Charlie asked.

"We're going back to get your goddamn girlfriend," Vance said, disgusted.

"Yay!" Charlie clapped his hands excitedly. Vance fumed.

They finally made it back to the general goods store, but Angela was nowhere to be seen. Vance and Charlie looked around nearby, but were unable to find her.

"Well kid, we might be out of luck. This is a big town, and I'm not going to spend all day looking for her," Vance said as he leaned up against the wagon.

"This is all your fault! You didn't turn around until we were halfway to New Mexico!" Charlie growled. Vance frowned and leaned down at him, as if warning him to watch his tone.

"There she is!" Charlie shouted, and pointed behind Vance.

Vance turned around, and there she was. About a block away, Angela was slowly walking around the corner, staring at the ground.

"Angela!" Charlie screamed.

The girl looked up, and started limping in their direction. Charlie ran up to her, hugged her, and helped her over to the wagon. Angela stared at Vance for a moment, who curled his lips up in irritation. Then

90

he nodded his head toward the wagon, as if saying "jump in". The three boarded the wagon and took off down the road.

"Now that we're way behind schedule, maybe we can still get some miles in today," Vance complained. Charlie and Angela were chatting up a storm in the back, as if they had been separated for a long time and had known each other for longer than five minutes. Traumatic events sure caused people to become close to one another very quickly.

***

Many hours passed by, and Vance had shrugged off the fact that he had wasted time going back for a girl just so Charlie could have a friend. It was over, and nothing could be done about it now. Now his primary concern was how quickly he could make it back to New Mexico, and with every mile his fear grew about what the conditions might be back home. He didn't want to return to a wasteland, or to a war zone. He wanted to return to the same nice, civilized place. But that probably wasn't going to happen.

By the end of the day, the group was about 20 miles southwest of Nashville. Vance made camp in a pasture, right beside a lake, far away from the road. He pulled out a few automatic fishing reels, tied them to small trees along the lake's bank, and placed a few snares around the lake. He caught grasshoppers as he went, and before long he had collected a jar full. He stuck some of the grasshoppers on the fishing hooks, then went back over to the camp and stuck the remaining grasshoppers on twigs

"Ew..." Charlie grimaced.

"They're a good source of protein, and they don't taste that bad," Vance said as he watched them cook over the fire.

"That's gross," Charlie continued.

"Go fill up the jugs. Remember to use the rags, like I taught you." Vance shooed him away.

Once the grasshoppers were done cooking, and Charlie was back

91

with a couple jugs of water, the group sat down and ate their supper. The grasshoppers were crunchy, and didn't taste bad at all. Charlie frowned every time he took a bite, simply from the thought of eating an insect. Angela struggled through it as well. Vance didn't have a problem eating them; he knew the nutritional value they contained, and he had eaten worse.

After supper there was only a half hour or so of daylight left. Vance went down to the lake and checked his lines. Two of the four had fish on them, so he pulled all of the lines and brought them back. He quickly cut off the heads of the two largemouth bass, gutted them, and ripped out their spines. He then peeled off the skin and placed the meat in a pan that was sitting in the fire.

"If we were in more dire need of nutrients, we'd be eating all of this," Vance reminded them as he tossed the waste off to the side.

The fish were done relatively quickly, and the group ate it more eagerly than they had eaten the grasshoppers. Vance felt nostalgic as he remembered going fishing before The Fall. It had been a good time, filled with lots of fun and beer drinking. Now it was just a method of survival.

After everyone was finished with the snack (the two fish hadn't provided much more than that), Vance ensured the horses got more water and that the group's own supply of potable water was in good standing. Charlie had remembered what Vance had taught him, and had done a good job of purifying the water he got from the lake. The water didn't taste all that great, since it was only filtered with cloth, but at least they wouldn't have to worry about parasites and bacteria since it had been boiled. They also still had a fair supply of more palatable water from when they were in Bowling Green.

Charlie and Angela snuggled up in the back of the wagon, while Vance remained outside. He had heard coyotes earlier in the night, and he wasn't about to let some mutt bite one of his horse's legs. That was the last thing he needed. But of course, if it hadn't been for chance, he would still be walking back to New Mexico. He probably would have only made it halfway across Kentucky by now, if it hadn't been for the horses. Vance put some more wood to the fire to keep it going, with the hope that it would deter any predators from coming close to the horses. After that he sat up against a tree, his M4 in his lap, and slowly nodded off to sleep.

7

Charlie and Angela were teasing each other, having fun, at the very start of the next morning. The two had become almost like siblings, and in an amazingly short amount of time. Vance's neck felt like it was frozen in place. Apparently he had slept in the same position all night long.

Charlie and Angela got the horses more water and brushed them down with rags, to help get some of the sweat and dirt off of them. Vance had told them to do this at least once a day, if possible. They also went down to the lake and retrieved more water, to pour over the horses and clean them up a bit. Vance prepared breakfast, which consisted of two rabbits he had discovered in his snares when he awoke and a few sliced up apples. Vance prepared the rabbits in an expert fashion, and placed them in a pot of water over the fire. Boiled rabbit wasn't a delicacy, by any means, but it ensured that the nutrients weren't lost during the cooking process. Once it was all done, Vance served Charlie and Angela their rabbit soup and apples.

"Make sure you drink the broth as well," Vance told them.

The three ate their breakfast, and it was becoming very obvious that the two younger members of the group felt very grateful to have Vance leading them. Without him, neither of them could even begin to imagine what sort of life they would have. Charlie would be back in

Charleston, probably wandering the streets and begging for scraps.
With any luck, Wild Bill would have taken him in and forced him to
work in exchange for food. Angela would be in Bardstown, if she
would even still be alive. Chances were pretty good that the gang of
men would have raped and killed her, or at least raped her.

"So what's your story?" Vance asked Angela as they ate.

"Born and raised in Lexington, Kentucky. My mother was killed
during The Fall. Dad and I stayed in Lexington until a year ago. He
was killed by some bandits. After that, I didn't really know what to do.
I heard there was a lot of work in Bardstown, so I went there. I lived
there for a few months, had to beg for food. You wouldn't believe the
number of men who want a girl to pay them with...you know...*her
body*. But I wouldn't stoop to that level. I managed to get by,
somehow. I never stole, never whored myself out, never conned
anyone. Looking back on it, I probably should've done *something*
immoral. I would've eaten better. But I don't have to worry about that
anymore, at least for now." Angela spoke quietly, dryly.

"You won't ever have to worry about it. We'll take care of you,"
Charlie said with a pat on her shoulder. She smiled at him, then
glanced at Vance.

"Did you know those guys in the alley?" Vance asked.

"No. Never seen them before. But guys like them are
everywhere. I don't know how I made it there that long without
something like that happening sooner. But I'm thankful you came
along, and I'm still thankful for everything you're doing." Angela
smiled at him, as if saying, *I wish I had more to give you for all you've
done.*

"What do you plan to do?" Vance asked, straight to the point.

"I don't know. I hadn't really thought about it. New Mexico
sounds nice." She smiled again.

"It's not. Whatever happened back West, it wasn't good. I don't
even know if there's much civilization left." Vance looked down at his
bowl as he spoke.

"What do you think happened?" Charlie asked.

95

"My best guess would be some sort of invasion. There was a pretty powerful group forming in California. They might have gone East and raided everything they came across. Could have caused mass panic and anarchy. Everything would be destroyed in the process as people rushed to move out." Vance continued looking into his bowl.

"Why would that make people leave? I mean...wouldn't they stay after it was over?" Angela asked. Vance looked up at her.

"It's a little different when you aren't anchored down. Look around you. Nobody really feels like they're 'home' anymore, no matter how long they stay somewhere. If a place gets too dangerous, you just pack up and move. And anarchy...well, anarchy takes quite awhile to die down." Vance looked back down and continued eating his soup.

"Why?" Angela asked.

"It just does. When mass chaos ensues, it takes a lot longer to settle down than it did to start. I'm guessing that group moved East and started scavenging for resources. Probably too powerful for anyone to fight off. Since it's not their home, they wouldn't be concerned with settling down and establishing order. They just want to push people out of the way—kill them, if they have to—so they can take whatever they want. People in the area would pack up and move. The ones who would stay and fight would be killed." Vance stared at the ground, trying his hardest not to think about what might have happened.

"Did you have family in New Mexico?" Angela was just trying to show that she cared, but it was unwanted.

"Let's get ready to move," Vance said as he finished off his food and stood up.

The three loaded up the wagon, hooked the horses up, and took off down the road. Angela and Charlie joked around in the back, and Vance listened intently. He pretended to not care, but the laughter and good conversation actually calmed him. A smile even formed on his face a couple of times. Around midday, the group came upon a body laying in the middle of the road. It was a man with a backpack, face-

96

down in the road.

"Is he dead?" Charlie asked.

"Not sure," Vance said, irritated. Knowing his luck, this man would be alive. Then he would be obligated to help him.

"Let's check," Charlie said as he started to get out of the wagon.

"No!" Vance said sternly. Charlie sat back down. The body could be a trap. Raiders or bandits could be hiding off of the roadway, just waiting for a lone traveler to come along.

Vance applied the brake and dismounted the wagon. M4 touching his shoulder, ready to be brought up if need be, he approached the man.

"You alright?" Vance asked. He looked around, away from the road. He didn't hear or see anyone.

Vance walked up to the man and nudged him with his boot. He didn't move. Now that he was closer he noticed that the man was African-American and had salt and pepper hair. Vance rolled him onto his side, and the man gasped for air.

"Great," Vance said to himself.

The man looked like he was in his late fifties or early sixties. His full beard had more gray in it than the hair on his head did. Tucked inside his waistband was a handgun. Vance leaned down and removed it, just in case. The old man slowly opened his eyes.

"Wa...water..." he managed to spit out.

Vance leaned down and poured some water into the man's mouth from his canteen. His lips were dry and cracked, with white forming around them. His eyes were sunken in and lifeless. Vance grabbed the man's hand, which was limp, and squeezed his fingertip. The flesh under his fingernail turned white, then very slowly started filling back in. This man was so dehydrated that he was near death.

Vance grabbed him under his armpits and dragged him to the back of the wagon. After removing his backpack, he loaded the man up and told Charlie to start rubbing small amounts of water across his lips. The old man barely moved at all. His tongue slowly came out and touched the droplets of water forming around his mouth.

97

"Is he going to die?" Charlie asked as Vance climbed in the back of the wagon with them.

"Don't know. Probably not, if his only problem is dehydration. I think we found him just in time," Vance said as he dug around in his backpack.

He pulled out an empty IV bag, along with some surgical tubing, an IV catheter, a syringe, and a container of salt. Vance grabbed a jug of water, poured it into a tin cup, and mixed a little salt in. He then sucked up the mixture with the syringe and shot it into the IV bag. He repeated this several times, until the IV bag was about half full. After wiping off the man's arm with iodine and wrapping a tourniquet around his bicep, Vance carefully stuck him in one of his veins. It wasn't easy, since the man was so dehydrated. His veins were hard to find, and they would surely roll every time Vance began to insert the needle. But somehow Vance got the needle into a vein on the first try.

Vance pulled the needle out and taped the catheter to the man's arm. He then tied the IV bag to the top of the wagon. Within only a few minutes, the man opened his eyes and groggily looked around.

"Hold still. I gave you an IV because you were severely dehydrated," Vance told him. The man stared at him blankly, then closed his eyes again.

Vance pulled out a small pipette squeeze bulb and soaked up some water. He lifted the man's eyelids and carefully dropped a few beads of water into each eye.

"Watch him. If he starts turning colors or he develops a rash, tell me. He should be alert by the time the IV runs out, and when that happens start giving him more water. Until then, keep swabbing water across his lips, eyelids, and forehead," Vance told Charlie as he climbed up front and got the wagon moving again.

***

After about half an hour, the old man was completely conscious and alert. Vance pulled the wagon over and removed the IV, which

98

was empty. The man started chugging water, but Vance took it away from him and made him sip out of a tin cup. Vance got the wagon moving again, and after another hour Vance told Charlie to give him an apple.

"Who are you guys?" the old man asked.

"Just travelers," Vance said from the front.

"Thank you for saving me. I would have died for sure," the man said.

"You were pretty bad. How did you end up in that situation?" Vance asked him.

"I was traveling, and this group picked me up in a wagon. I feel asleep, and the next thing I know, they're trying to steal my things. I fought them off, but I fell out of the wagon and they kept going. So I walked the road for awhile, but they had managed to take my satchel. It had my food and water in it. I guess I just got so dehydrated that I passed out." The old man raised his eyebrows as he spoke and slowly shook his head, as if the situation had been nothing more than a simple occurrence.

"Where were you coming from?" Vance asked.

"Back West. Things are terrible that way. I'm moving East to get away from it," the old man said.

"Actually, you're heading back West as we speak," Vance told him.

"What? You all are going back West?" The old man was quite alarmed.

"Yes. What happened there?" Vance took his eyes off the road and turned to face the man.

"Bad stuff, my friend...bad stuff..." the old man shook his head slowly.

"What kind of bad stuff?" Vance asked him.

"There's this group—more like a militia, really—from California. They're becoming pretty powerful. They started spreading like a wildfire, consuming everything in their path. No one knows much about them, other than they're ruthless and merciless. People join them because they're strong. They don't think about what they might have to do. But the way they train their people—the things they force them to do—change them completely. If people speak out against them, they die. If their soldiers try to leave, they die. If you don't give up your food and water, you die. It's sad stuff, son."

So, Vance's fears had been true. This group—whoever they were—was trying to take over everything. But they weren't helping the people. They had a chosen few who reaped the benefits. Everything else was just in the way. Vance shut his eyes tightly and cringed. War was supposed to be over. It now appeared that it was beginning again. Damn humanity, and everything about it.

"I can't turn around, but I'll drop you off at the next town," Vance told him.

"You can't go back West, son. You'll get caught up in it and die." The old man spoke coldly and leaned forward so he was right behind Vance.

"I don't have a choice." Vance kept his eyes on the road, thinking about the things to come.

***

Several hours passed, and the group arrived at the intersection of Interstate 40 and Highway 48. Vance dropped off the old man, who thanked them kindly and assured them that he could manage the short walk to Centerville. Vance and his two companions continued West, traveling until the sun was barely above the horizon. They made camp in a large pasture, eating only bread and apples for supper. The next morning, Vance managed to catch a few bass with his automatic fishing reels. The small group ate the fish quickly, enjoying the meal. They set off on the road with full stomachs, and everyone was content...except for Vance. The nagging fear of what was going on back West tore at him, forcing his mind to think about things he didn't want to think about. He battled this all day long.

Vance's only break from his horrible thoughts was when he

100

managed to shoot a deer while they were traveling on the road. As he cleaned the deer, thoughts of the events back West escaped him. It was mid afternoon when they decided to take a break, and the group ate large venison steaks while the horses grazed. Vance now let the horses free roam when they took breaks during the day, so long as they were deep in No Man's Land. The horses had developed a bond with everyone in the group, especially Vance. All he had to do was call for them and they would gallop over to him. It paid off, because toward the end of their break Vance noticed one of the horses eating from a tree. Upon further inspection, Vance discovered that it was an apple tree. Vance refilled his bag of apples, thankful for the horse's discovery. Without any salt, the venison would spoil by the next morning. However, the group had a large bag of apples and two loaves of bread left. They were fine, for now.

8

It was the group's second day since saving the old man, and the weather was less than ideal. Rain poured from the sky nearly all day long. The wagon pressed on down the road, fighting through the heavy rain and wind. Vance could barely see the road, but decided to keep going until it was too dangerous. Angela and Charlie sat in the back, protected by the wagon's cover. Vance was completely soaked, but it didn't deter him. He had suffered through much worse weather. It wasn't until the cold rain soaked all the way through his clothing and began to chill his bones that he became uncomfortable. But he continued on.

"Just pull over!" Charlie yelled over the storm.

"We've got to keep going as long as we can!" Vance yelled back.

Another hour passed, and the storm intensified. Vance finally pulled the wagon off of the road, but not too far. The last thing they needed was to have the wagon sink in the mud. Vance unhitched the horses and tied them to a tree, not allowing them much freedom to move. He didn't want them to get spooked by thunder and take off. They would never find them in this weather.

After the horses were secured, Vance climbed in the back of the wagon with Charlie and Angela. Water was coming in from the back and the front, even with the canvas covers pulled down. But it was

102

better than being out in the storm.

"How long do you think it will last?" Charlie asked.

"Hard to tell. Probably another couple hours, at least." Vance stripped his wet clothing off, leaving only his pants on.

"What happened?" Angela asked as he looked at Vance's bare chest.

"Got shot a few days ago, before we picked you up. Cannibals." Vance gingerly touched the wound. It was healing up pretty well. There was still a nasty bruise around it, but the broken skin was scabbed over and didn't appear to be infected.

"Oh my God!" Angela said, covering her mouth in horror.

"It's not a huge deal. I had my bullet-proof vest on," Vance told her as he looked at it one more time.

"Vance is a bad ass!" Charlie informed her.

"Hey," Vance snapped, "Watch your mouth."

"Yes sir." Charlie looked down at the floor of the wagon.

Angela looked over Vance's bare skin. Feelings of admiration, sexual appeal, and sadness hit her all at once. Vance's body was toned almost to perfection, his complexion was almost olive, and his face was strong and stoic. But his body was covered with numerous scars. Not hideous, just by looking at them. They added character. But the thought of *how* he got those scars made Angela sad. This man had been through so much...yet he still found compassion within him. Countless men—who had experienced many less horrors than James Vance—had taken a very different path after The Fall. Perhaps that was why James Vance remained a good man, while the others chose to live their lives in sin.

"Have you been shot before?" Angela asked as she looked over Vance once more.

"Yes. I took a bullet here," Vance touched his left side, the one that had a large scar, "and another here. But this one was stopped by my bullet-proof vest."

"What is that scar?" Angela pointed to a linear scar on Vance's left shoulder.

"Stab wound," he said casually.

"How did you get that?" Angela's eyes were wide now.

"Clearing a building in Syria. Went through a doorway and a bad guy was waiting on the other side. All he had was a knife and a sidearm. Knocked my weapon down and the fight was on. Almost shot me in the head, but luckily I walked out of there with nothing more than a knife in my shoulder." Vance started wiping himself down with a dry towel.

"And that one?" Angela pointed to another, smaller linear scar on Vance's right side, "Did you get that one in war, too?"

"That?" Vance looked down, "No...that's from a bar fight."

"And what about that one?" Angela pointed to the last scar she could see, at the base of Vance's neck on the right side.

Vance chuckled slightly.

"That one's from my brother, when we were kids. We were sword fighting with sticks and he accidentally stabbed me." Vance smiled. Nostalgia set in as he automatically thought back to his time as a young child. Thoughts of his brother raced through his mind. They had been very close.

Angela felt bad for Vance. He had seen so much, been hurt so many times. She wanted to get closer to him, but knew she'd have a hard time doing it.

"Tell me a story," Angela said, changing the subject.

"A story?" Vance asked.

"Yeah!" Charlie got excited.

"Yes, a story. Whatever you want to tell." Angela leaned forward and rested her elbows on her knees.

"Well...I'm not a very good storyteller," Vance said as he grabbed the sack of apples and pulled three of them out. He handed one to Angela and another to Charlie.

"Please!" Charlie begged.

"What kind of story?" Vance asked.

"Anything. We don't care." Angela laughed as she looked over at Charlie, who was bouncing up and down on the bench.

"Story! Story!" Charlie demanded.

"Alright...alright..." Vance leaned back and thought for a moment.

"I remember—years ago—when President Walters was elected. My buddy Scott was so excited about it that he wanted to throw a party. I had just gotten home from my first deployment ever—Iran—and I was a little apprehensive about going out. But my...well, somebody I knew...they told me I needed to spend time with my friends. So I reluctantly went out. My brother came along, too.

We got there and I was pretty surprised with how many people showed up. My buddy had a two story house, and it was practically packed. I remember feeling so nervous being around all those people. I mean, here's a guy who just got home from some pretty intense combat, and now he's being thrown into normal life again with all of these people. A lot of them I didn't know. But my brother assured me that everything would be alright, so we stayed.

Halfway through the night, Scott—the guy throwing the party—got incredibly drunk and started trying to get everyone to go down to the basement. My brother tried to help him out, make him calm down. Scott got mad, tried to fight my brother. I didn't interfere at first—my brother could certainly hold his own—I didn't need to get involved in something like that. But then Scott pushed my brother down the stairs. I heard my brother roll all the way down, so I rushed over, almost threw Scott through a wall, and ran down the stairs. My brother wasn't at the bottom, and the lights were off, so I was a little confused.

All of a sudden, the whole party started running down the stairs after me. The surprise and noise was almost too much for me, but then the basement lights turned on. The room lit up, and hundreds of pictures were hung up all over the walls of me and my family, me and my friends. My brother—who was perfectly fine—smiled and said, 'Welcome home, bro.' Scott pushed through the crowd of people and hugged me. Then all at once, the whole group shouted, 'Welcome home!' I looked around the room, and felt tears filling my eyes. Pictures of float trips and parties with friends, holidays and birthdays with family. It was such a simple action, yet it meant the world to me. That memory is forever ingrained in my mind, and I am thankful that it is."

Angela smiled through the whole story. Vance's tone and enunciation of words had a way of captivating people. Charlie seemed a little distracted. Vance bit into his apple, avoiding eye contact with either of them. Angela noticed the emotion deep within Vance's eyes. All the pain and torment and the constant struggle to remain somewhat normal.

"That was boring. I want another one," Charlie said, after concluding that the story was over.

"Charlie!" Angela tapped him on the arm.

"What?" Charlie genuinely didn't know what the big deal was.

"It was a wonderful story. And you lied...you do tell stories well," Angela said to Vance.

"Wish this storm would go away," Vance finally said as he pulled the canvas flap back to look up at the sky.

***

Hours passed by, and the storm was finally beginning to lift. Angela and Charlie had taken a nap during the bad weather, while Vance cleaned his firearms. Once the rain was little more than a sprinkle, the group dismounted the wagon. Vance allowed the horses to roam freely and began setting up camp. There was only a couple hours of daylight left, so there wasn't much use in getting back on the road.

The sun started to set, and Vance tied the horses up as per usual. The group ate bread and apples for supper, since Vance's automatic reels had failed to catch them anything. Hopefully the snares he had set up would get them something else to eat in the morning.

About an hour or so had passed since sundown. Charlie had fallen sound asleep, and Vance and Angela sat quietly around the fire. It was sobering, watching the flames dance around, the humid air, the

106

very gentle breeze. Finally, Angela broke the silence.

"I really thought you'd leave me in Bowling Green," she said.

"I had planned on it," Vance said bluntly.

"Why didn't you?" she asked.

"Charlie wouldn't shut up about it. I didn't have much of a choice." Vance looked over at a sleeping Charlie and shrugged.

"You're telling me that an 11 year old boy made you change your mind? I don't see anyone changing your mind, James Vance." Angela chuckled at the end.

"He had a lot to do with it. He made me see what was right and what was wrong. It's funny how a child can do that, when we're the ones who are supposed to be teaching *them*." Vance laid down on his side and propped himself up on his elbow.

"I'm glad you came back for me," Angela told him.

"So you keep saying." Vance continued looking into the fire.

"So what did you do in the Army?" Angela asked him.

"I was originally a Combat Engineer—a guy who specializes in explosives—but then I joined the Special Forces," he told her.

"Wow. Special Forces, huh? Did your loyalty remain with the government after The Fall?" Angela genuinely wanted to know everything she could about James Vance. Probably more so, she simply wanted to know everything she could about the Old World.

"I wasn't in the Army when it all happened. I'd been out for a little over a year. Got out because I saw all of this coming, or something like it." Vance sipped on his canteen, still staring at the fire.

"So where have you gone? For the Army, I mean."

"Iran once, Syria twice. I participated in operations in other parts of the Middle East, as well as ops in South America and Africa, but those weren't publicly sanctioned by the U.S. Government." Vance kept his answers short, still not very trusting of this girl.

"Was it exciting?" she asked.

"I suppose some of it was. Exciting is such a general term. To me it implies approval of the situation, or having a good time. The vast majority of my experiences with the Army were neither of those

107

things."

"I'm sorry. So how long were you in?"

"Fifteen long years. Seven of those years were spent with Delta Force." Vance finished his canteen and tossed it toward his backpack.

"I've heard of Delta," Angela said.

"Everyone has. Well...at least those who were old enough before The Fall," Vance said, finally looking over at her.

"You've seen so much...I'm surprised you still have some of your humanity left." Angela scooted a little closer toward him.

"In the end, that's all we can really hold onto. Don't get me wrong...the shit I've been through changed me. Some of it made me better, stronger. Most of it just made me more bitter and indifferent, more selfish and uncaring." Vance pretended to not notice that Angela was getting closer.

"I don't believe that," she said, staring at the side of Vance's head.

"Well, you don't have to. I know who I am, and who I'm not."

"I wouldn't want anyone else watching over us." Angela turned away and looked into the fire once more.

She was certainly attached to Vance now, but not infatuated with him. Her appeal for him extended beyond his physical appearance, or even the fact that he had saved her. She respected him, and didn't want to push too much. Her feelings for him were scattered, hard to consolidate. She certainly felt drawn to him, but not in a way that made her overlook the things that made James Vance truly great.

"So what did you want to be when you grew up?" Angela asked after a few short moments.

Vance chuckled.

"I don't really remember," he said.

"Everyone remembers what they wanted to be," Angela said.

"I guess I wanted to be an astronaut, when I was a kid. Then when I got old enough to start understanding the world it changed to a lawyer." Vance looked down at the ground, feeling a little awkward. He certainly didn't look like the lawyer type.

"You, a lawyer?" Angela laughed.

"Then I realized that I wanted to make a difference, so I decided I wanted to be a scientist. I went to college to study biology." Vance looked over at her to see her reaction. She started giggling.

"You don't seem like a scientist, either," she joked, "So did you graduate?"

"Eventually, yes. I started college when I was 17—I had been bumped up a grade in school—and had just completed my sophomore year when I enlisted with the Army."

"Wow. You must be pretty smart. Why did you join the Army?" Angela asked.

"No, not smart. I remember getting bored with everyday life, so I dropped out of college and joined. I ended up taking classes online with the same college and got a degree in biology when I was 24." Vance sat up and stretched his arms.

"Why'd you get the degree, if you didn't want to get out of the Army?"

"I've never been much of a quitter. And I decided it was a good idea to have something to fall back on," Vance explained.

"I'm sure you would have made a great biologist," Angela said with a smile.

"Yeah. So what did you want to be when you grew up?" he asked her.

"Oh, you know...the normal occupations that young girls are always drawn to. An actress at first, then a model, but then right after my 16th birthday—just before all of this happened—I decided I wanted to be an archaeologist. Digging up old stuff seemed exciting to me. Something about finding treasures from long ago...things people held hundreds or even thousands of years ago...really appeals to me. I still want to be one. Maybe after this is all over..." Angela's voice trailed off as she stared deeply into the fire, as if she didn't really believe her own words. The world as it currently was didn't seem likely to change anytime soon.

"Who says you can't be one now?" Vance asked her. Angela quickly snapped her focus on him.

109

"What do you mean?" she asked.

"Well...you can't very well go dig up old relics and carbon date them, but who says you can't collect old things and learn about them?" Vance jumped up and walked over to his backpack.

"I don't think that would make me an archaeologist..." Angela argued.

"Not literally, no," Vance said as he sat back down with his backpack in his lap, "But archaeology is the study of what people did in the past. Learning about the tools they used, the items they held close to them, the things they did for fun, those all teach you how people lived." Vance started digging through his backpack.

"I suppose..." Angela watched intently as Vance started pulling things out of his pack.

Finally, Vance pulled out a small cloth bag with drawstrings and tossed it over to Angela. Angela gently opened it and pulled out what was inside. It was a small piece of stone, chipped away to a fine point and had sharp, jagged edges.

"This is an arrowhead..." she said as she studied it.

"A spearhead, actually. I found it near a creek one day when I was out hiking, back in 2033 or 2034. It was partially sticking out of the hillside that was arching down into the creek. I took it to an expert, and he said it was likely around 6,000 years old." Vance smiled a bit as he told the story.

"Wow. This is beautiful. Just to know that a person from thousands of years ago held this and used this...I'm in awe." Angela was fixated on the arrowhead.

"Keep it," Vance said. Angela looked up at him, eyes wide.

"I can't..."

"Hey now, I'm Sicilian. Never refuse a gift from a Sicilian," Vance playfully warned.

"Thank you. This means the world to me," she said quietly. She tightly clinched the arrowhead in her hand as she brought it to her chest, right next to the gold necklace hanging from her neck.

After a few more minutes of talking, the two of them finally fell

110

asleep. It hadn't been a very productive day because of the storm, but Vance planned on hitting it hard over the next few days. They had traveled nearly 150 miles since parting with the old man, and were camped just East of Memphis. Tomorrow they would ride on through the large city and hopefully make it to Arkansas.

9

Three more days passed, and the group was now about 40 miles away from the Oklahoma border. They were making decent time. Much better than if Vance had been walking. He still would have been walking through Kentucky, probably.

They had picked up some good supplies in Memphis. Vance had traded Ricky's gun, a pair of boots, and one of their hatchets for several loaves of bread, a large pack of tea leaves, half a bushel of corn, three jugs of fresh water, and a small water-tight container. The three had eaten well over the last three days, especially when Vance had caught some fish and a couple of rabbits. Now they needed to make it to Oklahoma City, where things were much more civilized and orderly. At least they had been the last time Vance was there on his way to Boston. Oklahoma City was known as a large, growing community, with plenty of services and amenities. Once they reached Oklahoma City, they still had over 500 miles to go until they reached Albuquerque. That was about a week or so, if everything went well. Realistically, it would probably take about a week and a half or maybe even a couple of days more than that.

The group decided to stay in Oklahoma City for a night, so they could enjoy real civilization for once. Parts of the city utilized wind power, so there was electricity in certain areas. At night, the main roads would light up brighter than any of them could have imagined. Vance squinted, but not from the bright lights. He forced back a few stray tears. There had been a time, not all that long ago, when street lights were taken for granted. Now just seeing the bright bulbs filled his head with countless memories.

The city had quite a bit of entertainment. One section of the city seemed to be devoted entirely to festivities. Carnival-type games were played, and Charlie was fascinated. He had never had the opportunity to take part in anything like that. Some of the games were free even, no doubt an act by the local governor to keep morale up. It was a smart decision. The community seemed to thrive here, and crime appeared nearly nonexistent.

"Can we stay?" Charlie asked.

"No," Vance told him.

"Please! Your package can't be *that* important," Charlie begged.

"It's very important," Vance said.

"But Vance...this place is great..." Charlie looked around and became sad.

"Yes it is, but I have to deliver my package. I have no other choice." Vance gently put his hand on Charlie's shoulder and led him down the road. Angela walked beside them.

"But it's already been so long. They probably think you're dead anyway," Charlie said.

"Probably so. But I'm not dead, so I still have to deliver the package."

"Listen to Vance, Charlie," Angela chimed in.

"Ugh...fine." Charlie began pouting.

The group ate at a very nice restaurant that evening. They were served steaks and mashed potatoes, and it was the best meal any of them had had for quite some time. It was expensive, of course. Several bars of soap, several pairs of socks and a portion of their tea leaves had been traded for the wonderful meals.

After supper the group went back to the area where the horses were being kept. Part of the park had been fenced in, and was

113

managed in a similar manner to how they did things in Bowling Green. Vance enjoyed the nice evening, put Charlie to bed early, and then took a few moments to be alone. He walked a few feet away from the wagon, backpack in hand, and sat down on a bench. He opened up his backpack and pushed a few things aside. In the very bottom was his package, and he gingerly pulled it toward the top. It was simple, really, but very important nonetheless. Vance had promised to bring it back to Albuquerque.

"Just another package..." he said under his breath.

"What are you doing?" Angela asked as she walked around the wagon toward Vance.

Vance stuffed the package back down to the bottom and closed up his backpack.

"Just going through the supplies I have in my pack," he said. Angela sat down next to him on the bench.

"Charlie thinks the world of you," she said to him.

"I've grown to like the boy, myself," Vance replied.

"He's not the only one. I think a lot of you, too." Angela stared at him, smiling as she did so. Vance turned his head toward her and stared into her eyes, searching for her true intentions. She was absolutely beautiful.

"Are you...I mean, do you...Is there a Mrs. James Vance?" Angela stuttered.

"I don't see why that matters," Vance said.

"What do you mean?"

"My family has nothing to do with what's going on out here." Vance stood up and took a couple of steps away.

"Well how's a girl supposed to know what she can get away with?" Angela joked.

"I'm forty-three years old, Angela. You're twenty-five. Regardless of what my family situation is, we're not an option." Vance was cold and blunt. Angela's smile faded.

"I see. I apologize." Angela got up and walked over to the wagon. She pulled back the canvas flap and crawled inside.

114

Vance leaned up against the fence, looking out over the park and all of the horses contained within. He took a bite of an apple and thought briefly about his life. This goddamn world had gone to hell fast. It wasn't all that pleasant before, but at least there had been some level of order. Now there was nothing, except in seemingly utopian places like Oklahoma City. And Canada, supposedly. But even at that, Oklahoma City was nothing like the Old World. Technology had taken several steps back, and it seemed like it would take at least twice as long to get back to where they had been. That was considering a stable government could be formed. Thus far, none had succeeded. Several had tried, but they fell apart within a matter of weeks or months. It seemed that regional powers and city-states were all that was feasible at the moment.

Vance threw his apple core toward the nearest horse, who happily picked it up off of the ground and ate it. He then got in the back of the wagon and snuggled up in his blankets. Charlie was snoring on the other end, and Angela was pretending to be asleep beside him. Vance felt a little guilty for shutting her down like that. She was a good girl, after all. He gently nudged her with his foot. She raised her head and looked down at him.

"If things were different, then perhaps. But they're not. It's nothing personal," he said to her.

Angela forced a smile, then laid her head back down. Vance wrapped his arms behind his head and stared up at the ceiling of the wagon. Sometimes- and the times seemed to come at random- he felt like he didn't even want to be alive. He hated the world at this point, and nearly everything in it. Especially out in No Man's Land, where the land was unforgiving and the people even more so. Every once in a while, however, he stumbled upon people like Charlie and Angela. They had basically been thrown in his lap, and he had no other choice but to ensure their safety until they were no longer his problem. When they would no longer be his problem was yet to be determined.

***

The group awoke early the next morning. Vance was already up when Charlie and Angela crawled out of the wagon. He had retrieved their horses and was hitching them to the wagon.

"Gotta get on the road soon. Might be able to travel over a hundred miles today, if we push hard enough. Got plenty of water and food now." Vance finished hooking up the horses and crawled up into the driver's seat.

"Do what you need to before we leave. That's assuming you're coming with me, of course." Vance slipped his gloves on. Charlie and Angela looked at each other.

"Why wouldn't we?" Angela asked.

"Just saying...this place is great. Safe, fun, clean...if you guys want to stay here, I don't have any qualms with it." Vance lit a cigarette and took a long drag off of it.

"No...we're coming with you," Angela said.

"Yeah Vance, we don't ever want to leave you," Charlie said.

"I don't know what lies ahead. It's bound to get a lot more dangerous down the road," Vance told them.

"We've got you to protect us," Charlie told him.

"If you're coming, then hurry up," Vance said.

Angela and Charlie quickly walked off toward the outhouses.

"That was strange," Angela said.

"Yeah...it's like Vance doesn't want us to go with him," Charlie told her.

"Maybe he's afraid of what might happen to us?" Angela asked, mostly to herself.

"He'll protect us. Vance wouldn't let anything bad happen," Charlie said with confidence.

"Charlie...listen," Angela stopped the boy, "Vance is just a man. He'll do what he can to keep us safe, but anything can happen out there."

"I know, Angie. I watched my dad die," Charlie said before

116

pushing her arm away and continuing toward the outhouses.

Once the group was ready to go, Vance hit the reins and off they went. Before they knew it, Oklahoma City was miles behind them.

***

Two days passed, and the group rolled their wagon into Shamrock, Texas. The town was small. An old sign, barely hanging on a pole, said the town's population was 2,029. Of course, that was before The Fall. Now it probably only had a few dozen inhabitants, maybe a hundred. Vance looked around as he steered the horses and saw clean streets, no people, and abandoned storefronts. As they got into the town a little more, he saw a couple of people in a park playing with an old baseball. A little further down the road was a small merchant's kiosk. An elderly man sat behind it, reading an old newspaper. When he saw the wagon he nearly dropped the paper, and stared at the wagon with wide eyes.

"Hello traveler!" he said, "Mind taking a look at my wares?"

Vance stopped the wagon and dismounted. As he approached the elderly man's kiosk, he saw old relics from a time long ago. Trinkets and toys littered the small counter.

"Where you from, Outlander?" the old man asked, paying special attention to Vance's tactical vest and assault rifle.

"Heading back West," Vance answered as he scanned the old man's items.

"Ain't nothing back West, friend." The old man wiped his brow with a handkerchief.

"That stuff looks pretty neat!" Charlie exclaimed as he jumped down from the wagon. Angela followed closely behind him.

"These things *are* neat, young man. Take a look at this." The old man gingerly picked up a snow globe and handed it to Charlie.

"Wow!" Charlie said as he watched the snow flakes fall inside the globe. Inside the globe was a white horse.

"Will you take a couple ears of corn for the snow globe?" Vance asked.

"That sounds fair," the old man replied with a smile.

Vance looked at Angela and nodded his head toward the wagon. She went back and retrieved two ears of corn, and handed them to the old man.

"Thanks, Vance," Charlie said, his eyes still locked on the snow globe.

"Looks like a pretty nice town," Vance said to the old merchant. The old man's face turned sour.

"It used to be," he said.

"What do you mean?" Vance asked him.

"Those bandits from the West Coast came into town a couple weeks ago. They've been raising all kinds of hell. Folks say it's only a matter of time before they burn this place to the ground and move on. If I were you, I'd move on down the road as soon as possible." The old man sat back down on his chair.

"How many of these bandits are there?" Vance asked.

"I'm not sure. I've seen four or five at a time. They're hold up in City Hall, just down the road. They come out every so often to harass us and take our things." The old man picked up his paper again and started reading.

"What kinds of weapons do they have?" Vance took this opportunity to find out all he could about these bandits. If they were part of the militia from California—and chances were pretty good that they were—he needed to get all the information he could.

"Most of 'em carry clubs and such. Usually at least one of them has a shotgun or pistol with 'em. Not sure what all they got inside City Hall. They came in the middle of the night, so none of us really know how many there are. Judging by the different faces I've seen, I'd say there's at least ten."

"Thank you," Vance said, and turned to walk away.

"What do they do to you?" Charlie asked, still standing in front of the kiosk.

"They throw us around, sometimes beat us. They mostly just take

118

our goods." The old man looked sad as he spoke.

Vance got back in the driver's seat of the wagon. Charlie and Angela climbed in back shortly after.

"We have to help these people, Vance," Charlie said.

"No," Vance said coldly.

"But Vance..."

"It's not our fight, boy. Be quiet and leave it alone," Vance said as he snapped the reins.

Just as the wagon began moving, the group heard laughter and shouting coming from down one of the side streets. Soon a small group of four men dressed like bandits or raiders appeared, casually walking down the street. Two of them had baseball bats, one had a logging chain, and the other had a handgun on his side and a crowbar in his hand.

"There they are!" Charlie said as he peaked his head out of the wagon.

"Get back!" Vance said as he nudged the boy back into the wagon.

Vance watched the men out of the corner of his eye. They began pointing at the wagon and talking amongst themselves. Vance got the horses moving a little faster, but the men ran up alongside the wagon and slowed the horses down.

"What you got inside that wagon, friend?" the man with the gun asked.

Vance remained silent.

"Why don't you get down and let us take a look," another said.

"Hold on. He's got firepower!" one of the others said with a laugh.

"Alright then...nice and slow," the first man said as he drew his handgun from its holster.

"I suggest you boys move away from my wagon and let me leave," Vance said calmly. Behind his dark sunglasses his eyes were jumping back and forth, noting details about the men in front of him.

"Come on cowboy, get off the wagon," the man holding the gun

119

said.

Vance slowly stood, allowing his M4 to hang in front of him. He casually dismounted the wagon on the side closest to the man with the gun.

"If you move at all, I'm filling you full of holes," the man said. Vance stared at him coldly. If the man had been able to see his eyes, he might have backed up a couple of steps. Unfortunately for the man, he couldn't see Vance's cold eyes looking into his soul.

"Take a look inside the wagon, boys," the man with the gun—presumably the leader—said with a smile.

"I wouldn't do that," Vance told him.

"And why's that, Outlander?" the leader asked.

"Because you'll die," Vance said.

The leader stared at him for a moment, then let out a guttural laugh. The other three followed suit. Vance continued staring at them, his face completely devoid of emotion. After several moments of laughter, two of the men began walking around the side of the wagon. The leader kept the gun down by his hip, the muzzle pointed at Vance's chest. He was only about two feet away. The other bandit stayed just behind the leader, watching Vance as well.

Vance drew his Glock from its thigh holster and fired two rounds from his hip before the leader could even pull the trigger. It looked like something out of a Western film. The bullets hit the leader square in the chest, and the man doubled over before crashing to the ground. Vance then transitioned to the man standing behind the leader—who was holding a baseball bat—and shot once. The bullet hit right below the man's chin, blood poured out from the gaping hole in his neck and he fell straight to the ground.

The two men who had just gotten to the back of the wagon came running around toward Vance, who quickly holstered his Glock and drew his tanto sword. There was no need to waste anymore ammo on these untrained bandits. The first man charged Vance with his baseball bat pulled back above his shoulder. Vance skipped forward and thrust his sword through the man's chest. The baseball bat fell to the ground,

and Vance pulled his sword out of the man's body. The remaining
bandit began swinging his logging chain around, building momentum
for his attack. Vance squared off with him, waiting for the man to
make his move. The logging chain had more reach than Vance's
sword, so it would have been unwise to rush in and attack. As heavy
as it was, it would cause devastating damage if it made contact with
any part of Vance's body.

The man jumped forward and violently swung the chain. Vance
stepped to the side and hurled his blade toward the man's head. It
lodged in the man's skull, causing him to fall to the ground like a rag
doll. His body convulsed and his eyes rolled back in his head. Vance
stepped on the man's face and forcefully removed the sword from his
skull. After wiping his blade on the man's pant leg, Vance sheathed his
sword and walked around to the back of the wagon.

"Everyone okay?" Vance asked as he pulled the canvas cover
back. Angela jumped a little, and was holding one of the shotguns
Vance had recovered from the cannibal's farm. Vance stared at her
calmly, and she lowered the weapon.

"Yes...yes we're okay," she answered.

"Did you kill them?" Charlie asked.

"They're taken care of. Stay in the wagon," Vance told them.

Vance walked down to the old merchant's kiosk. The old man
was hunkered down behind the stand, shaking from fear.

"It's alright. They're dead," Vance told him.

"Boy, I don't know if you did this town a favor or not. Those men
needed to die, but now the rest of 'em are gonna rain hell down on
those of us who live here." The old man slowly rose to his feet with
Vance's help.

"I know. I'm going to take care of it. Do you have somewhere my
companions can stay until this is all over?" Vance asked.

"What do you mean you're going to take care of it? You're one
man. You may have gotten lucky with those four guys, but next time
there will be more. Maybe seven or eight." The old man brushed
himself off.

"I said I'll take care of it, and I will." Vance started walking back to his wagon.

"We'll need to have a town meeting first. Hide somewhere and meet me down at the community building in an hour or so," the old man told him.

"Where's the community building?" Vance asked.

"Just down the road here," he pointed, "It's a big sheet metal building. You can't miss it. Hopefully they won't send out a posse for awhile."

***

Vance, Angela and Charlie were parked behind an old shed on the outskirts of town. Vance wasn't happy about the situation. It not only delayed him, but he now had to put himself in harm's way. He couldn't just leave, though, not after killing those bandits. He couldn't allow them to harm the people of Shamrock because of an altercation he had with them. After about forty-five minutes, Vance topped off his canteens and got out of the wagon.

"Stay here until I get back. I mean it. Don't even get out of the wagon. If any of those bandits happen to come across the wagon, shoot them with the shotgun." Vance checked his magazines and then stared at Charlie and Angela to make sure they understood.

"Okay. Hurry back," Angela said reluctantly, fear in her eyes.

Vance began walking into town, trying to stick to the small side roads as much as possible. Infiltrating a small town that only had a handful of people to watch out for might not sound too difficult, but Vance was unsure if the bandits were looking for the people that killed their friends.

Vance arrived at the community building without incident. About two dozen people were sitting down inside, and they silently stared at him as he entered. The old man motioned for him to come up to the front.

"Good folks of Shamrock, this is the man who killed the bandits in the street today," the old man said. The people of shamrock began whispering amongst themselves, presumably discussing Vance's appearance, where he might have come from, and if he could be trusted.

"I know you are all concerned that the group of bandits who invaded our town will kill us to take revenge, but this man says he is going to take care of the problem." The old man spoke matter-of-factly, and when he spoke everyone became silent.

"How do we know he can deliver on his promise, John?" a man asked.

"We don't. But we don't have many choices now. We have to let him try." The old man—John—was obviously in favor of Vance trying.

"They'll be pissed off when they find those guys dead, but think of what they'll do if this stranger causes anymore damage," another man said.

"At least then there will be less of 'em," John argued.

"True," someone said.

"Fuck 'em. Let this guy at 'em," another blurted out.

"He killed four of them. Perhaps he can actually do what he says," someone else in the crowd said.

"I can't let these men take out their vengeance on you people," Vance interrupted, "not because of something I did. I started this, and it's only right that I finish it. With or without your blessing, I'm going to City Hall and killing them. I just came here to respect your customs."

The people murmured amongst each other. Vance stood at the front of them with John, getting slightly irritated as time passed. All of a sudden, one of the townsfolk rushed through the door.

"They're comin'! They're comin'!" he said quietly.

"Quickly! Pray!" John said to them. Everyone bowed their heads, almost in unison.

"Get to the kitchen!" John told Vance.

Vance ran out of the large room just as he heard the double doors

123

fly open in the front. He ran around to the kitchen and took off his tactical vest, as well as his bullet-proof vest, backpack and M4. He hid them inside a cabinet and quietly made his way back out into the hall. Now he was only wearing his thigh holster and sidearm, but he could blend in with the local populous a little easier. Even though John had told him to go to the kitchen, Vance couldn't just hide somewhere and risk letting more harm come to these people.

Vance sneaked up to the end of the hall and peeked around the corner. Three men were standing in the middle of the room between the two sections of folding chairs. The townsfolk still had their heads bowed in prayer. John was standing at the front, reciting a passage from the Bible. Vance quietly ran forward when the three men were busy looking around the room and took a seat next to one of the people. He bowed his head as well.

"Yea, though I walk through the valley of the shadow of death, I shall fear no evil, for thou art with me. Thy rod and thy staff, they comfort me..."

"Enough!" one of the bandits—presumably the leader—shouted.

"Amen," John finished. The townsfolk said amen as well.

"What are you all doin' here?" the leader—a large, burly man with a baseball bat in his hands and a shotgun on his back—growled.

"Having church," John told him.

"On a Thursday? In this place?" the leader asked.

"We're very religious. We have church whenever we feel we need to. Normally we'd do it in the church down the road, but we didn't feel like it would be proper without our preacher. He's still recovering from what you boys did to him a few days ago..." John spoke softly.

"Shut up, old man. You know what's going on here. My boys got killed right down the road from your shitty little stand. Who did it?" The man's voice was deep and loud.

"I'm afraid I don't know what you're talking about," John told him.

"Bullshit. You know exactly what I'm talking about. Now tell me or I'll start killing your friends," said the bear-like man, as if he had

124

done something similar before.

"Please...just let us be. This is our town, damn it!" John became angry.

The leader stepped to the front of the room and smacked John with the back of his hand. The frail old man tumbled to the ground. Vance felt his legs jerk out of instinct, wanting to push his body up and rush to John's rescue. But he stopped himself and waited. Rushing into things was how men got killed. The leader's two companions were watching the crowd, and both of them had firearms. One had a hunting rifle, the other had what looked like a little semi-automatic .22 rifle.

John pushed himself off the ground and sat on all fours. Blood dripped from his mouth. Vance began breathing hard, his heart started to race. Rage engulfed him.

"Now you'll tell me who did it," the leader said as he approached the first row of people, "Or I'll kill this fucking bitch!"

He grabbed a woman and dragged her to the front of the room. Out of his pocket he pulled a knife, and he placed the blade against her throat. Vance started getting up out of his seat, but the man next to him forcefully grabbed his leg and pushed him back down.

"If you get killed, then we have no hope of saving this town," he whispered to Vance.

"No one wants to tell me, huh? Then I guess this bitch needs to die!"

A single shot echoed throughout the building. The townsfolk threw themselves to the ground, and the leader's thugs reeled back out of instinct. The leader fell to the ground, a bullet hole in his forehead. The woman ran off to the side, safe and sound.

Vance turned his attention to the two thugs, who had just figured out that their leader had been shot dead and Vance was the one who did it. Vance fired twice at the closest one, who had the .22 rifle. The man screamed and fell to the ground like a ton of rocks. The second man brought up his rifle and attempted to aim through the scope, probably because that was how he had always done it. Vance started

125

walking toward him, watching as the muzzle swayed back and forth while the man tried to get his target in his sights. As close as they were, it would be nearly impossible.

Vance shot the man in the leg, making sure not to kill him. The thug dropped his rifle and fell to the ground, screaming in pain. Vance walked up to him, holstered his Glock, and grabbed the man by his collar.

"Meeting's over," he said as he dragged the thug toward the kitchen.

Vance threw the man on the floor, while a couple of the townsfolk brought John to the kitchen and started cleaning up his lip.

"How many men do you have?" Vance asked him.

"Fuck you!" the thug said through clenched teeth. Vance stomped on the man's wounded leg and let him scream.

"I can get real nasty, boy. Now tell me what I want to know," he roared.

"Okay, okay!" the man whimpered. Vance left his foot pressed against the man's wound.

"We had thirteen, but now I guess we only have...two...twenty...or...eight..." The man wasn't being difficult...he was going into shock. Vance removed his boot from the man's wound and grabbed him by his face. If there were originally thirteen of them, then they only had seven left. Six, after Vance got through with this guy.

"What kind of firepower do you have?" Vance asked him.

The man's eyes rolled back in his head as he said something inaudible. Vance glanced down and saw a massive amount of blood gushing from the man's leg. He must have grazed an artery.

"Shit..." Vance threw the man's head down and walked over to the cabinet where his gear was stored.

"So what now?" John asked. His lip was beginning to swell.

"Now I kill these bastards." Vance still felt the rage pumping through him.

"Six left. Those aren't good odds," John said as someone else

126

patted his lip with a towel.

"I've faced worse odds, against worse enemies. I'll manage," Vance said as he zipped up his vest.

"Need someone to go with you?" John asked him.

"No. They'll just get in the way," Vance said as he picked up his M4 and threw the single point sling around his neck, "Besides...it wouldn't be right for me to put anybody else in harm's way. You going to be okay?"

"I'll be fine," John said.

Vance walked out of the community building and scanned the surrounding area. The chances were pretty good that the three men he had faced were the only men that had been sent out, but he remained cautious nonetheless. As he made his way to City Hall, he thought about what he was going to do. These people disgusted him. But it wasn't simply what had gone on in Shamrock that had gotten him so worked up. He was also thinking about what was going on back West, and the idea that these men were from the same group was stuck in his mind. The reality of what was going on had finally set in, and Vance was going to kill as many of these people as possible. He wouldn't run and hide, he wouldn't lay down and die, and he sure as hell wouldn't join them. This was a glimpse of things to come, in his mind.

Vance was about half a block from City Hall. He had thought up his plan while walking, and now it was time to put it in motion. He surveyed the building, looking for snipers or guards. There didn't appear to be any. It was a small, one story building. The front door was propped open to let fresh air in. These guys apparently weren't too worried about someone attacking them.

Vance nonchalantly walked inside the building. Directly to his right was a man sitting at a table reading an old magazine with his legs propped up. When he saw Vance, his eyes widened and he kicked his feet off the table. He opened his mouth to scream but Vance silenced him with a bullet to the head. Vance heard yelling coming from the adjacent room, and brought up his M4. Two men rushed through the doorway, but were immediately put down by several bullets from Vance's assault rifle. If the boy had been right, then there were only three left. Vance waited several moments, but no one else came through the door. He cautiously approached, his M4 still shouldered. At the last moment he rushed through the doorway, and found the remaining three men. One was sitting at a desk smiling, hands empty, the other two were standing on either side of him and were unarmed. Vance kept his rifle trained on them.

"Well done," the man behind the desk said, and started clapping.

Vance wanted answers, and as much as these people needed to die, he couldn't help but ask some questions.

"Who the hell are you people?" he asked, M4 still up and his finger on the trigger.

"I'm David Grider. The men you killed were under my command," the man answered, not a hint of fear on his face.

"Where did you come from?" Vance asked.

"West. We're with Xander's Army, a growing militia from California. We were tasked with pushing East and taking control of small towns." Grider poured two glasses of water, pushing one to the edge of the desk toward Vance.

"What's going on in New Mexico?" Vance's adrenaline was pumping.

"Same thing, except there are more of us. We take over cities, get what we can from them, send the supplies back West, and move on. We could use someone like you." Grider casually took a drink of water.

Vance shot the man on Grider's right, then put down the one on his left. Now it was just him and Grider, who was leaning back in his chair. Fear had finally taken over, and it showed on his face.

"Stand up with your arms raised," Vance ordered. Grider did as he was told.

"Now turn around and back up toward me."

Grider obeyed, and when he got to Vance he was pushed down to his knees. Vance took off his backpack and pulled out some 550 cord. After tightly tying the man's hands behind his back and doing the same thing with his feet, Vance dragged him outside.

"Have you been through Albuquerque?" Vance asked him calmly.

"Yes," Grider answered.

"What's going on there?" Vance lit a cigarette and offered one to Grider, who accepted. Vance placed the cigarette in his mouth and lit it for him.

"We took it over," Grider told him, "Listen, my commander will pay a lot for my safe return. I'm a valued asset to Xander's Army. Let me go, and I'll make sure you are paid."

"Alright," Vance said, "You tell me what I need to know, and I will let you go."

"Xander's Army is strong. There are maybe five or six thousand of us. We're scattered out, of course, and the strongest forces are in California." Grider squinted through the smoke as he spoke, obviously confident that he was going to make it out okay.

"What kind of weaponry do you all have?" Vance asked.

"As you have probably seen, the majority of our forces use melee weapons. Firearms are in short supply, and ammo is hard to come by. Xander has started manufacturing his own ammunition, though. In just a few months, every soldier in Xander's Army will be supplied with firearms and ammo. We're taking this country back." Grider believed in the cause, whatever it might be. Vance didn't care much about that part.

"Who is Xander?"

"Alexander Thompson. He goes by Xander. He started this militia about six years ago, and he's obviously done very well for himself..."

"By enlisting the scum of the earth and promising them free reign on innocent people..." Vance interjected.

"That's how you see it. We see it as making people stronger. In time they'll come to respect us," Grider quickly responded.

Vance turned his back on Grider and finished smoking his cigarette. His blood was boiling as he thought about the state of affairs in Albuquerque. If Grider was telling the truth—which he probably

129

was—then Vance's home city probably resembled Shamrock, or worse.

Vance dug more 550 cord out of his backpack and pulled a long strand of it out. He left it connected to the rest of it, and wrapped the end around Grider's neck.

"What are you doing?" Grider protested. Vance ignored him.

After tying a knot and pulling the cord tight, Vance picked up the rest of the cord and took off walking. The cord became taut, and Vance jerked Grider along behind him. Grider began to snort as he tried to breath, but the cord had tightened to the point that breathing was impossible. Vance continued walking, his destination only about twenty yards in front of him. There was a decorative arch in the middle of the town square, with a tree and some benches. When he reached the arch, Vance loosened the cord around Grider's neck a little so he could breath. Grider began gasping, and had been on the verge of losing consciousness. Vance threw the other end of the cord through the metal arch, gripped the cord tightly over his shoulder, and forced himself forward. It was not an easy task. The 550 cord was thin, and hanging onto it was difficult. But Vance managed, and soon Grider's body was hanging from the archway. He swayed from side to side, kicking his bound feet around. His eyes were bulging out of his head, his face was turning purple, his tongue poked out through his lips. Vance tied the cord to the tree in front of him and walked away.

Several of the townsfolk appeared from around the corner. They cautiously looked around, and quickly saw Vance walking away from a man hanging by his neck. They slowly approached the dying man, who was barely moving at all now. Grider's body finally went completely limp, and calmly swayed from side to side. The people of Shamrock were horrified, but were glad that the terror was finally over. The relief was evident on all of their faces. They all knew that this man deserved it, whoever he was. One of them caught up with Vance and touched him on the shoulder.

"Who's that guy?" the man asked.

"His name was David Grider. He was in charge of the people

who took over your town. You might be able to save him, if you cut the cord now. He'll probably have some brain damage, though. I'd let him hang," Vance said as he kept walking. The man quit following and stared as Vance walked away.

Vance walked in silence all the way back to his wagon, which wasn't far. When he arrived, he found Charlie and Angela still sitting inside the wagon, as he had told them to.

"Is everything alright?" Angela asked, "We heard gunshots."

"Everything's fine. Those men won't be bothering these people anymore."

Vance drove the wagon back into town a little ways so he could get back on the main road. A few townsfolk—old John was among them—were standing on the street corner talking about what had just happened.

"Stranger!" John yelled. Vance stopped the wagon and looked over at John.

"We're mighty grateful for what you've done here, Outlander. Care to stick around?" John asked.

"I've gotta go back West," Vance replied.

"Well at least stay for the night. It's already after noon, and you folks might as well have a nice place to sleep and some good food to eat." Vance could see the hope in John's eyes. Hope that this mysterious stranger with all his gratitude would stay a little longer.

"I suppose we can do that," Vance finally said.

The group was led down the road to John's house. It was a medium sized house, with white vinyl siding and a picket fence around the yard. Vance unhitched the horses and led them through the gate into the yard.

"Don't worry about getting them horses water, I'll have my boy do it," John said. For a moment, Vance wondered if the old timer was referring to his actual son or to a "colored" person. Soon a man who appeared to be about thirty came walking out of the house.

"Chance, get these horses some water. There's an old trough down at Billy's house. Go get it and have a couple of your friends fill

131

it up with water from the well." John spoke with authority. He was probably the oldest person in town, which would make him the patriarch in a way.

Chance hurried over to a cart and wheeled it down the road. John led the group inside his home, sat them down, and served them tea.

"You all can have our beds for the night," he said.

"That won't be necessary," Vance told him.

"Of course it's necessary. You're our guests." John looked at him sternly.

"No offense, but I don't like sleeping in someone else's bed. Not to mention the fact that you're being kind enough to take us in for the night, so we don't need to take your beds as well." Vance sipped at his tea and began taking off his gear.

"You never told me your name, stranger," John said.

"James Vance. Everyone just calls me Vance."

"I'm Charlie," the boy piped up.

"And I'm Angela. Thank you for letting us stay in your home."

"After what this man did for our town, he's welcome to stay here permanently." John nodded his head as he spoke.

"What happened to Grider? Did your people cut him down?" Vance asked.

"Hell no. One of 'em was about to, but I told 'em to let him hang." John frowned at the mention of Grider.

The afternoon was spent talking, drinking tea, and Charlie playing with some of the old man's toys. There were several moments of nostalgia. The house was completely furnished, as if it had been taken straight out of the 90s and dropped into an apocalyptic wasteland. Pictures still hung on the walls, furniture was still in good condition, and the wallpaper wasn't peeling. Vance was especially taken aback by all of it. It reminded him of his grandparent's house.

"So why are you heading out West?" John asked as he lit several candles around the living room.

"I'm a courier. I have a package to take back to New Mexico," Vance told him.

132

"A courier, eh? It's nice to see a few of those still around. Since those bandits have been pushing East, we don't see a lot of couriers around here anymore." John took a seat in his recliner and kicked the feet up.

"I'll probably retire after this one," Vance said.

"Retire? Ha! I haven't heard anyone say that for quite some time." John chuckled.

"So what happened to everyone else in town? Where did they all go?" Angela asked.

"Most of 'em packed up and moved on after The Fall. A lot of 'em died from starvation, disease, violence. We lost about a dozen here recently, when those men came into town." John spoke softly, his eyes cast down at the floor.

"Did you lose anyone?" Angela asked.

"My wife was diagnosed with cancer about a year before everything collapsed. After The Fall, we couldn't get her the medicine and treatments she needed. She died three years ago. One of my boys—Daniel—was killed by a bandit while out scavenging about a year after The Fall." John's voice was monotone, but there were no tears, no trembling in his voice. Most people had become hard as stone since The Fall, especially the old timers.

"I lost both my parents," Angela said.

"Me too," Charlie said as he looked down at the floor.

"And what about you, James Vance? Have you lost anyone?" John asked.

"We've all lost something. That was true even before The Fall." Vance pulled out a pack of toothpicks and began chewing on one.

"I think it's time for supper," John said as he rose from his chair.

The group was served fish, potatoes, and green beans. It was a lovely meal, and John was a good cook. Even without the luxury of spices and herbs, the meal tasted wonderful. They even had apple juice to drink. John's son Chance was a quiet man, with gentle features and a simple way of talking. Vance enjoyed the time because it resembled some level of normality. Charlie and Angela also seemed to

133

be enjoying themselves, teasing each other and playing with John's old toys and nick-knacks. Vance stayed quiet most of the evening, listening to John tell stories and watching Chance flirt with Angela. He was handsome, but lacked charm and charisma. Angela didn't seem to mind. She was probably just happy to have some attention.

As the hands of the clock on the wall moved closer to 10 o' clock, Vance felt his eyes getting heavy. Charlie had fallen asleep on the floor, and Angela was sitting down beside him with her back against the couch. John was still rambling on, telling a story about one thing or another before The Fall. Chance and Angela seemed to be listening, but Vance was lost in thought. Finally, he got up and retrieved the group's sleeping gear and laid it all out on the floor. After placing Charlie inside the blankets and putting a small pillow under his head, Vance laid down next to him. John wished them a good night's sleep and went off to his bedroom. Chance and Angela stayed awake, and now that Vance was laying down to go to sleep, he found himself surprisingly energized. His eyes were wide open, no longer heavy, and his legs did not want to stay still.

"So you're a pretty tough guy?" Chance said all of a sudden.

"We're all only as tough as we choose to be," Vance said, still staring at the ceiling.

"James Vance...always cryptic." Angela smiled.

"Where'd you learn to shoot so good?" Chance asked. He had been sitting nearby when Vance shot the guy in the head in the community building.

"I suppose I've always been a decent shot," Vance said as he sat up and leaned his back against the other couch, "but being in the military certainly helped. I didn't get real good until I experienced combat. Even better once I joined the Special Forces."

"You were in the Special Forces? That explains it. I wanted to be in the Special Forces when I was a kid." Chance's voice radiated with excitement.

"It wasn't all it was cracked up to be, I promise you." Vance pulled out his canteen and took a drink from it.

134

"Did you do anything exciting?" Chance asked him.

"Heh..." Vance chuckled slightly. He was always asked that question, "I suppose that depends on your definition of the word."

"Well...did you?" Chance asked again.

"I took out Bassel Al-Kalif, if you remember him," Vance said as he turned his head and looked at Chance.

"No shit! He was the Syrian President, right?" Chance's eyes widened as far as they would go.

"Yep. Pretty much ended the war with Syria, and subsequently Iran." Vance decided to divulge some interesting information to this guy. He looked like someone who would appreciate it.

"Wow. How'd you do it?" Chance leaned forward, resting his elbows on his knees.

"Sniped him from nearly a mile away while he was giving a speech. Probably a lucky shot, looking back on it. It took a lot of preparation and the help of people 7,000 miles away. Hit him right in the head with a .50 caliber round, then I hightailed it out of there and traveled about two hundred miles in the trunk of a car." Vance threw his blanket over him, an attempt to hopefully make himself a little sleepier.

"Damn...that's crazy. I wouldn't believed you, if I hadn't seen what you did today," Chance said honestly.

"Hell, I don't expect you to believe me now. It's a pretty fantastic claim." Vance didn't really care if anyone believed him. It made no difference to him. He knew what he had and hadn't done.

"I don't mean to offend you, but I'm curious. What's war like?" Chance asked softly.

"What's war like? It would take hours—even days—to fully answer that question. And even then you wouldn't have a true understanding of it," Vance looked past Angela and Chance, staring off into space, "War is cold, dark, empty. A man can take another man's life outside of war, but it's not the same. For some reason war itself changes everything about the simple action of killing someone. The time spent away from everything familiar to you, the foreign

135

environment you are forced to call home, the strange people you are fighting, it all plays a part in the experience. And killing a man...that's easy. The easiest part, probably. It's how a man handles it after the fact that defines him.

Anyone can kill another human being. But only certain people can do it and live peacefully with themselves afterward. It doesn't matter if the person you killed deserved it, or they were a sworn enemy of your people...you still took a life, and you have to live with that. Living in this new world, you probably know what I'm talking about. But in war you don't get to go home that night after killing a man and snuggle up in your bed, or sit down with your family and take comfort in the fact that they're there for you. In war you get to go back to your hut, or your tent, or your sleeping bag, and think about the things you've done without those feelings of normality keeping your boots on the ground. You alone are left to struggle to keep your grasp on reality, to not let your emotions run rampant. It takes a special breed to be able to do that effectively, especially after the first time."

"You're apparently one of those people," Chance said after a brief moment of silence.

"I never claimed to be," Vance said as he broke from his trance, "I struggled to keep my head on my shoulders during my first deployment. Hell, I even struggled off and on for years after I came home. There were still times of grief and feelings of emptiness even after I joined Delta Force. You just finally reach a point of collapse, where your mind no longer views those things as taboo. But the memories...they never go away. To this day I have dreams about the things I've done, and if there is a Hell—which, fortunately for me, I believe there isn't—then I am surely going there. War forces you to do things that sometimes go against your moral compass. And the more you think about them, the more you analyze it, the more you begin to question your actions."

"What do you mean?" Chance interrupted.

"Would that kid have pulled the trigger?" Vance looked right at him.

"Huh?" Chance cocked his head to the side.

"Would he have pulled the trigger? Or did that guy really look like he had a detonator? Those are the kinds of questions that eat at you. Yes, I have killed children. Children who were not much older than Charlie. They had guns, but would they have used them? Some of them would have, there's not a doubt in my mind. In fact, I've been shot at by kids before. But I *know* that some of them would *not* have. And I killed a man once because he pulled something out of his pocket that resembled a detonator. We had come upon an IED—an Improvised Explosive Device—sitting next to the road. A guy strolled up, stopped in the middle of the road about two hundred meters away, looked right at us, and pulled something out of his pocket that looked like a detonator. I shot him dead, and when we went up to his body, I discovered he had a pack of cigarettes in his hand. Hindsight is a bitch, and like I said, your mind can't help but to break everything down and second guess itself."

"Damn. I'm...I'm sorry..." Chance began.

"Don't be. I don't need pity. I'm telling you these things because you asked, and I want you to understand. Never envy a man who can kill without mercy, because deep down he's probably a sociopath." Vance stood and slowly walked toward the front door, pulling a pack of cigarettes out of his pocket as he did so.

Once outside, Angela came up behind him. She leaned against the railing on the porch and stared at Vance.

"I don't think you're a sociopath," she said.

"I know I'm not. At least not fully. I still care about things," Vance replied.

"Sometimes good men are forced to do terrible things," Angela told him.

"I know. I don't need a helping hand, but thank you. I've dealt with these things for years, and I've sat through countless hours of therapy that didn't help. In the end, I had to help myself. I'm at peace with my past, for the most part." Vance took a long drag off his

137

cigarette.

"For the most part?" Angela asked.

"There are still things that bother me, from time to time. Mostly random things, at random times. It just depends on the day of the week. But I know how to deal with it when they start bothering me. I've conditioned myself to simply decide what I allow to bother me and when. I'm not foolish enough to believe I can keep it bottled up forever, so I just choose when I want to think about it. I'm too stubborn to allow something to control me." Vance's deep, raspy voice told Angela he was telling the truth.

"If you ever need to talk, let me know," Angela said. She stared at Vance—who didn't reply—for a few moments longer. Then she went back in the house.

***

The next day the group was treated to a wonderful breakfast of bacon, eggs, and fresh milk. Again Vance felt nostalgic, but the old man and his son probably did most of the time as well. When they were finished, Vance began packing things up and getting ready for the road.

"You know you're welcome to stay," John said to him.

"I appreciate it, but I've got to head West." Vance continued throwing bags into the back of the wagon.

"We're going to need some law and order around here before too long. More bandits will probably come." John stared at the back of Vance's head.

"Now's the time to get your people ready. Make sure they're armed and ready to defend the town," Vance said.

"You're gonna take that boy and that girl with you into New Mexico? You're gonna put them in harm's way?" John asked. Vance stopped what he was doing.

"I know. I've thought about that." Vance stared at the two bags still laying on the ground, the ones that belonged to Angela and

138

Charlie.

"You're not planning on taking them, are you?" John asked him.

"No. If you'll allow it, I'd like to leave them here. I know you people will take good care of them," Vance said.

"They're more than welcome to stay here. They get along together fine, and I think my boy Chance has taken a liking to Angela." John chuckled at the last part.

"Thank you."

Vance walked back inside the house and found Angela and Charlie sitting on the living room carpet. They were playing with some old cars. The two were unaware that he was there, and Vance stared at them a moment. After a couple minutes he walked up to them and knelt down.

"I've got to get going," he said, "But I want you two to stay here."

"What?" Angela asked.

"I'm not staying. We're both going with you," Charlie said.

"No you're not. I need you to stay here. It's dangerous where I'm going, and I can't drag you two into it." Vance actually felt his throat knot up.

"Why do you want to leave us?" Charlie asked, tears forming in his eyes.

"I don't want to. I care a lot about both of you. But I don't want anything to happen to either of you." The knot in Vance's throat tightened even more.

"You'll protect us! Don't leave us!" Charlie shouted as he threw himself into Vance's arms and began crying. Tears were welling up in Angela's eyes as well.

"I'm just a man, Charlie. I can't keep anything bad from happening." Vance felt his eyes glaze over, a feeling unfamiliar to him.

"But I love you, Vance..." Charlie sobbed.

Vance hugged the boy, tightening his lips and frowning as he did so to keep the tears from coming.

139

"I love you too, Charlie..." The words forced their way out. Vance hadn't spoken those words for quite some time, and that made them all the more sincere. Angela was sitting next to them, and tears started rolling down her face as well.

"It's the right thing, Charlie," she said.

"No it's not!" Charlie yelled, his faced buried in Vance's chest. He tightened his arms around Vance's neck.

"Charlie, I'll come back. You'll see me again." A single tear rolled down Vance's face.

"I don't want you to go..." Charlie began sobbing again.

"I have to. Now pull yourself together, boy," Vance said as he pulled Charlie off of him, "You've gotta be strong. Angela needs you."

Charlie stared at Vance, his lip quivering and his face covered in tears. He looked down at the floor and started shaking his head.

"It's not fair," the boy said.

"Nothing's fair in this world." Vance swallowed, trying to get rid of the knot in his throat.

"I know you want to keep us safe, Vance. But the three of us—we're all we have. Without each other there's no reason to keep going." Charlie, once again, spoke words well beyond his years.

"That's not true, Charlie. You two will stay together." The knot in Vance's throat returned.

"But we'll miss you. We need you, Vance. I don't care how dangerous it is, or if something happens to one of us. At least we'll be together." Charlie wiped his face off on his sleeve and stared at Vance.

"I'm sorry, Charlie. I have to go now. You two take care." Vance gave the boy a quick hug, and had to pull him off when he stood up. Angela wrapped her arms around Vance's neck, standing on her toes so she could reach. Vance quickly hugged her—not feeling near the bond with her that he did with Charlie—then left the house. As he walked away, he felt the knot in his throat return. His face flushed and tears threatened to roll out of his eyes and down his cheeks.

"Are they staying?" John asked.

"Yes," Vance said, then started leading the first horse to the wagon.

"Are they alright with it?" the old man asked him.

"Not really, but I have to do it." Vance grimaced, shaking off the feelings of sadness.

"They're like family, aren't they?" John took off his straw hat and fanned himself.

"The boy is, yeah. I care about the girl's safety, of course, but her and I aren't bonded in the same way that Charlie and I are." Vance finished hooking up the horse to the wagon and retrieved the other one.

"Them horses got names?" John asked him, trying to change the subject.

Vance froze for a moment.

"Yeah. Maggie and Daisy."

"Those are fine names." John smiled.

"The boy named them," Vance said, and finished hitching the horse.

When he was done, he said his goodbyes to the kind people of Shamrock. As he climbed up in the driver's seat, he looked at John's house and saw Charlie peering through the living room window with a sad look on his face. Vance turned away, snapped the reins, and headed off down the road.

<u>10</u>

Vance drove the horses down the road. He was about five miles away from Shamrock, and as he got further and further away, Charlie's words churned inside his head.

Without each other there's no reason to keep going.

Vance argued with himself, agreeing with the boy and then telling himself why the boy was wrong. They had only known each other for just over two weeks, but the bond they had formed was incredibly strong. Vance felt a connection to Angela as well, but it was completely different and not as strong. Charlie was the one who Vance really cared about. And what the boy said had made sense. Safety is important, but what is the point of being safe if you can't be around those you care about? Vance thought hard about it, and ended up stopping the wagon on the side of the road.

"Goddamn it..." he said to himself.

He quickly turned the wagon around and started heading back toward Shamrock.

Vance couldn't really explain why he did the things he did. He had made Angela and Charlie stay in Shamrock because it would be safer for them there, yet here he was heading right back to the very town he had left them in. Now he would allow them to join him once more, to ride West and hope they wouldn't be killed by bandits. It was stupid,

142

and he knew it. But why did it matter if they wouldn't be happy without him? Angela would surely be alright staying in the town, but Charlie would probably never get over it. Vance had saved him from the raiders in Charleston, buried his father before killing his murderers, kept the cannibals from eating him, and prevented the bandits in Shamrock from potentially harming him. In Charlie's eyes, Vance was everything.

***

Charlie was still sobbing, even nearly two hours after Vance had left. Angela was trying to comfort him, but the boy didn't want to have anything to do with her. Old John tried to divert the boy's attention by throwing some toys out on the living room floor, but Charlie didn't care about any of that, either. He just sat in front of the window, staring down the road and whimpering. But then he saw a wagon being pulled by two horses off in the distance. He momentarily stopped his crying and froze. As the wagon neared, Charlie recognized the man driving as James Vance.

"Vance! It's Vance!" Charlie yelled.

Angela nearly jumped out of her skin. She got up from the couch and peered out the window. It was indeed James Vance.

"He came back! I knew he would!" Charlie jumped up and down in excitement.

"Charlie...don't get your hopes up. He probably just forgot something..." Angela said, trying to prevent the boy's heart from breaking once more.

"No...he came back for us!" Charlie ran out of the house as the wagon pulled up.

Vance jumped from the wagon just as Charlie raced through the gated picket fence. Some would say that Charlie jumped into Vance's arms, but it was really a mutual thing. They held each other for several moments before either one said anything.

"I knew you wouldn't leave me, Vance..." Charlie cried, but this

143

time they were tears of happiness.

"I decided I couldn't do it, Charlie," Vance said, "You're all I have right now."

The two regained their composure and walked back inside the house. John and his boy Chance were standing in the kitchen, while Angela got up from the couch and approached Vance.

"I had to come back. I couldn't turn my back on you guys," Vance told her.

"I'm glad," Angela said, then turned toward the kitchen, "But Vance...I'll be staying here."

"What?" Charlie asked.

"This is a nice town, Charlie. I don't have any reason to go West," she said.

"But...I don't want to leave you..." Charlie had tears forming in his eyes again.

"You go with James Vance," Angela said, "I'll always be with you in your heart, Charlie."

Angela knelt down and hugged the boy.

"You sure, Angie?" Vance asked her.

"I'm sure. This is a good town, and these are good people. I've finally found a place I would be proud to call home." Angela smiled, although tears were forming in her eyes as well.

"Alright then. Charlie, get your things." Vance approached John and held out his hand.

"I'll wish you good luck one last time," Old John said as he shook Vance's hand.

Once Charlie had his backpack ready, and had hugged Angela as much as he could, him and Vance were headed out the door.

"Angela..." Vance began, "Don't forget what I said about your dreams. The world still needs people who can inspire hope."

"I haven't, and I won't," Angela replied, and pulled out the old arrowhead from her pocket.

Vance smiled, then exited the house and loaded Charlie up in the wagon.

144

***

By the end of the next day, Vance and Charlie were only ten miles or so from Amarillo, Texas. There were about thirty minutes of daylight left, and the sun on the horizon in front of them was a beautiful sight. Outside of town, Vance spotted someone sitting off on the side of the road. As he got closer he could hear a harmonica. It was an old man—wearing little more than rags—playing a somber tune with long, sad notes. The old man didn't even acknowledge that Vance and Charlie were approaching.

"What's wrong with him?" Charlie asked as they neared.

"I'm not sure."

But Vance's attention was more on the horizon, where he could faintly see several trails of smoke in the sky off in the distance. With where the sun had been on the horizon, Vance's vision had been limited before now.

"Are you okay?" Charlie called out.

"Hush!" Vance ordered as he pushed Charlie back into the wagon. They continued on past the old man.

Just after the wagon had passed by, the old man stopped playing his harmonica.

"Wouldn't venture into Amarillo if I's you..." he said. Vance stopped the wagon.

"And why's that?" he asked.

"Bunch of soldiers there. Go on around."

"What kind of soldiers?" Vance hopped down from the wagon and approached the man on foot, cautiously checking his surroundings as he did so.

"Mean ones."

Vance looked over the old man for a moment. Although the old man never looked directly at Vance, Vance could see turmoil in his eyes. It was as if Hell itself resided in the old man's gaze. His clothes were torn and dirty, his beard ratty and stained.

145

"Anybody left alive?" Vance asked as he swallowed the knot in his throat.

"Sure...but they been turned into slaves. Xander's Army really did a number on Amarillo. Governor's men didn't stand a chance. They marched on in and took over, killing anyone who stood against them. Governor's men lasted about...oh...three days, I'd say. Even the ones who surrendered were shot dead. Any civilians who tried to flee the city were shot dead, too. Everyone else is slaves now, they are." The old man looked down at his harmonica as he spoke.

"So how'd you make it out?" Vance asked.

"Oh...I'm a pretty resourceful fella. But don't you go into Amarillo, boy. By the looks of ya, they'll shoot you on sight. Go on around, if ya gotta go West." The old man slowly rose to his feet, his legs shaking beneath the weight. He was a skinny old man, yet his knees seemed like they were about to give out.

"You need any help?" Vance asked.

"Help? We all need help, son. You'll need help, too, you keep heading West." The old man picked up his burlap sack, slung it over his shoulder, and slowly walked East.

"You can come with us, old man. I'll keep you safe," Vance offered.

"Ain't nobody safe, boy..."

The old man kept walking, and began playing his harmonica as he went. Vance stared at him for several moments before climbing back on the wagon and taking off.

"So what are we doing?" Charlie asked as Vance hit the reins and moved the wagon forward.

"We're going around," Vance answered.

"But there's people who need help in there. That man said they had been turned into slaves," Charlie protested.

"Nothing we can do about it."

"But Vance, we can't just..." Charlie was cut off by Vance's sharp gaze. Vance snapped his eyes to Charlie and stopped the wagon.

"We can't save everyone, boy. Life isn't about saving everyone.

146

We have to keep ourselves alive. Those people...their fate is sealed...and there's *nothing* we can do to change that. Nothing."

Vance stared at Charlie for a few moments, noticing the boy's sorrowful look. He snapped the reins and continued on, going into unknown territory to bypass Amarillo.

***

After about two hours, Vance and Charlie were directly South of Amarillo, still heading West. They had taken a couple of highways and numerous back roads, and Vance's map was of little use. They had just turned West only a few minutes ago, all of their time being spent going South to get around the large city. The Harvest Moon above them provided quite a bit of light, but still they were struggling to navigate. It was easy to know which direction they were going, but determining what road would take them where was more challenging.

They were now just outside the town of Canyon. Vance couldn't tell if the town was deserted or not. There were no lights, no sounds. He didn't want to go through any sort of settlement, especially at night. He was currently traveling down Highway 217, and could take Interstate 27 if he wanted to avoid the town. However, the interstate appeared to veer back Southeast, and Vance didn't want to backtrack.

Vance slowed the wagon down, giving himself time to think, observe, and listen. The air was still and brought no sounds of violence or smells of death, and he still did not see any lights. Using the moon to his advantage, Vance carefully looked all around them for small glints of light. With as bright as the moon was, someone could easily reflect its light off of any shiny surface. Vance saw nothing. Then, all of a sudden, Vance began smelling something strange. He stopped the wagon and froze, as if the slightest movement would cause him to lose the smell.

"What are we..." Charlie began.

"Sh!" Vance hushed him.

He smelled it again. It was food...cooked food. Vance wasn't certain what kind of food, but something was definitely being cooked, and it was strong.

"Someone's cooking food, and they're close," Vance whispered to Charlie.

"How do you know they're close?" Charlie asked.

"Because there's no wind and I can still smell it," Vance told him.

Vance pulled the wagon off the road about twenty yards or so and hopped down, keeping his M4 shouldered. He had a tactical flashlight on the assault rifle's rail, as well as a flashlight on his vest, but he didn't want to create any light unless he had to.

"Get inside the wagon," Vance quietly ordered. Charlie obeyed.

For some reason, Vance had a very bad feeling about this. His soldier's sense was setting off alarms, the spot on the back of his neck buzzing like a hornet's nest just beneath his skull. He knelt down in the grass, so low he might as well have been lying down.

The smell concerned him. Normally, the smell of rabbit, squirrel, or venison being cooked doesn't linger, nor are the smells particularly strong. Vance could smell the unknown odor perfectly well now, his senses heightened. He couldn't put his finger on it, and he couldn't wrap his mind around the burning question (no pun intended): why was there such a strong smell in the air.

Then it hit him like a ton of bricks. It was human flesh. Human meat being burnt had an undeniable odor, and it stayed in the nostrils for quite some time. Vance had seen and smelled burning human beings on numerous occasions, and the memories had stuck with him eternally.

Vance made his way back to the wagon and motioned for Charlie to jump down and follow him. He led the boy away from the wagon, over to a small grove of trees, and placed him in the center of them. Brush surrounded the grove and would conceal him well.

"I need to scout up ahead and see what's going on before I take you any further," Vance whispered.

"Don't leave!" Charlie said, a little louder than Vance would have liked.

148

"I have to, Charlie. You'll be safe here. Take this canteen of water," Vance removed a canteen from his vest and handed it to Charlie, "Stay very, very quiet, and *do not* move under any circumstances. If anyone comes around here, flatten yourself to the ground. Don't peek through the bushes. I'll be back soon."

Vance took a half-step away from Charlie, but the boy wrapped his arms around him for a moment.

"Be careful..." the boy said.

Vance wrapped his big arm around Charlie and squeezed him tightly, then slid out of the boy's grasp and cautiously made his way across the field.

The former special forces operator stayed off of the road, moving in short, quick bursts between hunkering down and scanning his surroundings. He was maybe two miles away from town. Moving through enemy territory was a specialty of James Vance's. Unfortunately, he wasn't exactly moving under the cover of darkness. A full moon provided plenty of light, and all it did was keep everything in grayscale. One could easily see a person moving around. But Vance was a professional, and he remained cautious. If anyone happened to see him, they would only catch a glimpse of him before he disappeared.

Quickly moving in a crouched position to a tree, Vance became certain that he would encounter *someone* up ahead. The smell was getting stronger. Still no lights and no noises, but Vance didn't take any chances. Each time he moved, he did so for only a few moments before taking cover or flattening himself against the ground. Structures were coming into view up ahead, and he could now make out the layout of the towns buildings. He passed a sign that read, "Welcome to Canyon, Population 17,890."

Now that he was moving into the town itself, and was approaching at a different angle, Vance could see a slight orange glow. It was coming from around the corner of a building, down the road from where he was. He moved toward the nearest building and waited. At first he thought he heard a man laughing, but it quickly ceased and

Vance wasn't certain that his mind hadn't played a trick on him. Animals make all kinds of noises, and it wouldn't have been the first time Vance had mistaken the sound of a critter as a human being.

Vance crossed the street and flattened himself against the neighboring building. Peeking his head around the corner, toward where the glow was coming from, he saw a fairly large fire way down the street. He rounded the corner and moved along the side of the building, stopping at every nook and cranny to hide and listen. As he neared, he heard the man laughing again. It was undoubtedly a person. A deep, guttural chuckle. Not hysterical laughter, but more like a maniacal, controlled release of sound. As Vance got closer and closer, he could see that the fire was a controlled one. *Things*—he wasn't sure what they were—were piled in the street, blazing away. He had a sneaking suspicion of what they were, but he banished the horrible thought from his mind.

Vance saw no one, but was certain that the fire was being supervised. He was now less than a block away, and after stopping at an entryway to a storefront and peeking his head out, Vance realized what was burning in the street: bodies. Human bodies. Just as Vance was about to pull his head back behind the cover of the brick wall, he saw two men coming out of an alleyway carrying a dead body. They nonchalantly approached the fire and heaved the dead person onto the mound of burning flesh. The two men then stepped onto the sidewalk and sat down on some boxes. Vance was about half a block away, and the men were on the opposite side of the street facing away from Vance's location. Vance meticulously scanned every nook and every hole, looking to see if they had any buddies with them. He absolutely *had* to find out who these men were, and what they were doing exactly. Perhaps they were citizens of Canyon, and were burning a mass grave of their fellow Canyonites who had been gunned down by Xander's Army? Unlikely, but the possibility existed.

Vance crossed the road without a sound, taking cover behind an old post office drop box. The two men were about twenty feet in front of him now, their backs to him. One was lighting a cigarette, the other

150

taking a drink from his canteen. The one on the left was a skinny, small framed white guy. The one on the right was big, burly black guy.

"Fuckin' shitty work," the one on the left said.

"Yeah, I'll be glad when we're done here," the other replied.

Vance tucked his M4 behind his back and pulled the tanto combat knife from his vest. He moved around the mailbox and slowly crept closer to the two men.

"Ya know...I don't really like killing people, but at least we get treated well. I mean...we'd be dead if it wasn't for Xander," the left one said after a long moment of silence.

"True. I don't really mind it," Right Guy said.

"Really? Why?" Left Guy asked, his cigarette dangling from his mouth.

"Survival of the fittest. We're at the top of the food chain now. Either people become a part of us, or they die because of us." Right Guy chuckled at the end. It was the same chuckle Vance had previously heard.

"I guess you're right, man," Left Guy took a long drag off his cigarette, "I'll just be glad when we don't have to rape and pillage anymore."

"You don't," Vance interrupted, and stuck the knife in the side of the guy's neck.

Right Guy jumped off of the box and stumbled backward, fumbling for the handgun tucked away in his belt. Vance forced his knife forward, cutting through and out of Left Guy's neck. In two quick strides he made it to Right Guy, who just now had managed to wrap his giant paw around the grip of his handgun. Vance drove his knife directly into the man's chest, twisting it as he did so. The mountain of a man released his grip on the handgun and instinctively curled both of his arms against his chest. He made no sound as he fell backward toward the asphalt, Vance pushing himself on top of him as he fell. The man hit the ground hard, and Vance twisted the knife once more to open the wound before pulling his knife out. Blood immediately gushed out of the man's chest, and he began gasping for breath. His eyes widened and his jaw opened as far as it could go as he gripped his chest, but no noise came out. Within seconds the expression of fear and pain was erased from the man's face. The stab wound to his heart had caused him to bleed out almost immediately.

Vance looked around and saw two rifles leaning against the building about ten feet away. He checked Right Guy's handgun and found that it was a .40 caliber. It wasn't a Glock, so the magazine was useless, but he removed all of the ammunition and put it in a pocket on his vest. Left Guy didn't have a handgun, and both of the rifles were lever-action .30-30's. They were useless to Vance, so he looked around for anything else that might be useful. He found nothing, and headed deeper into town, gladly moving away from the burning bodies of men, women, and even children.

At first, Vance thought that perhaps these two men had been sent down here to clean up the mess that the army had created earlier in the day, but he quickly dismissed it as unlikely. They were probably part of a larger platoon, sent from Amarillo to recruit soldiers and slaves and cleanse the town of those who fell into neither category.

Vance moved further down the street. He was going a bit slower now that he knew what was going on here. It was very likely that anyone he ran into in this town would become an enemy very quickly. After going a couple of blocks, Vance took a brief breather to evaluate the situation. What was his plan? What was he going to do if he found people who needed help? So far he had not encountered anymore soldiers. He also hadn't seen any civilians, either, but he was certain that *some* had to be hiding. He also strongly believed that a large portion of them were probably being held captive to be used as slaves. If that was indeed true, then Vance had to accept the disheartening realization that there was nothing he could do about it. Sure, a couple of soldiers here and there was no big deal. But a whole squad? A whole platoon? Not a chance. No matter how much training and experience Vance had, he was still just one man. It didn't matter how proficient you were when you had twenty barrels slinging lead in your direction. Vance had experienced that before, more than once, and each time he had been very lucky to escape alive.

Vance rounded a corner at the end of the block and saw movement down the road a ways. Probably four blocks, maybe more. He could see several bodies standing erect, and there appeared to be a group of people hunkered down in front of them. The question was...who were they? Vance guessed that the men standing up were part of Xander's Army, and the people sitting in front of them were former residents of Canyon. However, he couldn't be sure without getting closer. It was also possible that they were just citizens who had taken up arms. If that was the case, then they could easily take Vance for the enemy and turn on him in a heartbeat. Either way, he had to be careful.

Vance slowly crept closer and closer to the group, moving from cover to cover. He finally came upon a building with a fire escape, a little less than half a block away from the group. Vance climbed the ladder slowly, quietly, not wanting to make any noise. He finally reached the roof of the two-story building and made his way to the edge. As he got closer, he squatted down and barely moved forward. The lip on the roof of the building was less than two feet high, so whoever was below would be able to easily spot Vance if he wasn't careful.

Peeking over the edge of the building, Vance looked down at the group below. There was no wind, and the moon was full, so Vance could hear and see just about everything that was going on. There were also two fires lit, both in large metal trash cans. Vance saw a large group of civilians—probably thirty or so—sitting down and huddled close together in the middle of the four-way's intersection. Mothers were clinging to their children, fathers were staring at the soldiers with rage burning on their faces. Children screamed and cried. Vance noticed that there were no infants, at least not any that he could see. The youngest child appeared to be about six years old. Soldiers circled the group, firearms at the ready. They didn't appear worried at all, like it was just another day at the office. Vance put their number at ten. Ten heavily armed men, possibly experienced, possibly well trained, well fed, and well supplied. Not the sort to mess with, and definitely not the sort to take on by yourself. It was out of the question, especially with so many civilians that would inevitably get caught in the crossfire.

Vance was barely peeking over the edge of the building, doing his best to stay alert and pay attention to where all of the soldiers were looking. None of them seemed to be on watch, really. They were mostly standing around in pairs, talking. Soon a very scary looking man stepped out from an alley and approached the group. He was definitely someone in charge. Vance could tell by the way the soldiers perked up when they noticed him. He was very large, muscular—probably standing at least six feet, five inches—with a clean shaven head and a thick beard. A black vest adorned his chest, to go with the black BDU pants. A charcoal gray t-shirt was under the vest, and it looked like the man was wearing no body armor. A single handgun hung from his right hip, a large knife from his left. The man climbed up on top of an old, burnt out car—a relic from days long passed—and raised his hands in the air. The soldiers quieted down, and the man spoke. His voice was deep, raspy, and loud. It demanded respect and authority...and fear.

"Do you all know what will happen to you?" he asked as he looked over the group of civilians, seemingly rhetorically.

"Do you know why?" Again, this appeared to be a rhetorical question. The man was attempting to prove a point or put on some great speech, it seemed. Or perhaps he just enjoyed all of the eyes looking at him in fear.

"Xander has called upon you—upon all of us. You will serve him now. In this world, no one can get by on their own. Nor can anyone get by if they are inherently weak. Be grateful! Feel fortunate! You have been chosen! You are weak, but you can be made strong!"

The man made a fist with his right hand and held it out in front of him to add emphasis to his words.

154

"As you have seen, many people have died here today. Some may have been your loved ones. I feel the loss as much as you do. But death is not always bad. Sometimes, death must happen to make way for new life, for new possibilities. The ones who have died were the ones who were inherently weak. The old, the sick, the dying. The ones who refused to throw down their arms and join us. And now the ones who are left—all of you—will live to see another day. You will live to serve Xander in whatever way he sees fit. Because you are the strong ones!"

He formed the fist again, and seemed to be gnashing his teeth. His eyes slowly scanned the crowd in front of and beneath him.

"Be proud," he said quieter, "Be thankful. We have spared you. In Xander's new world, only the strong survive. And when only the strong survive, humanity thrives!"

His voice boomed at the end. The man was certainly charismatic, even if what he was saying was absolute insanity. Vance could tell that this man actually believed the words coming out of his mouth. Who was this Alexander Thompson? How had he succeeded at duping so many people? Was the human race truly that desperate? Or was it that homo sapiens were truly that *violent* by their very nature? Or perhaps it was just that people needed someone strong to cling onto, something that was steadfast and unwavering, whatever it may be...

The leader jumped down from the wrecked car and walked straight through the crowd of cowering civilians, presumably demonstrating his dominance. The group of slaves or conscripts— Vance wasn't exactly sure which, yet—all leaned out of his way and moved their bodies so the large man could get through unimpeded. Vance looked over the group of civilians and the soldiers one last time, then moved along the rooftop to follow the large leader as he walked away. He was heading south, down the middle of the street, and no other men accompanied him. This man looked mean. He looked like he could give Vance a run for his money. It would have been very simple for Vance to just shoot him from his vantage point on top of the roof. Honestly, none of the soldiers would have probably

155

known where the shot had came from and Vance could have made it out before anyone even started looking. But that was a huge risk. The man was getting further and further away, and Vance was running out of rooftop. If he shot and missed, then his action would only serve to heighten the wits of his enemies. Even if he hit the man, there was no guarantee that the shot would be fatal. More importantly, Vance had no idea how this force would react to such a direct provocation. They could very well shoot the group of civilians without even blinking an eye, and Vance didn't want that amount of innocent blood on his hands all at one time. He also had to worry about Charlie. What would happen to him if Vance never returned? He was already taking a risk by leaving the boy in the grove and heading into hostile territory, even if he hadn't been certain it was going to be hostile when he set out.

Vance stopped when he reached the very back of the building's rooftop. The man walked to the intersection at the end of the block, and stopped right where he was with his back to Vance's position. He seemed to be waiting on something. Vance looked on as the large man placed his hands on his hips and stared into the night. Even from this distance, because of the bright light emitted from the moon, Vance could see how large the man's biceps were. Certainly larger than his own. The man looked like a tank, but certainly with more mobility. Everything about him—from his chiseled face, to his large chest and arms, to his wide stance—told Vance that this man was as agile as any predator in the wild and as strong as a gorilla.

The man suddenly turned around and focused his attention toward the rooftops above him. Not where Vance was, but about one building over. Vance ducked his head down a bit more, but kept his eyes on the man. What was he doing? The man scanned the rooftops, finally directing his gaze almost exactly where Vance was hiding. There was no way that the man could see Vance, even with the full moon. Vance was nearly half a block away, and less than half of his head was above the roof's lip. Nevertheless, the man stared at the corner of the rooftop where Vance was. Vance squinted his eyes, his primal subconscious viewing the man's act as a challenge without him

156

even being aware of it. The man did not react in any other way...he just kept staring with his hands resting on his hips. For some reason, Vance felt some sort of connection with this man. Some sort of bond between the two of them, perhaps predetermined by fate long ago. If Vance believed in fate, anyway.

"Captain Wolf!" a voice let out, but Vance couldn't see who it was. *Wolf...what a fitting name...*

The man—presumably "Captain Wolf"—turned his attention to his right, down the street. A building blocked Vance's view of whoever had called out to the man.

"Sir, I have a message from General Xander himself," a man said loudly as he jogged up to Captain Wolf, "You're being recalled to Albuquerque."

"I see," Wolf said as he looked down at a piece of paper, his deep tone barely audible to Vance, "I'll leave at once."

The soldier ran off the same way he came. Wolf turned around once more, looking in Vance's direction. He then scanned the rooftops around him, as if he was aware of some sort of idle threat that he knew he would have to deal with in the future. Vance watched him walk away, out of sight behind the next row of buildings. He let out a brief sigh before making his way down the fire escape.

***

Vance made it back to the area where he had left Charlie without incident. He hadn't even encountered any more of Xander's soldiers on his way out. A small knot formed in his throat as he approached the grove, halfway expecting Charlie to not be sitting in the center of it. Vance pushed some branches aside and stepped in. Charlie was hunkered down with his knees pulled up to his chest, his eyes wide with fear because he hadn't been sure it was Vance coming through the trees. When the boy saw him, he jumped up and hugged him. Vance squatted down on one knee and hugged him back.

"I knew you'd make it!" Charlie said in a loud whisper. Vance could feel the boy's cheeks expand and a smile forming on his face as they embraced.

"Charlie," Vance began, "We need to go. Quickly. It's extremely important that I get to Albuquerque as soon as possible."

"Okay. To deliver your package?" Charlie asked. Vance stared into the boy's eyes for a moment.

"Yes...to deliver the package."

11

Vance and Charlie were now traveling in a more westerly direction. They were still going out of their way just a little to avoid the main roads. There had to be a lot of activity between Canyon and Albuquerque, or so Vance assumed. If someone like this Captain Wolf fellow was in Canyon, then Vance saw the town as sort of a front line. Or perhaps the front line had not yet come. All Vance knew was that a man like Wolf didn't get sent on simple missions like raiding a town. Not unless that town happened to be the precipice of Xander's Army and their goals. But why had he been called back? Was Xander experiencing problems back West? Had a serious resistance formed, perhaps? Vance could only hope.

Then it struck him like a ton of bricks. Vance's good friend, Logan Finley, was still out West...somewhere. Vance had helped him set up a small regional government shortly after The Fall. It had been about the only thing Vance had done to influence the fate of many. Finley's nickname was "Red", even though his hair was more auburn than red. He was of Scottish decent, and he had served with Vance for a short time in the Army. Was Red being a thorn in Xander's side? Red was a good man, and if there was anything he could do about this Xander guy, then he would most certainly do it. The trouble was...Vance wasn't certain that Finley was still around, or if he even

159

had a fighting force anymore. The two of them hadn't seen each other since Vance had helped him establish power in southern New Mexico. Last Vance had heard, Finley had had a falling out with a couple of municipal governments and picked up his roots to move elsewhere close by. Or so Vance had heard, but rumors like that were unreliable. With any luck, Finley would still be around somewhere close and Vance could track him down. Between the two of them, they could surely help to dismantle Xander's force, or at least push them out of New Mexico and away from Vance's home. Whatever was left of it. Vance just hoped that Finley still had a strong force of loyal soldiers.

***

Vance and Charlie crossed over into New Mexico. They still had a ways to go, but they were definitely on the home stretch. Not much further now. A little more than two hundred miles separated Vance from his home and the successful delivery of the package he was carrying in his backpack. They weren't exactly traveling the most direct route. Taking the wagon as the crow flies would have been too risky, so they were actually a little south of the ideal route. Charlie stayed in the back of the wagon for most of the time, playing with a couple of toys that Old John had given him, before falling asleep. They had traveled throughout the night, and the sun was starting to come up. The sky was clear, and as it rose from the west it became very difficult for Vance to see where he was going. He pulled off the road and decided to let the horses rest. They were starting to slow down quite a bit anyway, and so was he. Admittedly, he had almost fallen asleep a couple of times during the journey.

Vance dismounted the wagon and unhitched the horses. There was a rather large field nearby, and it was fenced in. Vance led the horses to it, cut the old barbed wire and bent it back, and put them inside. He then tied the barbed wire back together and let them roam. They probably wouldn't have gone too far if Vance had let them roam free, but he didn't want to take that chance. He had no idea what was going on back home, and the last thing he needed was for his only two horses to run off and not come back in a timely manner.

Charlie was still asleep in the back of the wagon, and Vance let him be. After watering the horses and petting them a little bit, Vance crawled inside the wagon with Charlie. The sun was shining brightly now, the whole of it finally making it above the horizon. Vance didn't bother with any blankets or pillows...he simply leaned backward against the side of the wagon. He fell asleep in just a few short minutes.

***

Vance woke up in relatively the same position he had fallen asleep in. He hadn't taken off his tactical vest or any of his other gear, besides his backpack, so there was very little preparation. Looking down at his watch, he realized he had slept for almost four hours. He rubbed the sleep from his eyes and looked over at the makeshift bedding that Charlie had used. The boy wasn't in the wagon, but it really wasn't that surprising since he had fallen asleep not long after they left Canyon. Vance hopped out of the back and looked around. Charlie was nowhere to be seen. A small amount of anxiety grew in Vance's stomach. He rounded the back of the wagon and immediately saw Charlie in the nearby field, petting the horses and feeding them something. Vance walked over to him and stepped through the barbed wire. He noticed that the pots he had given them were completely empty.

"Didn't feel it was necessary to give them anymore water when you got up?" Vance asked the boy.

Charlie turned around and looked at him with a big smile on his face.

"Naw...there's a pond down there over the hill that they can get to," the boy said. Vance smiled a little, but couldn't see the pond over the hill.

"That's good. Get ready to go, okay?" Vance told him. Charlie

161

nodded.

Vance took this opportunity to check his weapons and ammunition, give his M4 and handgun a quick cleaning, and feed himself and Charlie bread and apples. It wasn't exactly the best breakfast, but it would suffice. He had sent Charlie to go fetch some water, even if they didn't have time at the moment to make it drinkable. They still had a couple big jugs of water, so that would last them awhile.

Vance hooked the horses back up to the wagon, giving them plenty of reassuring pats as he did so. He knew they would be slower now. The break they had wasn't exactly sufficient, but he didn't have a choice but to push them as hard as he could. It would still take them another four days to make it to Albuquerque, maybe more. Vance wasn't happy about that, but there was nothing he could do about it.

Vance and Charlie had been on the road for about three hours when they came upon a small camp. Initially Vance had stopped the wagon and gone up ahead to scout out the area, but when he found out it was a small gathering of refugees he went back for the wagon.

The group looked no worse for wear, really, even if there was a general sadness and feeling of exhaustion that enveloped the whole group. No one paid much attention to Vance and Charlie as they approached with their wagon. The group had a few tents and a fire going with something cooking. Only a couple of men gave Vance a second look. Vance stopped the wagon and approached them, leaving his M4 on the wagon. These people didn't have any visible firearms, and even though that really didn't mean anything, Vance was positive that they weren't going to be a threat.

"Howdy, Outlander," a man sitting by the fire said. He had long, ratty hair and dirty clothing, and was probably around 40 years old.

"Where are you people from?" Vance asked them as he walked right up to them. The hot New Mexico sun was beating down on him, and he was already sweating from all of his gear, so he didn't get too close to the fire.

"Santa Rosa," the man replied.

162

"That's just East of Albuquerque," Vance said. Then, "You wouldn't happen to know a Logan Finley, would you? Goes by Red? Used to be in charge down in the south part of the state."

"That it is. Or what's left of it, at least." The man took a sip from his cup and stared into the fire. Vance could see pain and hopelessness etched deep in his eyes, "Don't recognize the name of the man you mentioned."

"What happened?" Vance asked quietly. His chest tightened as the words came out of his mouth.

"Same thing that seems to be happening everywhere else around these parts. Xander's Army happened." The man continued staring into the fire, the same look of overwhelming despair on his face and in his eyes.

Vance waited for a moment and looked off into the distance for no particular reason at all. After a few short moments of silence, he said in a raspy whisper, "And Albuquerque?"

The words had not been meant to come out of his mouth in that manner. The way he asked the question had been very revealing. His voice had been soft and shaky, probably just barely loud enough for the man to hear him.

The man broke his own gaze and looked up at Vance. He stared at him for a moment, then took another sip from his cup.

"Albuquerque's still standing, for now, but it's only because that's Xander's new headquarters."

A feeling of relief passed over Vance, even though he knew that what the man said really meant nothing. Just because Albuquerque was still standing didn't mean that people hadn't been slaughtered. But the way the man had said it made Vance feel a small amount of relief, no matter how misplaced it was. After another moment, Vance regained his grasp on reality and continued probing for more information.

"Have you been to Albuquerque, or have you just heard stories?" Vance asked him finally, this time in a more normal tone.

"Stories from people who managed to escape. They said it wasn't

163

easy. They have that city pretty locked down, with Xander there and all," the man told him.

"So Xander's really there?" Vance's tone immediately turned into a more ruthless one, and it got the man's attention.

"Well, I don't know for sure," he said, "but I would say so. I've talked to folks who say they've seen him in person. They talk about him like he's the devil himself. Even without the stories, I would guess he probably is there. They have a pretty strong presence around Albuquerque, patrols all over the place and such. Not sure why they're so interested in Albuquerque. Maybe because it's such a large city and there isn't one quite like it for a long ways?"

"And the people there...what's going on with them?" Vance asked, this time in a more shaky tone but not quite as revealing as before.

"Well, I've heard a lot of stories. Guess they're not treating them as bad as elsewhere. I've heard of them storming through towns and stripping them dry of both people and resources, like locusts. From what I hear, they're still letting a lot of people live and even move about. Maybe because there's so many of 'em? Heard a lot of bad things, too. Same horrible stories about shooting people in the streets and stealing goods. Killing children, things like that."

Vance looked like a totally different person by the time the man was finished. He blinked rapidly a few times. His mouth was twisted to the side a little. His right hand had been gently resting on his handgun, but now it was clenched around it so hard that his knuckles were white. Vance stared on, lost in his own thoughts. He finally looked down at the ground for a brief second, then snapped his head up and looked off in the distance to the west, away from the group of survivors.

"I take it you have people in Albuquerque?" the man asked.

Vance looked back down at the ground again, fighting back the tears in his eyes. He knew it was a futile attempt. Tears weren't yet running down his face, but his vision was blurred and he could feel his nose starting to run. His throat was knotted so tightly that he couldn't even reply to the man.

Vance turned around and walked back to the wagon without giving the man an answer. Once he made it to the wagon, he leaned against it with his left forearm and stared down at the road's asphalt.

Damn this world and everything it's become, he thought to himself.

Still staring at the ground, he watched a single tear fall from his face and hit the man-made terrain beneath his feet. He could see the soles of his boots. They were torn from all of his walking on rough terrain.

Sort of like me, he thought.

"Vance?"

The seemingly stone structure that was known as James Vance snapped his gaze in the direction of the little voice to his left. It was Charlie. Vance turned away from him and wiped his eyes and nose.

"Are you okay?" Charlie asked.

"I'm fine," he said, then turned around.

Charlie approached him, and Vance placed his hand on top of the boy's head. Charlie stared at Vance with an obvious expression of concern on his face. Vance smiled reassuringly and rubbed Charlie's head before turning away from him.

"Time to get going, boy," Vance said, resuming his normal tone and persona as he climbed up into the front seat of the wagon.

***

"So what are we doing?" Charlie asked after they had been on the road for another couple of hours.

"We're trying to find a man I used to know," Vance told him, not taking his eyes off the road.

"Who is he?"

"His name is Red. At least, that's what everybody used to call him. I haven't seen him for about eight years." Vance took a long drink of water from the canteen sitting in the front seat with him.

165

"Why are we looking for him?" Charlie persisted.

"He used to have an army. He can help guarantee us safe passage."

It was a lie, even if Charlie had no way of knowing it for sure. Vance did indeed intend to get safe passage by finding Red, but not in the way that he insinuated. He meant it in a, *He's going to help me kill people*, kind of way. What Vance was going to do with Charlie was still unknown to him. He wasn't about to take him with him through battle. That wasn't an option. He started second-guessing himself for going back for him. He did care for the boy—quite a lot, as it seemed—but it was ultimately a very irresponsible thing to do. There was no way that Vance could guarantee Charlie's safety. But then again, neither could Old John or anyone else, for that matter.

Vance's plan was to continue traveling West, but just a little bit south of Albuquerque. He figured that if Red had anything to do with Xander's problems—if there were actually any problems to begin with—then he would most likely be operating in the area. Vance knew that there was no chance that Red could have a force equal to Xander's, but at least he had a hell of a lot of experience, and whatever following he had would definitely be well trained. Red was a lot like Vance, but they were also very different in a few fundamental ways. They were both smart, cunning, and ruthless—when they needed to be—but Vance always saw Red as a little bit of a wild card. He was a hell of a nice guy, but he often flew off the handle and pursued goals that were more personal than business. Vance saw plenty of that when he had helped Red establish himself in the south. Hell, he was probably the sole reason why Red hadn't ended up dead, or failed to keep his priorities in the right order, at the very least. Vance had played a pivotal role in Red's rise to power, even if it had been short-lived. He could have easily stayed with Red and been his right-hand man, or even his equal. Red had offered. But James Vance had little interest in such endeavors, and had other concerns to deal with anyway. He wanted to pursue a much simpler life delivering packages as a courier. And now here he was.

166

Vance took the wagon off the roadway and through a flat field. He didn't stray too far from the gravel road he had been traveling down, but this way was easier on the horses and not so out of the way, since the road had started to turn south. Besides, if Red really was around here, he would have a camp or outpost somewhere that was hidden to some extent. Somewhere Xander would have trouble finding him, or anyone else, for that matter. Vance knew Red like the back of his hand. Of course, that didn't mean that he would get lucky enough to choose the right area.

***

The sun was beginning to set, and Vance turned back south a little so he could hit the highway coming out of Santa Rosa. He had no desire to go to Santa Rosa, but he would get on the highway and keep going south so he could bypass that whole area. Another highway ran east to west a little bit further south, and he would hop on that one to continue his journey to the more immediate area surrounding Albuquerque.

Once the highway appeared to be in sight, Vance stopped the wagon in the middle of the field he was driving through. It was getting a little too dangerous to navigate, anyway. He didn't want to risk driving the wagon off into a ditch or ravine. That would slow their progress significantly. They could unhitch the horses and travel on their backs, but Vance wasn't sure how the horses would act and he didn't want to leave their valuable gear behind. Besides, running them off into a ditch or something would almost guarantee that one or both of the horses would suffer from a twisted ankle or something else debilitating. Better to just play it smart.

Vance and Charlie hooked the horses to the back of the wagon, but gave them long leads of 550 cord so they could move about a bit. Vance opened another one of his MREs, and he shared it with Charlie. Then they ate nearly a whole bag of stale crackers and drank just about all the water they could. Vance worked on purifying the water they had throughout their meal. That night they decided to sleep under the stars...at Charlie's request, of course. It was possibly the clearest night they had seen during their journey. One of those nights that are truly beyond "clear", and move into the realm of awe-inspiring and magnificent.

"Do you think he's up there?" Charlie asked after several long minutes of absolute silence.

Vance didn't say anything at first. He knew exactly who Charlie was talking about, and playing dumb would have been pointless. After a few moments, he turned his head away from the night's sky to look at Charlie.

"I think so," he finally said in a quiet, deep tone.

It wasn't true. Vance didn't believe in a soul, nor did he believe in any sort of afterlife. When you die, you just...die. The lights go out.

"I don't think he is," Charlie said, and it surprised Vance.

"What makes you think that?" he asked the boy.

"I just don't think he is. My parents always taught me that all that stuff is real, but I don't think it is." Charlie continued staring straight up at the stars.

"You don't think that your father would want you to keep believing?" Vance asked softly.

"Yeah, he would. But I just can't believe in that stuff anymore. Look at all the bad things that have happened, Vance. How can God let all that happen?" the boy asked. Vance looked up at the sky and thought for a moment before answering.

"Well, you're kind of asking the wrong guy. But I guess that the only answer—the only thing that really makes any sense—is that we can't even begin to understand what a being like God is capable of, or what he has planned, or *how* he has it all planned. I mean, he's such a *big* thing, ya' know? We can't really compare his logic and reasoning to ours. The truth of the matter is...for something like a divine being—a god—the bad stuff that happens to us mortals would really be insignificant."

"Well it shouldn't be," Charlie quickly replied.

168

Vance looked over at the boy once more and stared at him gently. He felt so much pain for him, so much regret that he wasn't able to do more.

"What happened to your mother?" Vance asked in a soft tone.

"She died when I was little. I don't remember why." Charlie said this without taking his eyes off the sky.

***

The two continued watching the stars, and their conversation turned a little brighter after they saw a brief show of shooting stars. There was a sudden burst of them, and there were so many that it made even Vance smile bigger than he probably had in months. Charlie seemed to almost be bouncing off of the ground throughout the whole ordeal. When it was over, the boy couldn't stop talking about what they had seen. He slowly inched his way over to Vance, and finally rested his head on his chest, his attention still fixated on the stars above them. Vance looked down and placed his arm over Charlie. The boy gingerly took his hand in his, without giving it any thought, and kept rambling on about the little pieces of rock they had just seen get burnt up in the atmosphere, miles above them. Miles above all of the tiny, insignificant mortals struggling to stay alive beneath them. For the first time in a long time, Vance thought happy thoughts, and he actually felt a level of compassion and love that had previously stayed locked away, deep inside him, for a very long time. And all was good with the world, if even for a very short while.

***

The two awoke early the next morning. Vance had to actually shake Charlie awake, who had ended up laying across Vance's chest with almost his entire body. Once both of them had rubbed the sleep from their eyes, they loaded everything up and headed toward the highway.

169

It only took a few minutes to get on the highway and turn south. Vance wasn't sure, but he guessed they were probably ten miles or so from Santa Rosa. Ten miles too close, as far as he was concerned. It was most likely a wasteland by now. Vance didn't care to go find out. He actually had no desire to investigate. There were more pressing matters to attend to, like trying to find Red. He wouldn't look for too long, though. If Vance couldn't find him soon, or at least get a clue from someone about his whereabouts, then he would just continue on to Albuquerque. He was still heading in the general direction, anyway.

"Son-of-a-bitch..." Vance said to himself as he stared at the situation before him.

They had only been on the highway for ten minutes before something snapped on the wagon and the whole right side dropped suddenly.

Two of the spokes in the right front wheel had snapped. Probably dried out, from what Vance could tell. Or perhaps they were just weak to begin with. Either way, as angry as it made Vance, he realized that they had been lucky to get this far without something breaking before now.

"That's not good," Charlie said as he stared at the wheel, "Can you fix it?"

"Maybe, but it will take awhile. Even if I *can* fabricate something that will work, we'll still have to take it to a water source and let the wood soak awhile. And that's *if* I can fix it. Albuquerque's still a long ways off, but we might be better just leaving it." Vance turned and kicked a small rock in the middle of the road. He couldn't catch a damn break.

"Can't we just ride the horses?" Charlie asked.

"Well, we can try. But we don't have the proper gear to do it, and even if we did they might not handle it well. I'm not sure they've ever done anything but pull a wagon. Riding a horse bareback is no easy task."

Vance took the opportunity to look at the hooves on the two horses.

"Shit!"

Just as he had suspected, they were starting to crack from all the hard traveling on asphalt. They didn't have horseshoes on, either. Hard surfaces like roadways were incredibly hard on a horse's hooves.

Vance placed his hands on his hips and started pacing. What would they do now? Walk? Not only was it slow and tiresome, but it was dangerous. They were in New Mexico now, where the sun beat down harder and the air was often very dry. They could only carry so much food and water.

"This isn't good, is it?" Charlie asked.

"No...it isn't," Vance said in a very angry tone.

Charlie walked to the back of the wagon and climbed inside out of the heat.

"Well, let's take this opportunity to give the horse's a little break while I decide what in the hell to do." Vance kicked the broken spokes in frustration.

After unhooking the horses and tying them up under a shady tree, Vance had Charlie fetch them some water while he evaluated the situation. He started going over what all he would need to fix this damn wheel, and how he would go about doing it. That was *if* he decided to fix it, of course. He hadn't quite yet made up his mind.

As Vance slipped into deep thought about what to do, weighing the pros and cons of all his options, he was interrupted by a strange noise. A noise he hadn't heard in a very long time. What the hell was it? It sounded like some sort of rumbling, and it was coming from the south. He stared at the hill in the road to the south of their position, and then he finally figured out what the sound was.

A vehicle! It was a fucking VEHICLE....

"Charlie! Out, now!" Vance yelled. He couldn't yet see the vehicle, but it was quickly approaching.

Vance happened to glance over at the horses, who were tied up under a tree that was about fifty feet off of the road. They were a little spooked by the noise. Vance ran to the back of the wagon as Charlie was starting to climb out.

"What *is* that?" Charlie asked, taking his time.

Vance grabbed him and almost tossed him out of the wagon.

"Run!" he yelled, and took off with Charlie off of the road.

Then he realized that he had forgotten something. Something very important. In his rush to get Charlie out of the wagon, he had forgotten his assault rifle...and his backpack. The backpack that contained a lot of their food and a fair amount of water. The backpack that held all of his dearest possessions. The backpack that had the important package inside. That package was more important now than ever, with everything that was going on.

"Keep going! Hide!" Vance yelled as he skidded to a stop and sprinted back to the wagon.

"But..."

"Just go, Charlie!" Vance ordered. He was already halfway back to the wagon.

Charlie kept running, looking over his shoulder every couple of seconds. His tennis shoes slid on the grass as he came to a stop, and he threw himself behind some bushes far away from the road.

***

Vance dove into the back of the wagon. The noise of the vehicle was getting closer. Normally a vehicle would be somewhat of a welcomed sight. But now, especially around here, Vance had no idea who was driving that vehicle. His fear grew as he couldn't help but think about how it was most likely soldiers from Xander's Army.

The vehicle was getting closer extremely quickly, its engine emitting a loud, deep noise. Now more than ever, the sound of a vehicle was deafening. In days past, most people wouldn't even pay attention to the sound of a car. But now everything was different. Now fuel was very rare—and mostly came from distilling alcohol—and only the most powerful groups were able to get vehicles working again.

Vance grabbed the backpack and threw it over his shoulder. His

172

assault rifle was sitting in the front seat. He crouched down and moved to the front, reached forward and snatched it into the back of the wagon with him. He started moving to the back when the noise from the vehicle changed quite abruptly. It was unmistakable...the vehicle had popped up over the hill.

Charlie looked on through the bushes, waiting for Vance to jump out of the wagon and run back to him. He kept waiting to see his big, heavily armed protector running to him to keep him safe. He waited for what was only a few short seconds, but seemed like an eternity. Then he saw a huge hunk of metal come up over the hill. It was a boxy thing painted in camouflage, with black wheels and a man poking up out of the top and a big gun in front of him. Charlie held his breath, flicking his eyes back and forth between the loud thing that must be a vehicle, and the wagon which still contained his only companion.

"Come on, Vance...."

***

Vance flattened himself in the back of the wagon. The vehicle was slowing down, and that wasn't a good sign. Whether the occupants were good or bad, he had fully expected them to stop and check the wagon. No one could afford to pass up possible supplies. Doing so could mean certain death later on.

Vance hadn't been able to see the vehicle, so he didn't even have a slight idea who might be inside it. He heard it come to a very abrupt stop. It sounded like several doors opened. Boots hit the pavement...several pairs of boots. Vance remained flat against the floor of the wagon, and brought his M4 up in front of him. He was extremely vulnerable. Both the front and the back of the wagon was open to the outside, so if these people checked both ends he would be completely defenseless either at his feet or at his head.

***

"Oh no..." Charlie moaned as he watched the vehicle stop and these scary looking individuals get out. They all had weapons. Charlie had no idea what the difference was between the various weapons, but anyone can identify things that kill. Even from this distance, he could see several men carrying clubs and guns. Charlie didn't even feel like crying. He was too shocked to cry. How was Vance going to deal with this situation?

***

Vance let go of his M4, instead opting to pull out his sawed-off shotgun from his backpack. He pushed himself off of the floor of the wagon, spun around so that he was facing the left side of the canvas cover, and sat straight up against the right side—the side that was on the edge of the road and in the grass. He sat the sawed-off 12 gauge shotgun at his feet, and pulled his .40 caliber Glock from the holster on his thigh. With his left hand he pulled out his .38 caliber snub-nose revolver from his vest, which was his backup weapon and he rarely used it. Vance then pointed one firearm at each of the exposed ends of the wagon, and stared forward.

***

Charlie watched as the men walked around to the back of the wagon. One of them walked around the front. The wagon was tall, so it would be hard for anyone to see inside from the front without climbing up at least a little ways. Charlie started to panic a little. He felt his heart start to race and his breathing became quick and shallow.

***

Out of his peripheral vision, Vance saw a man appear to his left at the back of the wagon. He was mostly certainly not a good guy, because he was dressed in the same fashion as the rest of Xander's soldiers whom Vance at ran into. Halfway through the man's surprised reaction at finding a person inside and raising his shotgun, Vance fired a single round with the .38. It hit the man somewhere in the chest, and he fell backwards. Almost simultaneously—no sooner than Vance had pulled the trigger—he saw another man climb up into the driver's seat and poke his head in. Had the man waited another second or so, he almost certainly would not have attempted it. Vance put a single round into his head with his Glock.

***

Charlie jumped as he heard two shots ring out and watched as the two men fell to the ground. The one at the front was as limp as a rag doll, and the one at the back was writhing around. Charlie heard him let out a single, blood-curdling scream. The boy flattened himself against the ground even more, now barely able to see through the bush he was hiding behind. Then there was noise. A lot of noise. The sound was deafening, even at this distance. A quick succession of what sounded like a very big gun firing over and over. And then Charlie noticed that the wagon's canvas cover was being torn to shreds.

***

Just a few seconds after Vance had shot the two men, he was startled by the sound of a large caliber machine gun firing. He instinctively flattened himself against the floor of the wagon. The gun kept firing, over and over. Pieces of canvas were raining down all over him, but no blood or pain so far. Finally, the shooting stopped. Perhaps they assumed they had hit him? Vance peaked up above and saw daylight shining through too many holes in the canvas to count. At this moment, all he could feel was concern. Concern for Charlie. The boy had been running in the same direction that the bullets would have

175

been going. Hopefully he went far enough, because the field started to angle down a little ways off of the road. If he had gone far enough, then the bullets would have most likely passed over him safely, right? Right??

"Light that thing up! You didn't get it all, dumb ass!" a man's voice said.

"I can't," a man—presumably the machine gunner—said to the other, "The gun doesn't aim that low! We're too close!"

That was all James Vance needed to hear. Apparently the vehicle had been parked close enough to the wagon that the machine gun couldn't angle down far enough to put any bullets any lower than about two feet above where Vance had been laying. It was time to get the hell out of Dodge before whoever was left decided to put more bullets into the wagon with small arms fire, or check through the wagon's openings again.

Vance launched himself out of the back of the wagon with a vengeance. He left the shotgun inside, and instead grabbed his M4. It would be more effective in this situation, and besides, there wasn't any time to think.

"Holy sh...."

***

Charlie looked up after the gunfire stopped. He could hear someone yelling, but it was faint and he couldn't tell who it was or what they were saying. He didn't think it was Vance. But it could have been. The boy just couldn't be sure. Charlie slammed his fist into the ground out of frustration, wishing he knew exactly what was going on and if Vance was okay. Then he saw Vance hop out of the back with his rifle shouldered.

***

Vance immediately regretted his decision, even though his

176

options were rather limited. Four men were now staring at him, and one of them was behind a .50 caliber machine gun that was attached to the top of a white SUV. Vance fired two rounds at the closest guy, who happened to be standing right next to the driver's side door. The soldier recoiled as at least one of the rounds tore through his upper body. The one who was behind the machine gun was well protected, so he would probably be the last to go. Besides, Vance was too close for the machine gun to do him any harm.

Vance managed to get off another round and hit one more of them who was standing toward the back of the SUV—probably in the abdomen, but Vance couldn't tell for sure. Then he was forced to retreat back behind the wagon to avoid being shot. Another guy unloaded on him with some sort of automatic rifle. Vance hadn't exactly had time to take note of what it was. As soon as the gunfire subsided, Vance peaked around the corner and saw the machine gunner climbing out. Vance pushed his rifle around the side of the wagon without looking, and fired five rounds blindly. Then he ran around to the right side of the wagon, which was parked far enough over that the wheels were in the grass. Vance waited a moment, but didn't hear the men saying anything. He crouched down beneath the wagon and could see the feet of one of them. Vance fired several rounds at the man's feet with his M4, but was fairly certain that he missed. The man appeared to run off to the other side of the SUV.

Vance scanned back and forth beneath the wagon, then looked to his left and his right to make sure no one was trying to flank him. He was obviously outnumbered, so it was probably in their best interest to rush him. And that's exactly what they did.

Vance was facing the wagon, so he could watch both sides as well as under it. He saw one of them come from his left, behind the wagon. Vance raised his rifle. Then everything went black.

***

Charlie looked on as the situation unfolded in front of him. He saw two of the bad guys come around either end of the wagon, almost at the same time. Vance aimed at the one coming from the back, the one who had a gun. But then another one holding some sort of blunt instrument came around the front and clubbed Vance over the head. Vance fell to the ground like a rock. Charlie couldn't help but scream at what he witnessed. He wasn't even sure what he said, exactly. It could have been *no*, or perhaps it was nothing at all. Whatever it was, he had said it loud enough that the two men took notice.

Charlie froze for a moment, tears already rolling out of his eyes. One of the men—the one with the gun—started walking in Charlie's direction. Charlie stared at him through the bush, bawling his eyes out. Then he regained control of himself to some degree and took off at a sprint. He ran as fast as he could away from the bush. The man was only a few feet away from the road, so Charlie had a huge head start on him. But he wasn't counting on getting shot at.

He heard the loud *crack* from the weapon. A clump of dirt seemed to explode about fifteen feet to his right and twenty feet in front of him. Charlie fell to the ground and covered his head with his hands.

***

Vance slowly opened his eyes. His head hurt. In fact, it was throbbing. Probably the worst headache he had ever had. Headache? Was it a headache? That didn't sound right. His vision was blurred, but he could have sworn that he was laying in grass. And in front of him was a road. Was that right? A road? As his vision cleared, he rolled his eyes up and saw the wagon. Right...the wagon. He was fixing it, wasn't he? What the hell had happened? His face was pressed into the grass. And then...then it seemed like someone was sitting on his back. Was Charlie messing around again?

Charlie...

Vance immediately remembered the situation. He tried to get up, but found that something very heavy was on his back. And then he realized that his hands were behind his back, and he couldn't move them. Were they tied? Where was his backpack?

"Settle down, big boy!" a man with a raspy but high-pitched voice said. He was apparently the one sitting or standing on Vance's back.

"Vance!"

He heard the boy's voice. He strained his head around and saw the boy being pulled along by a man with a gun. The same man Vance had almost shot right before losing consciousness.

"Quiet!" Vance told Charlie. The boy was extremely stressed. Vance could see it all over his face. But he didn't want the boy to get himself even more worked up, or indirectly antagonize their captors.

"Get up!" the man standing over Vance ordered.

Vance rolled over and sat up. His head felt like it was barely attached to his neck. His vision blurred even worse, and the world looked a little wobbly. The man tugged on Vance's arm. He wasn't big enough or strong enough to pick Vance up on his own, but Vance cooperated. He slowly stood, trying to take a moment to get his balance before walking. His captor was having none of that, though, and pushed him in the back with his billy club. Vance staggered forward. He noticed that his backpack was no longer slung over his shoulder, so he looked to his left at the man standing behind him. In his left hand was Vance's backpack. As Vance was forced to walked around the front of the wagon, he watched the other man with the gun walking toward the two horses. Both were extremely spooked, tugging at their leads and rearing up every now and again.

"No!" Vance yelled.

The man kept moving toward them with a fast and determined walk. As he got a little closer, he raised his gun to his shoulder.

Vance screamed again at the top of his lungs. A single gunshot rang out, and the closest horse—Maggie—dropped to the ground. The man took aim once more, this time waiting because Daisy was doing her best to pull free. Once she finally left all four hooves on the ground for more than a couple seconds, the man fired again. She, too,

179

fell straight to the ground.

Vance was nearly foaming at the mouth. The sheer ruthlessness set him off. He jolted forward toward the man who had killed his two faithful horses, his captor pulling on his vest with all his might to restrain him. Vance inched forward through sheer willpower and anger, letting out an angry and frightening war cry all the while. The man pulling on him finally had to hit him in the back of the knee with his billy club. Vance's right leg gave out from the blow, and he fell to the ground once more. He looked on as the man who murdered his horses commenced to field dress them and turn them into food. As he cut into them, Vance was pulled away and escorted to the SUV. Propped up against the rear driver's side was one of the men Vance had shot, still breathing. He was holding his stomach in pain, blood oozing between his fingers.

"I'm still alive," the injured man said to the one escorting Vance.

"*Fuck you!*" Vance screamed, and kicked the man in a fit of rage as soon as he was close enough.

He got struck between the shoulder blades for his act, but he honestly barely felt it. His adrenaline was pumping. His head hurt even worse from all of his straining and yelling, but it didn't bother him. He was too furious to care. He was now beyond the point of all pain compliance. It was as if rage itself was a drug that had been injected into him and was now coursing through his veins. He was now the epitome of wrath.

The SUV moved down the road at a quick pace. They were heading north, toward Santa Rosa. Vance was sitting in the back seat on the driver's side. He was staring out of the window, lost in a trance of hatred and bloodlust. Beside him was a dead body, and laying across his lap was a dead body. Sitting on the passenger side in the back seat was yet another dead body. Three total—all men he had killed. But it still wasn't enough to satisfy his rage. Charlie sat in the front seat. His hands were bound behind his back, just like Vance's were, and his mouth was covered with a bandana.

Behind Vance, in the cargo area, was the man who killed the

horses and the other whom he had injured. The one who had hit Vance in the head was driving. Vance looked on as if he had no emotion. But inside he was burning. Inside he felt as if he was going to rip a man's head off at the first opportunity. He actually felt fortunate for the ride, though. It gave him time to cool down and think about this situation rationally. Going off half-cocked and full of blind fury would only get him so far. He had to remain smart.

"This is going to taste real good..." the man behind Vance said, almost in Vance's ear.

Vance didn't reply. The horse meat was next to the man in the cargo area, and there was a lot of it. But the man had still wasted a lot because he didn't know how to dress an animal. At least not properly.

***

They were only driving for few minutes before Santa Rosa came into view through the front windshield. It was a small town, only having just a couple thousand residents before The Fall. Now it was home to just a couple hundred people, and that was only because the huge city of Albuquerque was a hundred miles or so to the west.

As the SUV grew closer, the form that the town had more recently taken on was becoming clearer. A security checkpoint was set up on the highway leading into the south part of town. But it was more like a defensive position, not a checkpoint. No one would be coming into Santa Rosa, or so Vance suspected. The men at the checkpoint seemed calm and casual...and heavily armed. It was becoming clearer that the further West Vance went, the more soldiers he saw and the better equipped they were.

The SUV slowly came to a halt at the south "gate". Vance noticed that on a road sign, off on the right side of the road, a large red "X" had been painted on it. A simple symbol for Xander's Army, perhaps?

"We have two prisoners. A boy and a man. Killed three of our guys and injured one," the driver said to the soldier who approached the SUV.

The soldier waved them through, and the makeshift wooden barricade was moved off of the road. The group slowly rolled through, and Vance looked on as the town opened itself up to them. As they continued at almost a crawl, he saw handfuls of soldiers here and there. None of them seemed to be alarmed. Vance also saw civilians occasionally, although their appearance was disheartening. Most looked like peasants. They were scurrying around, almost running. All of them were carrying something or performing some task. Slaves?

The SUV came to a stop a few blocks into town. There was quite a bit of activity for such a small town, but most of it involved Xander's Army. As best Vance could tell, it looked more like military activity. An outpost, of sorts. Large tents were set up in a grassy area off to the side, and people were moving in and out of it. Most were carrying papers. Small groups of soldiers were gathered around in places, usually with one man talking to them. A leader giving out orders to his soldiers, perhaps? That's certainly what it looked like to Vance: a mission brief. Or several briefs, apparently. Maybe inconsequential, maybe not. He had no way of knowing, and it wasn't exactly the foremost concern in his mind.

"Get out," the driver said as he opened Vance's door.

Vance gave a quick glance to Charlie, who was staring at him with eyes wide. He slowly stepped out of the vehicle, his mind now calm and his common sense restored. The overall atmosphere around him was calm. A lot of soldiers weren't even holding their weapons, instead propping them up nearby so they could talk with their hands. Vance estimated that the number of soldiers in his immediate vicinity was close to three dozen. That's a lot of soldiers, especially for an unarmed man and an 11 year old boy who both had their hands tied behind their backs.

Vance and Charlie were led into the closest tent, the same original soldiers escorting them. Inside the same military order was very apparent, and also the same military chaos. It was fairly noisy. Desks had been pulled out of buildings to be used by Xander's forces. Maps hung on the tent's walls. Several men were sitting at the desks,

182

writing things down. Two men were standing in front of a large map of New Mexico, pointing around and talking quietly. Beside them was yet another map, but this one was of Texas. Two more men were looking at it, one of them nodding his head in agreement with whatever the other one was saying. They were all dressed relatively the same as all the others that Vance had encountered: boots, BDU pants of varying colors, simple t-shirts, some had vests...they all had that "survivalist" look about them, like you would expect to see with a former military man out in the woods.

And then...

Vance saw him, standing above all the others at the back of the tent. He was listening to another man, nodding his head slightly. His hands were resting on his hips and his gait was wide in that same hard, defiant stance. An immovable object, always prepared to demonstrate his power. Captain Wolf.

"Wait here," the one who had been driving the SUV said to Vance. The other soldier stood behind them.

The driver approached Captain Wolf, who was about fifteen feet away, and waited for him to finish whatever he was doing. After a few brief moments, Wolf turned and looked down at him. He stood about six inches above the man. Wolf leaned in a little as the soldier spoke too quietly for Vance to hear. About halfway through, Wolf rolled his eyes upward and stared at Vance. No emotion was on his face. Finally, Wolf stepped past the man and slowly approached Vance and Charlie, stopping directly in front of Vance about a foot or so away. The boy stepped back a couple of inches, obviously terrified of Captain Wolf. Vance stood his ground, looking as dangerous as ever. The rage was burning in his eyes. Blood covered his clothing from the dead man who had been laying across his lap. Wolf glanced at Charlie, then stared directly at Vance, nodding his head slightly for no apparent reason. Now that Vance was close to Wolf, he could see that his assumptions had been correct. Wolf was terrifying to most people. His unmistakably firm stance and calm mannerisms alone would make most men cower in fear. His muscles were just as big as they appeared

183

before, the sleeves of his gray t-shirt stretched to their limit around his biceps. Lines on his t-shirt marked his pectorals. His face was rugged and hard. A scar on his left temple marked a previous brush with death, and now it only served to make him appear more menacing. The man's beard was dark brown, almost black, and it was full from ear to ear. It was maybe an inch long—not too long to grab onto. He must have recently shaved his head, because there wasn't a single hair on it. Vance could see the faint shadow where hair grew, but it was shaved down to the skin.

Wolf looked deeply into Vance's eyes for several long moments, his head no longer nodding. He squinted slightly, as if he could see deeper into Vance's soul by doing so.

"Have we met?" Wolf asked quietly, his deep, ragged voice cutting through the air like knives, "Perhaps on some distant plane?"

The question seemed odd to Vance. Philosophical, almost. *Some distant plane?*

"What's your name?" Wolf asked after Vance didn't answer.

"Vance," he replied calmly.

"And you're quite sure we've never met?" Wolf asked again.

"I never said that we hadn't."

"Well...have we?" Wolf continued staring deep into Vance's eyes.

"No," Vance finally said. The single word seemed to set the air on fire, for some strange reason.

Wolf smiled slightly, but it wasn't a smile that symbolized humor. It was more of a spiteful smile, and an evil gesture to show Vance that he was to be feared.

"So, what shall I do with you?" Wolf asked as he stepped away and approached a table, "You've killed...how many of my men?"

"Three, sir, and injured..." the driver said.

"Quiet!" Wolf barked, his eyes still locked on Vance, but he didn't yell. He didn't need to. His voice was booming and terrifying even without raising it. Then to Vance, he asked once more, "How many?"

"I don't recall," Vance answered quietly, but it wasn't a form of

184

submission. His words were still laced with poison.

Wolf smiled again, the same way as before.

"And will you serve Xander?" Wolf asked him.

Vance continued staring at him. Wolf slowly walked back over to him, a slightly larger smile on his face now.

"You won't, will you?" Wolf asked. Then, without taking his eyes off of Vance, he reached with his large bear paw of a hand and grabbed Charlie by the hair, "But this one will..."

"Don't!" Vance let out as he took half a step forward, his voice slightly raised. His reaction had been very revealing.

"I'll tell you what, stranger," Wolf began, letting go of Charlie's hair, "You are obviously a very capable individual. After all, you've killed at least three of my men all by yourself."

Wolf turned and walked over to a table, briefly looking over a piece of paper that was seemingly unrelated to the current situation.

"Do you know our ideology? Do you know what Xander's Army is really about?" he asked.

Vance remained silent. Wolf turned his attention away from the table and back to Vance.

"We are about survival of the fittest. The weak die, and the strong thrive. We are brutal and unwavering, but we treat each other with respect. Why? Because everyone you see in Xander's Army has earned it in some way. They have proven they are the strong ones. And you...you're strong. Oh yes, I can see it in your eyes. You have fought in many battles, killed many men. The mark of violence adorns your face, a mark only I can see. You're a mortal who should already be dead countless times over, but here you are." Wolf chuckled slightly.

"And what are you? The way you speak, it would seem that you think you are something more than a mortal." Vance spoke normally, calmly.

Wolf chuckled once more, and briefly glanced at the two soldiers who had escorted Vance and Charlie inside the tent.

"Some of my men would say that I am, though I have never claimed such a thing," he said with a grin.

185

"And if you're something more, then what does that make Xander?" Vance asked.

"Again, I never claimed to be more than a mortal. Nor has Alexander."

So...it seemed that Wolf was close to Xander, at least somewhat. He called him by his first name, instead of how everyone else referred to him.

"You won't fight for me, or for Xander. I can already see that. So you will fight for yourself."

Wolf approached Vance once more, this time stopping just inches away. His gaze was now a couple of inches above Vance's own, something Vance wasn't used to.

"Take him to the pits. Tomorrow he will fight for his freedom, or for his death. I'm guessing it will be the latter. Leave the boy here. In the morning he'll watch his friend die a terrible death."

Wolf growled as he spoke. Vance displayed no emotion, even though inside he was struggling to remain calm. He wanted to snap Wolf's neck.

"Be calm, Charlie," Vance said as the two soldiers started pulling the two apart.

Vance was escorted outside, while Charlie stayed inside the tent with Wolf. Vance wasn't overly concerned about Charlie's safety. He honestly didn't believe that Wolf would let any harm come to him, at least not yet.

186

12

Vance sat in his cell, focusing all of his attention on varies ways that he wanted to kill Wolf. And Xander, whoever he was. Vance looked around at the bars that held him captive. It was indeed a real jail cell. The police station sat right across the street from the town's swimming pool, which had apparently been converted into "the pits", whatever that was.

Vance picked at the couple slices of bread he had been given. He knew he needed to eat, but he had absolutely no appetite. Nevertheless, he ate all of his bread and drink nearly all of the water in his canteen. He needed to keep his strength up if he intended on making it out of this. Whatever "this" was. When he was finished he laid down on the cell's only bunk. His head still hurt like hell. It wasn't debilitating, but it was definitely distracting. He reached his hand around and could feel a small bump. It was surprising that it wasn't much larger, really. The guard sitting at the desk on the other side of the bars was busy reading an old magazine, not worried about Vance at all. Why should he be?

Vance was no stranger to sleeping in stressful situations. He actually slept better during those times than when he was home and there was no danger. Perhaps it was because he instinctively knew that his survival depended on it? On all the deployments he had been on, he had always had the uncanny ability to fall asleep practically whenever he had the time, seemingly at will. And when he would wake up, he didn't feel groggy or slow. Even when he had only gotten a couple hours of sleep. At home, however, it was a different story. He had insomnia, and it was a constant battle nearly every night to fall asleep and stay asleep.

***

Vance awoke the next morning completely alert. He had practically sat straight up before he was even fully awake. His watch had been taken, so he wasn't sure what time it was, but light was shining through the windows. His internal clock was telling him that it was sometime around 6:00 or 6:30, but he could've been off by an hour or even two.

Within thirty minutes, a soldier came in and brought Vance his breakfast. He then relieved the other soldier who had been guarding Vance. The food he had given him wasn't anything special: a couple small slices of chicken breast and more water. Vance ate the chicken, but after drinking down about a quarter of his water he made himself sip on it after that. The last thing he wanted was a big stomach full of water, and he wasn't sure when he would be "fighting for his freedom, or for his death," so he wanted to play it safe.

About an hour later, two more soldiers entered the police station. One of them apparently had some rank, because the soldier who had been guarding Vance jumped up quickly so he didn't look like he was slacking off.

"It's time," one of them said.

The three soldiers removed Vance from his cell and told him to walk out of the front door.

Vance thought about his options. There wasn't much he could do. He was outnumbered three to one, and two of them had firearms. Besides, Charlie was still here somewhere. He couldn't leave him behind. As they walked outside, Vance looked up at the bright morning sun. He raised his hand to the horizon and judged how high the sun was based on how many times he flipped his hand over before he reached the sun. As best as he could tell, it was about 8:00am or so.

The four of them made it across the street and entered the swimming pool area through a gate in the chain link fence. Vance immediately noticed that the pool had a makeshift fence all the way around it, and several dozen men were all gathered around. There didn't appear to be any water in the pool, not that Vance had really expected it to be full of water. As soon as the soldiers saw Vance, they raised their arms and began cheering. But not like they were cheering for their favorite football player. It was more like they were cheering at the sight of a bar brawl. Vance felt the uneasiness build in his stomach.

Vance was taken over to the edge of the pool. There was a break in the makeshift fence, and a ladder had been lowered down the inside of the pool. One of the soldiers ordered Vance to climb down it, which he reluctantly did. Once at the bottom, there was already a man inside. But this man didn't look like a warrior or battle-hardened soldier. He was just a man, with long frizzy hair and dressed in dirty clothes. His eyes were wide. Even from all the way across the large swimming pool, Vance could see the whites of his eyes.

"Quiet!" roared the unmistakable voice of Captain Wolf. The soldiers immediately silenced themselves.

Captain Wolf climbed up on top of the perch of a lifeguard and took his seat.

"As you all know, in Xander's Army we value life. But we also value death. Death separates us from the weak. How we die defines how we lived as men. The weak suffer, and the strong prosper. It seems like a bleak existence, but that is how the world has always worked. Because of weak beings, society collapsed. But now we have risen. With Xander's guidance, we have all come to realize how important it is to cast away the weak, to encourage the strong! We will ensure that we never have to endure another Fall! And now we have another strong being before us. He has killed our men, and injured

189

another yesterday. There is no denying his strength. But yet he doesn't see the light of our ways. He has refused to become enlightened. So now he will fight in the pits, not as punishment but as a lesson! If he falls, then so be it. If he lives, then he will have earned his freedom."

The soldiers cheered at Captain Wolf's charismatic words. Vance stood quietly the whole time, staring at the man across from him almost constantly. What was he going to do? Soon he noticed another soldier climbing up the lifeguard chair, and he was carrying Vance's backpack with him. It even still had his tanto sword in it.

"Here you are," Wolf said as he removed the sword from its sheath, "This shall be your weapon of death. Unleash Hell until I am satisfied, then I shall let you go."

Wolf threw the sword down to Vance. It hit the bottom of the pool with a decisive *clank*. Vance approached it and picked it up slowly, staring at it as he did so. Then he noticed a machete being thrown down to the man he was supposed to fight. The man slowly walked over to it, his eyes still locked on Vance. He began reaching for the weapon, but then stopped.

Vance watched him, noticing the man's hesitation. He walked closer to the man, stopping about ten feet away. As he neared, the man's eyes lost their wide stare. He started blinking, tears soon falling from his face. The man fell to his knees a couple of feet away from the machete and started openly weeping.

"Kill me," he said, "Please..."

Vance stared at him, clenching his jaw and both of his fists as he did so.

"I can't fight," the man sobbed, "My wife is dead. Both of my children are dead."

Vance was in shock at the man's words. He had never faced such emotion when he was supposed to kill a man.

"Please...let me be with them..."

The man buried his face in his hand, the other was formed into a fist. Struck with grief, the man could do nothing but weep.

Vance dropped his sword.

190

"He forfeits," he said, "I have won."

Wolf stared down into the pool. Fury fell over his face, and he stood up quickly.

"No! *KILL HIM!*" he screamed.

"No," Vance said, "I will not. Kill him yourself."

Wolf stared at him for a moment longer before looking down into the crowd and motioning with his hand. Soon Vance saw a soldier dragging Charlie to the base of the lifeguard's chair, the thing Wolf had made his throne.

"Kill him, or the boy dies," Wolf growled.

The soldier holding Charlie pulled out a handgun and held it to the boy's head. Vance froze for a moment. A life hung in the balance. Charlie, or the stranger? If Vance killed the stranger, then Charlie would live. If he didn't then Charlie would die and the stranger probably would as well, afterward. He was obviously "weak" and would not be kept around for long, and even if he was he would be a slave.

"Decide!" Wolf yelled, and drew his own sidearm. He aimed the gun at Charlie, his finger on the trigger.

Vance grabbed his sword from the pool's concrete floor, took three big steps toward his sobbing opponent, and wrapped his hand around the back of the man's neck as he thrust the blade into the center of his chest.

The man gasped as his mouth hung open and his eyes grew so wide that they looked as if they threatened to pop out of his skull. Vance had pushed his sword all the way through the man, the hilt pressed against his sternum. The man's face was less than an inch away from Vance's own. Vance stared on over the man's shoulder for a brief moment, then stepped back and removed his blade. A horrid suckling sound was heard as the blade slipped out of the fatal wound. The man sat there, hunched over, for several moments before falling to the side and letting out his last death wheeze. A large pool of bright red blood formed beneath him, its color exaggerated by the baby blue paint that coated the inside of the pool.

191

The spectators roared, screaming their satisfaction. Vance turned away from the man and looked up at Wolf. He dropped his sword and began breathing heavily. Wolf put his handgun away—as did the soldier holding Charlie—and began clapping. The rest of the soldiers quieted down.

"Very good!" he said with a smile, "Now for round two."

"I've done what you asked!" Vance yelled.

"No, my friend, you have not. I am not yet satisfied." Wolf sat back down in his tall seat above everyone else.

Vance turned around and saw another man entering the pool. This time, his opponent was not a blubbering mess. This man was mean. He wore a makeshift breastplate made out of bones. Whether the bones were human or animal, Vance couldn't tell for sure. His face was covered in black paint, and he had tattoos covering both arms. He stood about as tall as Vance, perhaps a little leaner, but still muscular and foreboding. His head had been completely shaved except for one thick strip of hair going down the center. For pants he wore black BDUs which were bloused into his boots. In his right hand he held a sickle, in his left some sort of bludgeoning tool that looked like a homemade mace. The man closely resembled some sort of crazed Native American warrior, and Vance thought of him as "the Wild Man," for some reason.

"Begin!" Wolf said decisively.

Vance's opponent screamed a war cry as he immediately charged forward, catching Vance by surprise. Vance jumped out of the way and hit the ground rolling just as the man wildly swung his sickle. Vance's sword was now out of arm's reach. He was deeply regretting his decision to toss it down after killing his first opponent.

The Wild Man quickly turned and advanced toward Vance again, swinging the sickle, then the mace, then the sickle again. Vance narrowly dodged the attacks each time, just barely hopping backwards as each weapon flew past him and threatened to mortally wound him in a single blow. The Wild Man stopped briefly and threw his foot out in front of him, his boot connecting with Vance's chest before Vance

192

could even react.

Vance fell back and hit the ground hard. The wind had been knocked out of him, and he was now frantically gasping to inflate his lungs. The Wild Man took advantage of his opponents weakened state and jumped at him, bringing his sickle down as he did. Vance managed to roll to his right and avoid the attack. He then rolled once more and jumped to his feet, just barely starting to get the air back in his lungs. His head felt fuzzy and seemed to be floating, and he quickly became lightheaded from the lack of oxygen and the exertion required to avoid being killed. He squared off with the Wild Man, who was now in a fighting stance and circling Vance. Vance kept turning with him, so as to always remain directly facing him. He was glad for the break. It allowed him to get his wind back.

Vance took a few steps back in the direction of his sword. The Wild Man stared at him with wide, crazy eyes, both primitive weapons held up and at the ready. Vance was about six feet away from his sword. The Wild Man charged forward once more, this time jumping when he got close to Vance. He brought down both weapons as his feet hit the ground. Vance raised his left arm and jumped to his right to avoid the attack, but he wasn't entirely successful. The mace had glanced off of his shoulder, and an intense pain shot through Vance's whole left arm. Vance did his best to ignore it, and took the chance at turning his back to the Wild Man to run for his sword. He scooped it up as he ran past, the Wild Man on his heels. Vance turned around and brought his sword up just in time to block an attack from the sickle. The two metals raked against each other as Vance used all of his strength to hold the sickle at bay. The Wild Man was just inches away from Vance's face now, and a strong odor of alcohol could be smelled through the man's exposed and clinched teeth. The Wild Man swung his mace while Vance's sword was locked with his sickle, and struck Vance in his right thigh. Vance stumbled and fell to one knee before rolling backward and narrowly avoiding a blow to his head from the Wild Man's sickle.

Vance got to his feet once more and squared off with his

193

opponent. He needed to end this quickly. Before long he would become tired and weak, and he wasn't sure if he could say the same thing for his opponent. The man had obviously been drinking, but probably just enough to give him a little courage and more strength. Certainly not enough to make him less alert or less agile. Vance brought his sword up, and the feeling in his other arm was beginning to come back. He didn't think anything was broken, but it certainly hurt like hell. A quick glance at his left shoulder revealed some blood trickling down his arm, but he could still move it so the injury couldn't be too terribly severe.

Vance decided that he was done being on the defensive. He charged forward, spinning to his right to add momentum to his sword's blow. He connected with the Wild Man's sickle, which had been thrown up to keep the sword from hitting him in the head. The Wild Man stumbled back, now taking on a more defensive posture. Vance stabbed at the Wild Man, who just barely turned in time for the sword to miss his abdomen. The Wild Man quickly slapped Vance's sword with his sickle, and followed up with a quick swing of his mace at Vance's head. Vance ducked beneath the attack, the mace missing him by a good foot or more. He brought his sword up in a stabbing manner, aiming for the lower exposed part of the Wild Man's abdomen. His opponent recoiled back, Vance's blade missing his target and its tip ending up only an inch or so from the Wild Man's face. Vance took a chance, and reached for the Wild Man's throat. Being close meant that the mace would have a hard time doing any real damage, and the sickle would most likely only create a minor wound if it managed to connect with Vance's body.

Vance was successful, and managed to grip the man's throat with his left hand. He squeezed as hard as he could and pulled himself close enough to the Wild Man that their chests and noses were touching. The Wild Man dropped his mace and grabbed the side of his opponent's head, trying to dig his thumb into Vance's eye. Vance repeatedly flicked his head to the side, avoiding a potentially blinding attack. He brought his sword up and thrust it downward, toward the

194

left side of the Wild Man's chest and just above the bone breastplate. But the Wild Man grabbed Vance's hand, preventing the sword from going any further. The tip was only an inch away from the Wild Man's left pectoral, its short 17-inch blade proving insufficient against his opponents long reach. Vance cursed himself for not having a longer sword, no matter how practical the one he owned had been.

The Wild Man dropped his sickle as well, either on purpose or on accident, and struck Vance on his left side with his fist. Vance ignored it, even though it had hurt like hell, and continued his attempt to drive his sword deep into the Wild Man's chest. It was now a battle for who was stronger. The Wild Man gripped Vance's sword hand tightly as Vance tried to force it forward. The two men spun in a circle and moved several feet closer to Vance's first "opponent", before the Wild Man punched Vance once more in the same spot as before. This time it couldn't be ignored, and Vance involuntarily jumped back from the blow. He looked up in time to see the Wild Man grab the machete that had gone unused in the last round. Vance recovered, even though he suspected that he had a broken rib, and squared off once more.

The Wild Man charged forward, swinging the machete when he got close enough. Vance jumped back, but this time he hadn't been quite quick enough. The tip of the machete's blade just barely slid across Vance's chest in a diagonal manner, cutting him from his right pectoral all the way down to his abdomen. Vance let out a cry of pain as he kept moving back. He felt the cut open up, and had no idea if it was superficial or a mortal wound. Either way, his opponent was dying.

Vance knew that his opponent was assuming that he would take a quick breather, perhaps look down at his wound. He knew that the Wild Man would probably lunge forward in an attempt to land the finishing blow. Vance didn't give him the opportunity. He skipped forward, intentionally aiming for the Wild Man's machete with his own sword. He knocked it down hard, out of the way of the Wild Man's defensive center, then drew his sword from left to right as hard as he could, letting out a war cry as he did it. The sword raced toward

195

the Wild Man with lightning fast speed. His opponent leaned back, to avoid the blade, but it was not enough. Vance's sword sliced through the entire front half of the Wild's Man's throat.

Vance took a step back as the Wild Man fell to his knees, a gaping wound now exposing the inside of his throat. Blood ran out of his neck like a fountain. The Wild Man's head fell back, his blank gaze now staring straight up at the sky, his hands limply hanging by his sides, his knuckles just barely touching the ground. In a fit of rage, Vance attacked again. He gripped the sword's handle with both hands and swung the blade from right to left as hard as he could. The razor sharp edge hit the Wild Man's neck once more, this time cutting clean through in one decisive motion. His opponents head had been severed from its body, and it fell to the pool's floor seemingly in slow motion. Vance looked on as the rest of the Wild Man's body fell straight forward. His head was now at his feet, sporting the same surprised, horrified expression.

Vance stumbled back and looked down at his chest. Dropping his sword, he brought up both hands to his chest and touched the wound on either side, pulling it open a bit. As luck would have it, it was not a deep cut at all. It was really little more than a scratch, even if it *was* bleeding like crazy. Vance grabbed his black t-shirt where it was already torn and ripped it the rest of the way, removing it from his body so he could check himself for anymore injuries. This was an instinctive act for him. He had been in combat enough to know that you should always check yourself over. Adrenaline sometimes had a way of hiding even the most gravest of injuries.

Vance found no other wounds, besides exhaustion. Even then he was still feeling enraged, bloodlust coursing through his veins. He looked up at Wolf, who was sitting quietly with his fingers touching his hairy cheek in a thoughtful manner. The spectators were not cheering now, not this time.

"What do you say, Wolf? Round three, you and me?" Vance asked, eyes locked on Wolf and breathing heavy.

"Bring him to my quarters," Wolf said in a monotone voice

before climbing down.

***

Vance and Wolf were alone now in Wolf's personal tent. It was large enough for two or three beds, but Wolf had the whole thing to himself. There wasn't much in the tent, besides a cot, a small table, a folding chair, a duffel bag, and Vance's backpack and M4.

Wolf poured himself two fingers of scotch before offering some to Vance, who didn't even acknowledge the offer. Wolf poured him some anyway. Vance had handcuffs and shackles on now, and his hands were in front instead of behind his back.

"Don't mistake the medical aid I provided as an act of kindness," Wolf finally said, "I just didn't want you bleeding all over my things."

Vance looked down at the gauze taped to his chest. The wound was over a foot long and it still hurt like hell. The medic had done little more than clean it up and bandage it.

"You are indeed strong, James Vance," Wolf began.

"How do you know my first name? The boy?" Vance asked him.

"No, not the boy. Something I found with your name on it," Wolf said.

There was only one thing in Vance's backpack that had his first name on it. An old photograph from long ago.

"I also found something else very surprising in there. Something I wouldn't expect a man such as yourself to have in his possession. No, not at all." Wolf grinned.

"Did you take any of my things?" Vance asked him.

"No, everything is still in your pack. Even the antibiotics, which my men can surely use."

"So now what happens?" Vance finally said.

"Now you will travel with me to Albuquerque. You see, I believe you can be made to see our ways, Vance." Wolf pulled the folding chair closer to his prisoner and sat down. He placed the second glass of scotch next to Vance.

"Do you know why?" he asked before taking a sip of his drink, "You were faced with a decision today. A decision that involved doing something inherently wrong to satisfy yourself."

Vance stared into Wolf's eyes.

"You killed an unarmed man. Not only an unarmed man, but an unarmed man who was completely incapable of harming you..."

"Only because you threatened the boy," Vance quickly interjected.

"Ah, but the 'why' is completely irrelevant, is it not? It boils down to you killing him in order to influence the outcome of your situation. Killing him so everything works to your advantage." Wolf leaned forward, now only a couple of feet away from Vance.

"I couldn't let you kill the boy," Vance said.

"And if I had threatened a stranger? Then what? Would you have still killed the man? No...you wouldn't have. Not even if I had threatened to kill two strangers. And why is that? I'll answer for you: Because you wouldn't have known them. Would their lives be worth any more or any less than Charlie's? To you, they would have been. To you they would be worth nothing compared to your adolescent companion. It would have came down to the blood of a stranger being on either your hands...or mine. And we both know what you would have decided. Explain to me why Charlie's life is worth more than the man you killed today." Wolf spoke softly, quietly. His raspy voice cut into Vance like an ice pick, his words were cold but deeply meaningful.

Vance stared at the dirt beneath their feet. After several long moments, Vance answered.

"It's not, but it's worth more to *me*," he finally said.

Wolf sat up straight, a slight smile on his face.

"That boy is my responsibility. His father was murdered right in front of me. I have an obligation."

"Now you see the bigger picture of all this," Wolf said firmly.

"I understand that the strong must lord over the weak. I get that," Vance said.

"You just don't like it?" Wolf asked.

"Perhaps."

Wolf stood and grabbed the glass of scotch that Vance hadn't touched. He threw back what little he had left and then poured Vance's portion into the bottle.

"I wish to take you with me to Albuquerque. Maybe Xander can figure you out and turn you. You would be a great asset to our cause, and Xander probably would have me killed if I disposed of you without at least giving him the opportunity. After what we all witnessed today, I mean." Wolf walked toward the flap of his tent to leave.

"Like he turned you?" Vance asked.

Wolf froze just before the tent's exit.

"Exactly like he turned me," he said without looking at Vance, and then left.

13

Vance and Charlie rode in the back of a minivan toward Albuquerque. Captain Wolf rode in the front passenger seat and didn't say much at all to the driver during the trip. Two more armed soldiers rode in the third row. The minivan was part of a convoy of four vehicles, two of which were deuce-and-a-halfs carrying a whole platoon of soldiers. Either Xander had other plans for the soldiers and was sending them elsewhere, or he needed reinforcements. Vance hoped that it was the latter, and further hoped that he needed reinforcements because Logan Finley was giving him hell. That was the only possibility he could think of, as far as any sort of resistance that would be able to put up a good fight.

***

The trip only took a little less than an hour and a half. The highway was straight and clear, so they traveled as fast as the deuce-and-a-halfs in their convoy could go. By the time they made it to Albuquerque it was only a couple of hours before sunset. Wolf had other things to do before leaving Santa Rosa, so Vance spent more time locked away in the jail cell. This time, Charlie had been with him. Fortunately, Wolf had allowed Vance to change into a clean pair

200

of clothes that he had in his backpack.

As the convoy entered Albuquerque, Vance saw a completely different scene than he had in Santa Rosa. There was less order here, less totalitarian control. Or so it appeared. He saw groups of civilians running around in the streets, seemingly committing nefarious acts that angered their army of oppressors. But this was a good thing, right?

The convoy came to a halt outside of the Bernalillo County Metropolitan Detention Center. How fitting. Vance was escorted past the six or seven heavily armed and armored soldiers standing guard outside, and through the front doors of the building. Inside the detention center, the scene was markedly different than the scene outside. It appeared to be the definition of order. Two guards stood watch just inside the front doors. A handful of other soldiers were scattered about inside, all armed. Vance and Charlie were taken through several doors and down a couple of hallways, Captain Wolf following closely behind them. Vance was still handcuffed, but they had taken off the shackles from his ankles for the ride to Albuquerque.

The small group entered a much larger area through a set of security doors. Tables and chairs had been pushed around into almost a half square, like what you would expect from some sort of committee or something. The room was practically empty, except for three soldiers standing guard. This was a secure area of the facility, so they were probably just standing there specifically to watch Vance. Wolf stepped between Vance and Charlie and walked around the tables, then through another door in the back of the room. Vance waited patiently. He looked over at Charlie, who was staring down at the floor. The boy hadn't said a word all the way to Albuquerque.

"You okay?" Vance whispered to him. Charlie shrugged his shoulders.

"What's wrong?" Vance asked.

"That man you killed. You killed him...because of me..." Charlie said shakily.

"Charlie, it's not your fault," Vance told him.

201

The door that Wolf had gone through flew open. Wolf came out and began walking back over to Vance and Charlie. Just as the door almost closed again, someone on the other side stopped it. It flew open once more. The room beyond was dark, and Vance could just see a silhouette of a man. The shadow stepped out into the larger area, behind the tables.

"Holy shit..." Vance said as he dropped his jaw and his eyes grew wide.

The man that stepped out into the light was tall and muscular, built almost exactly like Vance and was the same height. He had short, dark auburn hair and a thick goatee. His skin was lightly complected, his skin smooth considering all the shit he had gone through. The man before them was none other than Logan "Red" Finley.

"Mean Jim Vance??" Red said with a smile as he walked around the tables.

Vance froze for a moment. What in the hell was going on here? What was Red's role in all this? How could he fight for this Alexander Thompson, a man guilty of such horrible atrocities?

"What in the hell happened? What have you been up to? Get him out of these handcuffs!" Red approached Vance before barking the order to remove his restraints.

"Red...can I speak to you in private?" Vance asked him quietly, leaning in closer and hiding his lips from Wolf's view.

"What do you mean? About what?" Red asked, like nothing strange was going on.

"I need to talk to you about your friend over there...Wolf," Vance whispered.

Red chuckled slightly.

"Come into my office, friend. Where'd you pick up the boy?" Red asked as he took off walking. Vance and Charlie followed.

"He's the newest addition to my magic show," Vance said dryly.

"Oh yeah? Well have him wait outside. I have a feeling our discussion is going to be about adult stuff," Red told him.

Vance looked down at Charlie, who wasn't really displaying any

202

emotion. He patted him on the head, then shot Wolf at mean glance. Wolf nodded his head, as if saying, *No harm will come to the boy.* Vance entered Red's "office" and remained standing as his old ally sat down behind a desk.

"Have a seat, Vance," Red offered as he stuck out his hand.

"No thanks, I'd rather stand," slipped out of Vance's mouth coldly. The old cliché had been uttered too many times to count in the old world.

"So what's going on? Wolf told me about what happened. Why are you attacking my men, Vance? I mean, don't get me wrong, I'll believe anything you tell me..."

"Then believe me when I say that your men are out killing innocent civilians," Vance interrupted, "Your men are enslaving people and stealing from them. Your men tried to kill me, and threatened to shoot that boy out there if I didn't fight in Wolf's twisted gladiator matches. I had to kill an unarmed man to keep Wolf from killing that boy. And your leader, or general—whatever his title is—Xander, is giving them these orders!"

Vance pointed his finger in disgust, as if he was frustrated that Logan Finley wasn't already aware of these things. Frustrated that Finley was helping these people, most likely giving out orders and training Xander's soldiers.

"Vance," Red said as he stood, "I don't have a leader."

"Well then who the hell is..." Vance froze mid-sentence. He slowly turned his head to the side, a look of shock stuck on his face, his eyes gazing through time and looking at nothing in particular.

"I'm Xander, Vance."

***

"How did you meet your friend Vance?" Wolf asked Charlie as he leaned against the wall right outside Red's office.

"He's not my friend," Charlie replied.

"Well...how did you meet him?"

203

"He stayed at my dad's motel in Charleston," the boy replied, his eyes still cast down.

"West Virginia?"

"Yes."

"That's a long way," Wolf said.

Charlie still stared at the floor, with no hint of expression on his face.

"Why are you with him, if your dad owns a motel in Charleston?" Wolf asked, although Vance had already explained the situation to him.

"My dad died when raiders attacked," Charlie said, "And Vance tried to save him. Then he saved me by taking me with him."

"Sounds like a friend to me," Wolf said.

"Not anymore. Vance is just like the raiders. Just like you. I didn't think so at first, but he killed that man when you made him fight."

"Well," Wolf began, "Vance didn't have much of a choice. Sometimes it's kill or be killed."

"Who was going to kill him?" Charlie asked, then, "Nobody can kill Vance. I've seen people try."

"Everyone can be killed," Wolf told him in a soft tone.

"Not Vance. He just kills other people. I thought he was good, but he's not. He killed that man for no reason at all."

"What about the gun I had pointed at you?" Wolf asked him, "Don't you think Vance killed that man because he felt the need to keep you safe?"

"Vance wouldn't have let anything happen to me. I mean, at least I hope not. He could've done something besides killing that man."

Wolf realized that the situation was beyond Charlie's grasp. Not only was the boy traumatized from the overall situation, but he had witnessed his hero brutally execute an unarmed man...to save his life.

***

"I don't think I can see things that way, Red," Vance said quietly.

"Vance...you, of all people, have to see it. I never would have expected you to be so damn stubborn. Not when it comes to killing people, anyway," Red—or Xander, apparently—said with a grin.

"Why'd you change your name?" Vance asked him.

"Alexander Thompson?" Red chuckled slightly and got up from behind his desk, "He was a Scottish man who was awarded the Victoria Cross a long, long time ago. In the 1800s. Quite fitting, isn't it?"

Red walked around the desk and stood right in front of Vance.

"I can't help you, Red," Vance finally told him, staring deeply into his eyes.

"Well, alright then. We'll just let bygones be bygones then...for old time's sake."

Vance could tell that Red wasn't happy about his friend's refusal to help him.

"How'd all this happen, Red? How'd you turn into this...Xander?" Vance asked him.

"Remember that force you helped me train? They were a hell of a team, even if our numbers were small. I had a couple people who tried getting me to expand, recruit more soldiers, make a big difference. But I didn't want that. I wanted to keep life simple. I was happy with the small territory I had claimed in southern New Mexico. I kept thinking about what you told me, about all the enemies I would make if I tried to get big. You said the people weren't ready for that yet."

"I still believe that," Vance said.

"Yeah, well you know what? I made enemies anyway. I tried doing the right thing. I tried being like James Vance, forever the hero!" Red turned and walked back behind his desk, "And you know what happened? I tried to take in some people who needed help. A group of about a dozen. Told them they could join my forces and work for me...never have to worry about surviving, ya' know? Well we had a disagreement shortly after I let them in. I didn't keep myself well enough protected. I allowed regular people—people who were weak—to become my soldiers, or guards, whatever you want to call

205

them. And I almost died because of it, Vance. One of 'em stabbed me, right in the back. Literally. I barely escaped Ruidoso."

"What about Reese? He was still with you, wasn't he?" Vance interrupted.

"Reese...you're protege. Yeah, he stuck with me. He was one of the only ones. Me and a handful of guys got the hell out of there and headed West. After I healed up, we went all the way to California."

"Reese was capable. So were a couple of others. I haven't seen them anywhere. What happened to them?" Vance asked.

"They're dead," Red said with cold eyes.

"Dead? Dead how?"

"Are you going to come with me, in these things I have to do?" Red asked after a moment of absolute silence.

"Can't do it, Red," Vance answered, "I have...people. In fact, I should have already gone to find them. I would have, if your henchman wouldn't have taken me prisoner."

"You're right. Go to your people. I saw them, not long after I came to Albuquerque." Red knew exactly who Vance was talking about.

Vance's mouth opened a little, but no words came out. His eyes glassed over a little.

"Wolf will take you wherever you need to go, friend," Red said quietly.

Vance stared at him for a moment before turning and leaving.

"Let's go, Charlie," Vance said.

The boy didn't even look at Vance, instead choosing to quietly walk beside him. Vance took his backpack from Wolf's hands, shooting him a menacing stare as he did so.

"Vance!" Red shouted, just as Vance and Charlie made it to the door.

Vance turned and stared at his old friend without saying a word.

"Thanks, for everything you did for me," he said, then turned to Wolf and whispered, "Take him where he wants to go, then kill him. He's too dangerous alive. Let the boy live."

Wolf stared into his superior's eyes, towering over him by about six inches. After a brief moment, Wolf nodded his head and walked away.

***

Vance and Charlie were standing outside the detention center, looking at the chaos around them. Buildings were falling down, people were running through streets yelling and looting, there were even a couple fights between civilians. The soldiers nearby stood idle all the while, apparently too burdened to deal with civil unrest. At least for now. Soon Wolf exited the building and walked up to the minivan they had all been riding in.

"Xander says to take you wherever you want to go. Hop in," he said.

Vance and Charlie got in the minivan, and Vance gave the driver directions to his destination. They only drove for about ten minutes before turning into a residential part of the city. A fairly nice neighborhood, or at least it had been before The Fall. It still was, all considering. The houses all looked relatively the same, as one would expect from a nice subdivision. Surprisingly, most of these houses had been occupied prior to Xander's Army moving in. Now Vance felt like he didn't know anything about the city he called home. It looked totally different. Albuquerque had been one of the few cities to remain nice. A lot of people still lived there, commerce thrived, and crime was actually relatively low. Lots of people came to Albuquerque with the hope of planting their roots there. Vance had felt fortunate to live there, especially in the nice house that he did. This city had not been his home until after The Fall.

The minivan pulled up in front of the two-story house Vance called home. It had a two car garage, although just like all the other garages, it was only used for storage nowadays. The house had tan vinyl siding, concrete steps that led up to the front door, and large bay windows off to the side. A single bicycle sat out front, off in the grass.

207

The only reason Vance was not surprised to find that it hadn't been stolen was because it was a pink child's bicycle, too small for an adult to ride. Xander's Army hadn't yet touched this portion of the city, so everything still looked relatively the same. Vance didn't notice any other people out and about, though.

"Here are your things," Wolf said as he removed Vance's tactical vest, bullet-proof vest, and weapons from the minivan's hatch. He placed them on the ground at his feet and walked back around to the passenger side. Vance approached his things, his backpack slung over his right shoulder and hanging off.

"I'm not going with you, Vance," Charlie said out of the blue.

"What?" Vance asked as he turned around and faced Charlie.

"I can't go with you. Not after what you did," Charlie said to him.

"Charlie...I can explain that to you. I promise. But for now you just have to trust me..."

"I did trust you, Vance. And you killed someone for no reason! You're just like the bad people who killed my dad!"

"Charlie," Vance said, "Please...I can provide you with a home. Food, safety, all that. We're home now, Charlie. We're *home*."

Vance placed his hand on Charlie's head and patted him. A few tears ran down Charlie's face as he fought the bad memories in his head.

Vance gave Charlie one last pat on the head before turning away from him. He slowly leaned over to pick up his things. Just as he was about to ask Charlie to help him carry it all, something hit him.

It was a sharp pain, in his back. Then he noticed his ears were ringing. There had been a loud, familiar noise, but it was as if his brain was just not playing it back to him. A loud, sharp cracking noise. Vance was still bent over at the waist, his arm still reaching out toward his things, a blank look spreading across his face. The pain spread from its point of origin and turned into a warm, throbbing feeling. Vance fell forward, sending the dust beneath his feet flying out in clouds as all of his mass hit it with a decisive *thud*. The left side of his face was pressed against the street's asphalt, the minivan's rear

208

passenger tire only a couple of feet from his eyes.

"NO!" he heard Charlie scream out.

Wolf stared down the sights of his smoking handgun at his fallen foe. He nonchalantly placed the firearm back in its holster before squinting at Vance and then crawling back in the minivan.

Vance watched the vehicle pull away. He tried lifting his head, but found all of his energy drained. He moved his eyes downward as much as he could, and saw his backpack laying next to him, the strap still looped around his right arm. A small trickle of blood made its way from underneath Vance and to the backpack, turning a tiny portion of the material deep red.

"Vance!" Charlie yelled as he nearly pounced on Vance's back, "Vance! Get up!"

"Ch- Charlie..." Vance managed to spit out.

"No! No, no, no!" Charlie began sobbing as he placed his hands on the uninjured portion of Vance's back. He laid his head down, coating Vance's gray t-shirt with tears.

"I can....I can get up, Charlie," Vance finally said, although it was a struggle.

Charlie got off of him and grabbed Vance by the arm, trying to help lift him up.

"We need...to get inside, Charlie..." Vance said as he raised his upper body from the pavement.

Charlie used all of his might to help Vance, his little arms straining. Vance placed his left boot on the ground beneath him, waited for a moment, and then stood.

"Come on, Vance..." Charlie whispered, never letting go.

"I'm...I need to..." Vance struggled, but he found it difficult to speak. The sensation of getting shot was quickly turning from discomfort to severe pain.

Vance put one foot in front of the other, staring at his house. He inched closer, with Charlie doing his best to hold him up. Truthfully, the child was doing very little to help. But Vance trudged on, hit feet becoming a little heavier with each step. He looked down and saw a large bloodstain on the front of his t-shirt, where the bullet had apparently exited his body. Vance placed his hand over it and applied as much pressure as he could. He let out a disturbing wince as he did so, but he knew that he would surely die if he wasn't able to stop the bleeding soon. Even then, there was a good chance he would die anyway.

Vance barely made it to the concrete steps leading up to the front door. He fell forward, catching himself with the hand that was clinging onto his backpack. He slowly crawled up the steps, Charlie doing his best to pull him up. Once they had reached the top, Charlie tried to open the front door. It was locked. Vance rose to his feet once more and approached the door. Without even looking at the small panes of glass next to the front door, he punched his left fist straight through one of them and reached around to the lock on the other side. After pushing the front door open, Vance collapsed on the white carpet. He could hear Charlie crying frantically, but barely felt the boy tugging on his free hand.

"Charlie..." Vance groaned.

"Vance!" Charlie yelled.

"We need to...we need to treat this wound," he said.

Vance lifted his head up and looked around, hoping to see other people in his house. He saw no one, and quickly noticed that something was very different about his house. He pulled himself to his knees and crawled toward the kitchen, which was just a few feet away. Looking around as he went, he noticed that things were missing. Pictures had been removed from their frames, and the frames had just been tossed on the floor. Boxes and containers that were normally sitting on the floor and kitchen counters were no longer there. The house smelled musky and empty, as if no one had lived there for a long time. Vance stared down the hallway, leading away from the kitchen and front living room. A large bloodstain covered the wall at the end of the hallway.

"No..." Vance said to himself, "What happened!?"

Vance let out a primal roar as he pulled himself into the kitchen.

210

Once there, he managed to slide over the tile and prop himself up against the cabinets. Charlie sprinted outside, quickly returning with Vance's rifle and sidearm. Vance tried to smile at the boy's smart decision, but wasn't sure if he had actually managed to do it or not.

"What do I do, Vance?" Charlie asked frantically, "Tell me what to do!"

"My...my family," Vance spat out, "What happened to them?"

Vance clinched his teeth together and closed his eyes tightly. In a fit of rage and pain and frustration he banged the back of his head repeatedly against the cabinets behind his head.

"Vance..." Charlie said desperately.

"Towels...get some towels..." Vance told him as he opened up his backpack and reached inside.

Charlie ran over to the bathroom and pushed the door open. Vance struggled to pull the small bottle of rubbing alcohol out of his bag, his fine motor skills refusing to work quite right. Soon Charlie came back with several hand towels.

"Op- open this, Charlie..." Vance said with considerable trouble.

He held the bottle out for Charlie to take, and noticed his hand shaking horribly. Charlie noticed, too, because he hesitated for a moment before grabbing the bottle. Vance held his bloody hand up, his elbow resting on his thigh. His hand still shook like he was a diabetic who had taken too much insulin. Charlie wrenched open the bottle's cap with some effort, and handed it back to Vance. Vance pulled his shirt up above his pectorals, the shirt being just tight enough that it wouldn't fall back down. He didn't even hesitate as he splashed the alcohol on the wound.

Vance let out a loud cry of pain, his back arching and one of his fists involuntarily punching the floor beneath him. As crazy as it was, placing the alcohol on the wound had woken him up a bit.

"Now the other side," he told Charlie, though still with some difficulty.

Charlie grabbed the bottle and Vance rolled onto his side as much as he could. The boy began shaking as he held the bottle over the

211

smaller wound on Vance's back, scared to hurt his one and only companion.

"Just...just do it," Vance said.

So Charlie did. He poured a large amount of alcohol over the wound, and Vance reacted almost the same way as he had before. He had known what to expect this time, so he didn't yell quite as loud. It still hurt like hell.

"Now go find...a small mirror," Vance told him.

Charlie ran back into the bathroom, and Vance could hear him rummaging around. While he waited, Vance took one of the hand towels and placed it on the wound on his chest. He looked down and got a better look at it, seeing that it was just to the left of his sternum. The bullet had to have just barely missed both his heart and left lung. He wouldn't still be alive if it had hit one of them.

Charlie quickly returned with a small hand-held mirror. Vance told him to hold it behind him, so he could see the wound on his back for himself. After several tries, Charlie managed to get it positioned good enough for Vance to see. The wound was small, and sat just left of his spine. It was just a few inches lower than his shoulder blade. The bullet had to have passed just beneath his heart and just to the right of his left lung.

"Alright, Charlie," Vance began, still struggling to speak, "In that front pocket on my backpack, there should...there should be some medical...supplies. Then put...put another towel on my back and...press against it hard."

Charlie opened the large pocket and pulled out everything inside. Vance fumbled through it while Charlie grabbed another hand towel and gingerly placed it over the wound on Vance's back.

"Press harder...Charlie. We need to...we need to stop the bleeding," he said.

Charlie pressed harder, and Vance winced a little from the pressure. Vance pulled out a suture kit, and didn't hesitate at all as he opened it up and looked at the needle and thread.

"Charlie...take this tape," Vance said to him as he handed him a

212

small roll of medical tape, "Wrap it around that towel as tight...as tight as you can, until we can get...to patching it...up."

Vance was finding it more difficult to talk and breath with each passing moment. The swelling and bleeding inside had to be pretty severe. Charlie quickly wrapped the tape around Vance's torso, pulling it tight so the towel would still serve it's purpose.

"Thread this needle...for me..."

Vance held up the suture needle and the thread, and Charlie put the thread through the needle's eyelet as quickly as he could. After two tries, he accomplished the task. Vance gingerly took the needle from Charlie's fingers, not wanting to accidentally poke him with it. His hand shook and swayed side to side a little as he brought it down to the small bullet hole on his torso. As he pierced the needle through his skin, it came as no surprise that it hurt very little. The area was throbbing now, almost numb besides the original pain. Vance slowly pulled the thread through, then stuck his skin again with the needle. He did this twice more before pulling the wound tightly closed and tying the stitching off as best as he could.

"Now I need...now..." Vance stuttered.

"Vance...tell me!" Charlie begged, tears rolling from his eyes again.

"You have to...do the one on the back, Charlie..." Vance said quickly.

"I...I can't, Vance..." Charlie cried even harder now, but never took his eyes off of Vance's.

"I can't do it, Charlie. You...you have to. I'll die if...you don't."

Vance noticed his vision fading. Everything was going black. *No, no...* Vance thought to himself. In his mind's eye he saw himself dying a glorious death on the battlefield, fighting for a noble cause. Not like this. Not from a cowardly gunshot to the back. Not without...

14

"You did *what!?*" Xander barked at Wolf.

"He must be dead, sir. I shot him in the center of his back," Wolf argued.

"You go back there, and you finish him off! I don't want any assumptions! You don't *assume* when it comes to men like *James FUCKING Vance!*" A vein pulsed on Xander's temple as he raised his voice. His normally pale skin turned red and his eyes seemed to bulge from his head.

"Yes, sir."

Wolf turned and began walking out of the detention center.

"And you go alone!" Xander added, "This is your fucking *mistake*, so *you* take care of it!"

Wolf paused before exiting the building and getting in the minivan.

Charlie sobbed as he pulled the thread through Vance's skin. He put in just as many stitches as Vance had on the front wound. Once he pulled it tight and tied it the best way he could, he placed a gauze bandage over it and taped it off. He did the same thing to the front before rolling Vance onto his back and leaning over top of him.

"Vance...*please*," the boy cried, "*Please* wake up! I didn't mean those things I said. You're not bad. I *love you*, Vance!"

Then the boy heard a car door shut outside. He got up and peered through one of the windows. It was Captain Wolf. Charlie ducked down and crawled over to the front door so he could lock it. Then he crawled on all fours over to Vance.

"Vance! Wake up!" he whispered loudly, "Vance!"

There was no reaction from the large man, and Charlie could barely tell if he was breathing. The boy began to panic, but quickly composed himself before grabbing Vance by his t-shirt and pulling as hard as he could. The slick tile allowed him to pull him a couple of inches before the shirt tore. Charlie fell backwards but quickly jumped back up on his feet.

"Come on, Vance!" he said in a loud whisper as he grabbed one of Vance's arms.

The small boy pulled on the limp limb with all his might, and Vance's body finally began sliding across the tile. Charlie's head felt like it was going to explode as he pulled and pulled, slowly making progress. He dragged Vance's body behind the kitchen's long counter, only stopping once he was positive that Vance's feet were no longer visible from the front door.

***

Wolf approached the front door with caution. Even though he was certain that Vance would die—or was already dead—he didn't want to take any chances. He had already seen what the man was capable of. Wolf peered through the small decorative windows around the front door, taking note that one of them was broken. He saw Vance's backpack and M4 laying on the floor in front of the kitchen. Large bloodstains coated the white carpet and tile. Neither Vance nor the boy were anywhere in sight. Wolf gingerly touched the door's handle, and found it was locked. After looking through the window once more, he violently kicked the door open with his massive brute strength. His sidearm in hand, he cautiously stepped inside and

215

scanned from left to right. On the floor beneath his feet was bloodstained carpet. The large man knelt down and touched the blood with his fingers. It was definitely fresh. In front of him, on the kitchen tile, was yet another small puddle of blood. Streaks of red went from just in front of the kitchen counter, all the way around to the other side. Wolf took a deep, quiet breath, exhaling slowly. His gut told him that Vance was on the other side, mortally wounded but still alive. But where was the boy? He had run off, most likely.

Wolf raised his 9mm handgun with both hands firmly holding it and slowly made his way into the kitchen. As his angle changed, he saw a pair of boots on the floor in the kitchen. They weren't moving. Wolf crept closer, finally seeing the whole body that was James Vance. Or used to be, at least. He appeared dead, his arms spread out from his sides and his eyes closed. Wolf took one step closer and stared at Vance's chest. It wasn't moving, that he could see. He decided it would be prudent to check around in case someone else was inside, someone who might present a more immediate threat. He slowly walked down the hallway and pushed open the bathroom door, which was the first room he came to. As he walked away from the bathroom, he heard a deep groan behind him. Wolf turned around and stared back into the kitchen. So...James Vance was alive, after all? Not for long.

Wolf walked back into the kitchen and stared down at the toughest man he had seen in a long while. James Vance was the poster child for rugged survival. It went against everything Xander stood for to kill him, even if he had refused to join them. Xander should have tried harder. A man like James Vance was an irreplaceable asset. Perhaps it was something personal?

"Sorry, brother," Wolf said softly in his deep tone, "You and I...we're not much different. We're exactly alike, actually. We kill when we have to. And that's why we have survived so much already. But...orders are orders. We'll meet again, in another life."

Wolf brought his 9mm up, took aim, and...

***

Charlie listened as Wolf walked away from the kitchen. He was shaking now, sitting next to pots and pans, hidden inside one of the cabinets. Just as he thought they might be in the clear, Vance let out a noisy moan. Charlie squeezed his eyes shut, terrified that Wolf had heard it. Apparently he had, because Charlie heard him making his way back to the kitchen. His heavy footsteps tapped hard against the tile floor in the kitchen. Soon he stopped and began talking to Vance, and it seemed almost genuine. Charlie listened for a few brief moments.

"...orders are orders. We'll meet again, in another life."

Charlie threw the cabinet door open and stuck out Vance's heavy handgun. He was directly in front of Wolf, with Vance between the two of them. The small boy fired the Glock repeatedly without even aiming down the sights. The weapon's flashes were all he could see. After firing about six rounds, Charlie stopped and stared on. He was breathing heavily, and his hand hurt from the weapon's recoil.

***

Wolf placed his finger on the trigger. All of a sudden, a cabinet door flew open. He saw the boy, Charlie, hiding inside. Just as he was about to say something, the boy unleashed all hell. He had a handgun, and he pulled the trigger rapidly. Wolf instinctively threw his arms up in front of him and ducked his head down. But something hit him in his side. It hit him hard. Wolf fell back against the drywall behind him, breaking it as he did. The boy was still firing. Wolf slid down the wall and forced himself to the side just before hitting the floor. He landed on the living room's carpet, right at the beginning of the hallway. But he was out of the boy's sight, for now.

217

***

Vance opened his eyes slowly, gazing straight up at the ceiling. Was he in his house? The décor looked oddly familiar. Had he made it home? Why was he laying in the...kitchen? There had been noises...and pain. What was going on? Then Charlie appeared, and it frightened him. He was saying something, Vance knew it. The boy's lips were moving, but Vance couldn't hear anything. It sounded like he was submerged in water.

"Vance!" Charlie whispered to him, "Wake up! Please!"

Vance heard it that time. Was Charlie holding his Glock? What in the hell was going on?

"Wolf is here! Vance! Captain Wolf is in the house! I shot at him!" Charlie whispered.

That got Vance's attention. He grabbed the handgun from the boy's small hand and struggled to sit up. He hurt...all over, it felt like. But he mustered all of his strength and grabbed the counter. He used it to pull himself to his feet, aiming his handgun out in front of him as he did so. As he came up over the counter, he looked into the living room and surrounding area. There was no one there. But Vance knew *something* had happened for sure...the drywall in the kitchen, next to the table, had a large dent in it with a crack running down the middle. It looked like blood had been spattered and then smeared all over the drywall, too. Looking closer at the living room, he noticed more blood on the wall leading down the hall.

"Did you hit him?" Vance asked quietly.

"I...I don't know. I think so," Charlie said, a worried look on his face.

"Hide!" Vance barked.

Vance limped out of the kitchen. He was only able to get up because of all the adrenaline and his extreme fear for Charlie's safety. His wound had been a clean flesh wound, but he had still lost a lot of blood. He wanted to tell himself that he had fought through worse, but...this was probably his worst injury ever. A bullet, right through his chest. It was a miracle he was alive at all, let alone able to get up

218

and walk around.

Vance held his left arm around his chest. It had already been hurting from the Wild Man's strong punches to his ribcage and the superficial laceration running down his torso, but those were the last things on his mind. Vance held his sidearm up as best he could and made his way down the hallway. Yet another patch of blood was on the wall of the hallway about halfway down, but this time it was nearly a perfect hand print. On the floor in front of him were several drops of blood. Vance briefly glanced at the large bloodstain that had already been at the end of the hallway when they arrived. He froze for a moment, wondering whose blood it was and halfway expecting to find the body of someone he knew in one of the rooms. Vance banished the thought from his mind, knowing that thinking such things would only distract him from the immediate threat.

Vance carefully scanned each room as he passed it. Then, at the end of the hallway, he pushed open the already cracked door on his right. A room with pale pink wallpaper revealed itself. They had chosen this house for that very reason. A bed sat against the opposite wall, its flowery blankets made neatly and the pink pillows propped up against the headboard. A white dresser sat a few feet away from the bed, small toys and trinkets resting on top of it. On the floor next to it was a stuffed animal. A white puppy dog. A relic from the old days. Vance was taken aback by it so much that he almost didn't notice the giant, bald man sitting on the floor propped up against the end of the bed. The elephant in the room.

Vance slowly stepped inside, forgetting all about his injury. Wolf stared at him, eyes wide, his handgun resting on the floor a couple feet away from him. It was still within arm's reach, but he didn't even try for it. Vance approached him and stopped a few inches away from his feet. The huge man snorted and coughed, a small amount of blood spraying from his mouth as he did so. Vance looked down at him blankly, half slumped over from his debilitating wound even though it didn't currently hurt.

"This is all I wanted," he said, waving his handgun around the

219

room, "Just to be here. Home."

Vance kicked Wolf's weapon away from him, even though the man showed no interest in it. He was in a bad way, his big paw holding his right side and his feet kicking at nothing for no apparent reason.

"Home," Vance repeated, "You don't look like you know what that word means."

He paused, looking down at the man who had fired a bullet into his back not long ago.

"Or maybe you do," he added softly.

Vance turned away from Wolf and looked around the room once more. Small paintings of animals still hung from the walls. A ballerina music box sat on a small child's table. Vance closed his eyes and briefly smiled.

"You and I...we're the kind of men who can never be kept around together. We're too much alike," he said, completely unaware of Wolf's previous words to him, "You were right. I did understand your ideology. I just didn't like it. The truth of the matter is...I'm not sure if we get to come back from the horrible things we've done. But I'm still gonna' try. And I'm still gonna' protect those who deserve to be protected."

Vance slowly bent over and grabbed Wolf's handgun, then shoved it in his back pocket. He then grabbed Wolf's boot with his free hand. He winced as he slowly pulled the large man around, dragging him out of the little girl's room by his foot and into the hallway. Wolf didn't resist. He couldn't really. Even if he had any fight left, he knew he had been mortally wounded. Charlie's aim might have been terrible, but a bullet hits a man the same way regardless of whether it's intentional or not. He had been hit on his right side, a few inches below his armpit. The bullet had torn across his chest, through his right lung, and exited through his left shoulder blade. It was amazing that he was still alive.

Vance continued pulling him. Slowly, methodically. It took great effort to pull the mountain of a man. He held his right arm across his chest, even though he was still holding onto his weapon. Vance stared

220

straight ahead, determined. Charlie was standing in the kitchen, watching with eyes wide. Vance didn't even look at the boy as he dragged Wolf across the tile, opened the sliding glass door, and muscled the heavy body outside.

Vance looked around at the backyard. A privacy fence surrounded it. It would have made a great home for Maggie and Daisy. Too bad this world was still a home to such cruel men. Ruthless men, like himself. But he knew that the difference between him and men like Wolf was that he only killed when it was necessary. The overall cause was noble and true, even if his actions had earned him an eternal spot in Hell.

"Do you know..." Wolf said quietly before coughing up more blood, "Do you know...why I followed Xander?"

Vance turned and looked at him calmly.

"He told me a story, about...about a man," Wolf coughed some more, his words only coming through great exertion, "This man...he was a brutal being. He killed...he killed all those who crossed...him. He trained Xander's...soldiers...to be...to be..."

Wolf had a coughing fit, and halfway through he groaned loudly in pain. He finally threw his head back against the concrete patio and stared up at the sky.

"...to be unforgiving. To always be...honorable and brave. Xander said...he said I could be like that man..." Wolf barely lifted his head and looked at Vance.

"And now...now I realize, that man...was *you*," Wolf almost smiled as he gave Vance a nod, "Finish me off. Give me a glorious death. A soldier's death."

Wolf's head fell back once more. Vance stared at him blankly. He limped over to him and stood above him, almost feeling pity for the dying warrior. Soon he shoved his own handgun in his waistband, then pulled out Wolf's 9mm. He removed the magazine from it and slightly pulled back the receiver, checking to make sure a round was chambered. He then placed the gun on the concrete about three feet away from Wolf but still within the man's reach.

"You're not going to make me kill another unarmed man," Vance told him, and stepped back.

Wolf chuckled dryly as best he could, blood running down the side of his face and beginning to pool on the concrete. Another, larger pool of blood had already formed from his entry and exit wounds. Wolf slowly reached for his weapon, finally wrapping his large hand around its grip. He stared at the gun for several moments, his eyes slowly blinking and his breathing labored. He finally lifted it from the concrete and into the air. In one slow, deliberate motion, he swung the gun's muzzle toward Vance.

Vance drew his own handgun from his waistband and fired two shots into Wolf's chest. The large man immediately dropped his firearm and took in one more labored gasp. Then he dropped his arm to the ground and his head fell to the side. The arm that had previously been laying across his chest rolled off and hit the hard ground. Vance stared at him for a moment before going back inside.

"Is he...is he dead?" Charlie asked him.

All Vance could do was nod as he fell into one of the kitchen chairs. He felt weak, completely drained and exhausted. His bullet wound was starting to throb again, and he felt a little less sturdy.

"Vance...what do we do now?" Charlie asked.

The boys words pulled him out of his trance. He slowly stood and made his way to the door, picking up his M4 and backpack on the way.

"Now? Now I end this thing. You stay here."

That was all he said. Charlie's lip began quivering as he watched his protector walk through the door and out of the house. Tears formed in his eyes, but he fought them back.

Vance approached the rest of his gear, which was still in the street and again sitting next to the minivan. He put on his thigh holster and placed his Glock in it, then threw on his bullet-proof armor and tactical vest. After checking his weapons and reloading them, he walked around to the front of the minivan. Standing over the hood, which had a large red "X" painted on it, he aimed his handgun at the windshield and fired a single round into the driver's side. Then he crawled inside and took off down the road. He knew what he needed to do, and even though he had suffered a serious injury, he found that he suddenly had an abnormal burst of energy. The adrenaline from being shot and finding Wolf in the house had subsided. He had slightly more control over his faculties now, and he could tell that his bleeding had at least slowed. The people he cared about—the people who were his *life*—were nowhere to be seen, and with recent circumstances as they were, it was likely that they were dead or at least far away from Albuquerque. Vance was now determined to kill Xander, or at least do as much damage as possible before dying.

***

"When Wolf gets back, I want you guys to head to the east side of town and put down those fuckers responsible for getting everyone worked up," Xander said as he pointed his finger.

"Yes, sir. How many of us do you want to go?" the soldier, Sergeant Phelps, asked his supreme leader.

"Just one platoon," Xander answered.

"But sir...there are at least a hundred people over there. Probably more..."

Xander stepped closer to Sergeant Phelps and stared deep into his eyes.

"Don't ever question me again, Sergeant. There's no room in this world for people who question their superiors," he said coldly.

"Yes...yes, sir," Phelps answered.

"Who the hell is that?" another soldier asked as he stared down the road.

"Looks like Captain Wolf," another said.

"That's his vehicle. I can't see the driver. The windshield looks like it took a round," yet another said.

Nobody thought any different, since they had all seen Wolf leave in the same vehicle. After all, it had the familiar red "X" painted on its

223

hood.

"Hey...he ain't slowin' down!" someone else shouted.

***

Vance pressed his foot against the accelerator. The minivan climbed past 40MPH. In front of him was a T in the road, and the Bernalillo County Detention Center. He stared on ahead beneath the spider-webbed windshield, barely able to see in front of him.

The soldiers standing guard out front watched as he sped toward them. They had barely seen him in enough time to react. Just as he hit the brakes, two of them jumped out of the way and another two flipped up onto his hood, slamming against his windshield. The minivan spun to the side and finally came to a stop after its back panel smacked into the brick building.

Vance pushed the door open, which hit the brick building but still gave him plenty of space to get out. He had his M4 up against his shoulder, ignoring the pain and the exhaustion and only focusing on killing Logan Finley. His family was gone, and he had no idea if they were even alive or dead. With no one to watch out for them, he didn't even want to think about it. But he couldn't help it. His reoccurring bloodlust fueled his wrath. It made him ignore his horrible injury and push on to exact his revenge. Directly in front of him, trapped under the back tire, was one of Xander's soldiers. He was still alive, the tire sitting on top of his abdomen. Blood poured from his mouth as he screamed in pain and fear.

One soldier walked around the front of the minivan with his rifle raised. Vance fired a single shot into his head. He stepped up toward the front of the vehicle and looked out over its hood. Three more men were before him. Vance resembled a robot designed to kill as he quickly and efficiently pulled the trigger on his assault rifle. All three men fell to the ground. Two more stood off to the side, and he could just barely see them through the broken windshield. Mustering all of his strength and willpower, he threw himself up over the hood and hit

224

the pavement on the other side. Bullets hit the environment around James Vance, but he didn't even flinch as he returned fire and took down the two soldiers. Only one remained. A single foe. Logan Finley.

Finley drew his sidearm as he dove to the side, taking cover behind some sandbags. Vance fired two shots as Finley ran, but both missed. Just then, two more soldiers came out of the front of the detention center and Vance saw them out of his peripheral vision. They had no idea what was going on. Gunfire meant very little in this city, it seemed. Vance put them down before they even raised their weapons. Then he turned back to where Logan was hiding and shot into the sandbags several times, just to keep him ducked down in fear.

"Alright! Alright!" Xander yelled over the gunfire.

"Let's finish this like men, Vance! You and me! No one else, and no guns!" the man roared.

A chance to take down Xander—the man responsible for countless deaths and possibly the deaths of his family—in a brutal and horrifying way? Challenge accepted.

"Come on out, then!" Vance yelled back, his M4 still up.

"So you can shoot me when I do? No thanks!"

"Fine, then," Vance said, "I'm putting mine down!"

Xander peeked up above the sandbags and saw Vance with his hands raised. He tossed his own handgun off to the side and stood up. He had only challenged Vance because he knew he had to be extremely weak from Wolf shooting him.

"I'm assuming Wolf is dead?" Xander asked as he stepped forward.

"Your assumption is correct," Vance answered.

"He was never as good as you, anyway," Xander said with a smile.

"But better than you," Vance replied, his face lacking any expression whatsoever.

"Let's do this the old fashioned way, Jim. For old time's sake?"

A handful of soldiers rushed through the front doors of the building, guns in hand.

225

"No! He's mine!" Xander ordered. What better way to boost morale than for the men to see their fearless leader take down a menacing foe like James Vance? After all, this situation was symbolic of the very ideology he preached to them. They didn't need to know that Vance was already injured.

"Alright then. Let's do this."

Xander approached Vance with his hands raised in a fighting stance. Vance let his harms hang down by his side, slightly limping as he walked to his left. The two men circled each other for a moment before Xander charged forward.

Vance reached over his shoulder and grabbed the handle of his sword. Just as Xander reached him, Vance pulled the sword out of its sheath and thrust it down with all of his might. Xander's body fell forward from the momentum of running. Vance's blade landed between Xander's neck and left shoulder. It had cut deep into his chest cavity. Xander fell off of the blade and hit the ground without a sound.

"You know why you should always fight dirty?" Vance asked as he stepped over his downed opponent, his feet on either side of his torso, "Because you must always expect your enemy to fight dirty."

Vance reached down and dug his hand between the pavement and the small of Finley's back. From underneath he pulled a push dagger, an efficient killing tool with a triple-edged blade and a handle that went horizontally so it could be firmly gripped in the palm of the hand, with the blade extruded out between the middle finger and ring finger. It had always been Finley's favorite melee weapon.

Vance stared at his fallen enemy and tossed the push dagger to the side. Finley wasn't even breathing, but his chest was frantically rising and falling in a futile attempt to draw air into his lungs. The wound had been a terrible one, and would kill him in just a few brief moments. But Vance brought his tanto sword up above his head and thrust it down into the center of Logan Finley's chest. He twisted the blade left and right, staring into Finley's eyes as the life drained from them. Once he was satisfied, he pulled the blade out and fell to the ground, exhausted now that his mission had been accomplished. In all

226

honesty, he had expected to die during his attempt. Especially with his injury.

The soldiers around him stared in awe as they saw Xander lying dead at the hands of a single man. Their ideology had been to always follow and support the strong. The weak died and the strong survived. And now their leader was dead. None of them rushed to his aid, or attacked Vance. None of them even acted like they were going to. With their leader dead—the preacher of their code—they had no reason to do anything to Vance. He had fought their fearless leaders and came out on top. Now *he* was to be feared and followed, if necessary.

Vance slowly rose to his feet and put the tanto sword back in its sheath on his backpack. Grabbing his M4, he drug his feet along as he walked around the minivan and opened the driver's side door. It seemed perfectly quiet now. The gunfire in the distance couldn't be heard over the shock of the situation. Vance put the minivan in gear and drove it away from the building. The handful of soldiers who had originally came outside to kill him now looked at each other in confusion. A couple of them threw down their weapons and took off down the street. The others ran inside to tell everyone the news. Xander was dead, and so was their cause.

15

Vance kept his foot on the gas, slowly creeping down the road back toward his house. As he turned into the subdivision where he lived, he felt his head become fuzzy. The light around him was turning dark again. His wound no longer hurt, and his hands and feet started to tingle. He finally stopped the minivan about two houses down from his residence. He could no longer drive. The broken windshield had made it hard for him to see in the first place, and now he was dizzy and his vision was blurred. His hands and feet weren't working right, and he would surely wreck if he continued on.

As he exited the car, he unzipped his tactical vest and let it fall off of him. Then he removed his bullet-proof vest, feeling like all he wanted to do was lay down and sleep. He sluggishly reached back inside the minivan and grabbed his backpack. The package was still inside. It had survived through all the hell, all the turmoil, all the bad decisions. And at this point, it was all that mattered. He looked down and saw that the recently applied gauze on his chest was blood-soaked. It was beginning to ooze through, and a tiny trickle of blood ran down his stomach. The bleeding had certainly slowed, but it hadn't been enough. Vance's life force was still leeching out, leaving him more and more weak with every passing second. Vance stumbled away from the minivan in the general direction of his house. As he

228

neared, he thought he saw Charlie sitting on the front steps, his head resting against his knees. Vance wanted to yell out to him, let him know he was back. But he couldn't. He barely had the strength to keep moving, and that was fading quickly. There was still no pain, not physically anyway. All of the choices Vance had made recently— trying to save Bob, hunting down his killers, taking Charlie under his wing, ridding Shamrock of Xander's bandits, killing that innocent civilian in the drained swimming pool, everything—they flashed before him like a movie. Vance smiled to himself as he saw his wife and little girl in his mind's eye. They were safe and happy, even if they weren't in reality. But he wanted them to be. He wanted them to be happy and safe more than anything. And Charlie...he loved the boy as if he were his own. It was too bad everything couldn't have ended differently. It was too bad Vance's sins had come back to haunt him. Even though he didn't believe in any god, he somehow felt like this was his punishment. But if his wife and daughter were alive after all— and if they weren't, at least Charlie was—then he had done them and everyone else a great service by killing the man responsible for so much pain and sadness. The man who he had once called a brother. The man who he had helped. The man who tried to have him killed.

Charlie lifted his head up as Vance inched closer and closer. For a moment he thought he was dreaming, but he rose to his feet anyway. Vance's torn shirt hung from his muscular torso. His handgun was still strapped to his right thigh, his backpack still hung from his strong grip. His face was rough and scratchy—he hadn't shaved in days. Blood soaked his ripped t-shirt and tan BDU pants. It was dried all over his arms and even on his neck and part of his face. Charlie jumped from the steps and ran toward Vance.

"Vance!" the boy yelled.

Vance smiled once more as he saw Charlie running toward him. Both of them had experienced so much pain, so much loss. He fell to his knees, then the rest of his body slumped over and hit the pavement.

"No!" Charlie yelled.

Vance's eyes were still open. He managed to roll over onto his back, his breaths were shallow and labored. As he looked up at the bright blue sky, he smiled once more. Charlie was now sitting down and leaning over him, yelling at him and crying. But Vance still smiled. He used the last bit of his energy to pull his backpack onto his chest and reach inside one of the pockets. From it he pulled a single photograph. It was an old Polaroid, but it had just been taken a year or so ago. Vance stared at it briefly, although it was blurry and he could barely see it. But he didn't really need to see it. He had looked at it so many times while on the road and out in No Man's Land. Even since he had taken Charlie with him, Vance had often waited until after the boy was asleep and would spend long moments of time just staring at it. As he looked on at the blurry image, he saw his wife and daughter smiling back at him. His little girl had been just barely six years old when this picture was taken. Her birthday was soon. Next month, actually. Vance brought the picture to his lips and kissed it gently before looking over at Charlie. He grabbed the boy's hand and placed the picture in it. Charlie was bawling uncontrollably now. Vance reached into the main pocket on his backpack and dug around some more. After several brief moments, he slowly pulled out the package that he had promised to deliver. Charlie stared at it with some confusion, but was more worried about his protector and companion. Vance looked at the package for a long while, or at least it felt like a long while. It was simple, really, but was so very important. Vance pulled it close to his face and took in a long, deep breath through his nose. It pained him to do so, but the smell was worth it. He pulled it away and handed it to Charlie, who gently took it and stared back at Vance in confusion.

"The package," Vance whispered.

"What do I..." Charlie choked as he cried, "What do I do with this? Who do I give it to?"

Vance grinned, then pointed to the picture he had given to the boy just moments prior. Charlie stared at it, then pursed his lips. The two things Vance had given him had made him even more sad.

Charlie heard footsteps rapidly approaching as he leaned over Vance. The boy didn't even look to see who it was. He just stared on into Vance's eyes.

"Jim!" a woman cried out as she grew closer.

Vance's eyes had been almost completely closed, but they sprang open at the sound of the feminine voice. A familiar voice.

"Jim!" the woman screamed again.

She finally made it over to Vance and Charlie and fell to her knees. Charlie looked down at the picture and immediately recognized the woman. She was beautiful, with dirty blonde hair and soft skin. Her features were perfect to Charlie, even if she was crying.

"Oh my God," the woman sobbed, "What happened? I thought you were never coming home!"

"I'm home..." Vance began, "I'm home...now..."

The woman cried even harder before looking over at Charlie. Vance grabbed the boy's arm gently and lifted it up. He pulled it across him and held it out in front of his wife. She looked at it for a moment, confused, but Vance tugged on it and she got the feeling he wanted Charlie to go with her.

"Daddy?" a soft, small voice said.

Vance's eyes widened once more.

"Daddy?" the little girl said once more.

Vance watched as his daughter came into his view. She knelt down beside him, her long hair touching his face as she leaned over.

"You're both...you're both...safe," Vance said with a smile, "Where...where were..."

The little girl—six year old Angela—seemed confused, but began crying at the sight of her father in so much pain. She looked over at the thing Charlie was holding—a small, pink teddy bear, the important package—and thought back to when she made her daddy promise to bring it back home with him. Charlie fell back and sat in the street, still bawling. Vance's wife and daughter leaned over him, their heads touching his body. Even with both of them laying on him, most of his large body was still visible. They were tiny compared to him. All three of them grieved as James Vance breathed his last breaths. The bullet had only caused a flesh wound, but the internal bleeding had sealed his fate. But Vance had known it was going to happen. He knew it was only a matter of time before he lost too much blood, even after treating the wound and slowing down the inevitable. Regardless, he used his last few moments to eliminate a very real threat. How many people would be saved from suffering because of him? No one would ever know. The selfless deed's effects were incalculable.

Epilogue

James Vance had such strength, such determination, such ability...he wasn't just a loss to Charlie, or to his wife and daughter, but a loss to the *whole world*. Even if the number of people who had known Vance was just a drop in the bucket, it didn't matter. What mattered was that a man like Vance had existed at all. He had already done so much to affect the course of human history *before* The Fall, but it hadn't been enough.

Some would remember James Vance as a brutal killer. Some would remember him as a savior. But *all* would remember him as the one who took down Xander and ultimately dismantled his army of thieves and murderers. That could not be ignored. Within just two weeks after Xander's death, all of his soldiers and followers had learned of the incident. No one rose to replace him, no one continued fighting in his memory. His legacy died with him that day. But not Vance's. He hadn't even set out to build a legacy, but he made one anyway. And isn't that how the best legacies are created? When good men act selflessly, with only the good of others in mind?

"And where would we be today Grandpa, if Vance hadn't taken you in?" James Frederick Jr. asked his grandfather.

"Well, no one can answer that. But you and your father's first names certainly wouldn't be 'James'," Charlie said with a laugh.

"I don't get it," little David said, "Why did he take that stupid doll with him?"

"You're too young to understand now, my boy, but when you grow up and have children it will make all the sense in the world to you." Charlie reached over and patted his youngest grandchild on the cheek.

"So...do you think the Federation would have still existed if it hadn't been for what Vance did?" Another question from James Jr., and Charlie didn't mind answering at all.

"No, I'm certain it wouldn't," Charlie said confidently, "Xander's Army was a force to be reckoned with, and it was only his death that started the negotiations between all of the cities and states. What he did was the worst thing to happen to the people of this nation, even considering The Fall. It seemed like everyone learned to appreciate one another a little bit more after that. And more importantly, they learned that they needed to join together to prevent something else like that from happening again. History repeats itself if we don't pay attention to it, you know."

Charlie slowly stood, his shaky legs barely supporting his frail body.

"Let me help you, Grandpa," James Jr.—who was 19—said to his elderly grandfather as he stood and took his arm.

"Thank you, son," Charlie said.

"Goodnight, dear. I'll be there soon," his wife said with a smile. Charlie gave her a peck on the cheek as he went by.

Charlie looked at the snow globe that sat on his night stand. It had a white horse inside of it, and like every night, that white horse made him smile warmly. He crawled into his bed, and gingerly touched the snow globe with his fingertips before turning out the lamp that sat on the same table. Growing up without electricity had made him appreciate it so much more now. His wife finally came in and laid down beside him. The two locked their hands together, staring up at the dark ceiling.

"Do you think my father would be proud of us?" Charlie's wife asked him.

"I *know* he would be, Angela."

www.ingramcontent.com/pod-product-compliance
Lightning Source LLC
Chambersburg PA
CBHW020606180626
46810CB00007B/2673